THE **BLOODLIGHT
CHRONICLES**

RETRIBUTION

D1214366

THE **BLOODLIGHT** CHRONICLES

RETRIBUTION

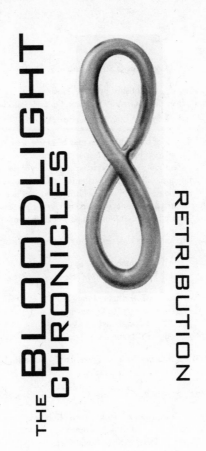

STEVE STANTON

ECW PRESS

Published by ECW Press
2120 Queen Street East, Suite 200, Toronto, Ontario, Canada M4E 1E2
416-694-3348 / info@ecwpress.com

LIBRARY AND ARCHIVES CANADA CATALOGUING IN PUBLICATION

Stanton, Steve, 1956–
Retribution / Steve Stanton.

(Bloodlight chronicles)
ISBN 978-1-55022-989-9
ALSO ISSUED AS:
978-1-77090-101-8 (PDF); 978-1-77090-100-1 (EPUB)

I. Title. II. Series: Stanton, Steve, 1956– . Bloodlight chronicles.

PS8587.T3237R48 2011      C813'.54      C2011-902914-6

Design and Artwork: Juliana Kolesova
Editor: Chris Szego
Development: David Caron
Printing: Webcom    1    2    3    4    5

This book is set in Garamond 3.

This is a work of fiction. Names, characters, places, and incidents either are the product of the author's imagination or are used fictitiously, and any resemblance to actual persons, living or dead, business establishments, events, or locales is entirely coincidental.

The publication of *The Bloodlight Chronicles: Retribution* has been generously supported by the Canada Council for the Arts which last year invested $20.1 million in writing and publishing throughout Canada, by the Ontario Arts Council, by the Government of Ontario through the Ontario Media Development Corporation and the Ontario Book Publishing Tax Credit, and the Government of Canada through the Canada Book Fund.

 Canada Council
for the Arts
Conseil des Arts
du Canada
 Canada
ONTARIO ARTS COUNCIL
CONSEIL DES ARTS DE L'ONTARIO

PRINTED AND BOUND IN CANADA

 FSC
www.fsc.org
MIX
Paper from
responsible sources
FSC® C004071
 ANCIENT FOREST ™
FRIENDLY

"He who hid well, lived well."

René Descartes

1596–1650

# ONE

Her house had been locked all day. Of that, Niko could be certain. She had standard webcam surveillance, touch-sensitive alarms, failsafe measures. She lived in suburbia, a single girl safely ensconced in the anonymity of urban sprawl, her illegal nest impregnable to all but the most violent means of forced entry, her vigilance meticulous. There was absolutely no way anyone could have infiltrated the perimeter without her knowledge.

A shock of paranoia carved through her consciousness as she returned home late in the afternoon with a backpack full of groceries. A faint glow emanated from her front window. She had not left any lights on; she never did. Electricity was too precious. Her alarm network and communications were solar powered. When she was out during the day, her system fed power back to the grid for brownout points. The front door was secure. She zoomed in with optical magnification in search of fingerprints or smudges on the handle. She checked for minute scratches around the locking mechanism. No sign of tampering.

Niko unlocked the door with a palm sensor and stepped quietly inside. She froze and listened for a few moments, dialling up frequency augmentation to her upper limit, but could sense nothing but her quickened heartbeat and a housefly in a washroom down the hall to her left. She crept forward carefully, catlike, sniffing the air for anything untoward. She caught a whiff of ozone.

A glowing vial was sitting on her coffee table in the living room, a bright white beacon with a subtle greenish tinge. She dropped her backpack and sat down with a thump as recognition dawned. This was the Eternal virus! This was the magic elixir, right here in her suburban hideaway. Panic pushed up into her throat. No way. She stared, not daring to touch it, her mind reeling with possibilities. Could her cousin Rix have sent it from the Eternal Research Institute? Some lab experiment? No way. There was no human technology available to transport the virus into a locked room. And besides, this was no diluted lab specimen. This was an activated sample, bright and vital. This was the real deal right from the Source. She could think of no other explanation. Her stomach began to churn.

Niko took her groceries to the kitchen, steady on her feet. She minced a veggie shake and downed it slowly. She put some cheese and fresh fruit in the fridge, a loaf of bread in the cupboard, trying to organize her thoughts against a tide of confusion. Her life would never be the same. The alien virus, the most sought-after treasure in the civilized world, right here in her living room. Eternal life.

What a rush.

*Okay, calm down.* She was on her own now. Her mentor, Phillip, stepfather one petri dish removed, was in a private rejuve clinic, brain-dead and just learning to drool again. Rix had been swallowed up by the ERI, newly Eternal himself. Perhaps she could contact him, suss it out somehow. His father, Zak, had journeyed offplanet to find an activated sample for his only son, had sacrificed his own memories along the way and who knew what else?

Niko stalked back to her coffee table and picked up the bright trophy lying there. She eyed it carefully. The vial was shaped like an infinity symbol, two lobes with a narrow causeway in between. It felt warm, alive, smooth like glass, perhaps some alien plastic, and was designed to be broken at the weak point and upended on the tongue. In a recent lab experiment, the virus had been diluted a hundred-fold and given to test subjects without a single successful contagion, except for Rix. Nor could it be transferred from person to person in any way. The transmission of the virus was the greatest biological mystery in the universe. Each activated sample was target specific to a single human host—in this case, to her alone. She had been chosen to live forever.

She tossed the vial to the table as though it were a burning ember.

No one could force her to accept the alien science, not while she lived and breathed. She had free will as always, she could still walk away and probably should. Viral contagion carried with it important obligations, both to other Eternals and the planetary environment in general—all that salvation of the world crap. She didn't need the extra responsibility for sure. Her life was complicated enough already. She could probably sell the virus to a rich but naïve buyer, or perhaps a research group with a new tack. She could retire on the proceeds and gulp veggie shakes on the beach in a tax-free haven for the rest of her days.

If she didn't get killed for it first.

The gentle glow held her attention like a magnet. This was the chance of a lifetime, her one invitation to immortality. How could she throw it away?

She touched it with hesitant fingers. She held the vial to her eyes under full magnification and tipped it back and forth, looking for bubbles of air, for movement. It seemed completely uniform and unchanging. She could almost see through it, but the steady glow obscured her close inspection. A liquid or gel, she could not tell. Perhaps it was gaseous. She put it back down.

Why her? Why had the aliens chosen her for contagion? She was a clone, a criminal by birthright. She was a smuggler by trade, and although she liked to think she had a good working relationship with the law of the land, she was always working from the wrong side of the fence of legitimacy. She was not a good candidate for infinite largesse. Was she being set up? Some conspiracy? She began to pace, prowling her home like a panther, thinking.

She was not worthy of blessing, but who ever was? The Eternal virus was not a reward for good housekeeping. It was not payment, but promise. It was a free gift from the gods, but at what future cost? Niko fancied herself a cynic, protectively paranoid. She questioned every assumption as part of her daily business demeanour, an ingrained survival instinct. She trusted no authority. What might the aliens demand down the road for the regenerative powers of the virus? Were they puppeteers, uploading purpose into willing subjects, perhaps even subconscious cognition? After the mortal humans died off, would the aliens sweep in for complete planetary domination? Were they just biding their time, setting a grand stage over the centuries?

Only one way to find out.

Niko picked up the vial for a third time and cracked it in half. It popped with the sound of a broken lightbulb and a whiff of spray wafted upward like smoke. She spilled a few drops, but poured the rest on her tongue without hesitation. It tasted like honey, rich and vibrant. She swallowed and felt warmth trickle down her throat. The taste lingered and grew, reaching up into her sinus with tendrils of pleasure. She swallowed again, the sweetness now cloying.

The warmth spread into her lungs and up her spine. She felt giddy for a moment and wondered if the virus had breached the blood-brain barrier so quickly. She was committed now. No need to panic. She sat down on her cushioned loveseat and made herself comfortable. Her stomach began to roil.

Poison, her body told her. Time to vomit. She resisted the urge. Maybe the virus had decided she was a bad candidate after all. Maybe it was testing her, reading her mind. *I will not serve you*, she subvocalized. But she knew in her heart that she had already pledged her allegiance. The virus was the only game in town, the only promise of longevity available to her species. Chemical rejuve could only do so much and was absurdly expensively. Cosmetic surgery, gene juice, steroids—all these options paled against the regenerative power of the virus. She had made the right decision.

A tidal wave of well-being surged up from her diaphragm, pushing her up and back into her seat. She tensed with alarm but forced herself to relax. She lay back and closed her eyes. She could feel her body tingling, every cell alive and kicking. Mitochondria, she had read, the target vesicles of the virus. She had never felt her mitochondria before. The thought made her smile, and she realized with a start that she was *already* smiling, grinning with elation like a fool on drugs. She barked a laugh.

So this was it, joy like a river. Pretty cool.

Niko drifted, delirious with a strange sensation of invincibility. She was being actively regenerated by the aliens. She could feel it. She *knew* it from within, by some new form of communication, some intuitive power.

Her surveillance alarm chirped three quick signals from somewhere in the distance, and she swam up through layers of perception and cognition to reach surface awareness. She opened her eyes and checked her wrist monitor. Her webcam showed three men at her front door. Damn. Just when she was getting a good buzz.

She apped for a webcam zoom on the three figures to check for guns. Nothing obvious, but really who would pull a gun on the street in suburbia? She apped the time, 4:49 p.m. Soon there would be returning commuter traffic.

They weren't dressed like cops but that didn't mean much these days. And why three? One man at the door might be selling insurance or some other scam. Two might be selling religion. But three meant nothing but trouble. Three could be an interrogator with two witnesses, or a point-man with backup. She had a bad feeling.

She apped for a full motion scan and got two hits in the backyard. She focused her cameras. Damn. Two goons with trank rifles inside her perimeter. Double damn. These guys were corporate hirelings, a mercenary squad. They had come to collect her for some reason. She reeled through recent memory in search of an explanation. Why her? She was not in play at the moment. She was supposed to be on vacation. Who might want her captured or dead? Sure, she had made adversaries in the past, but never by direct intent. Competition was just a natural part of doing business, playing out a temporary role. Next month her enemies might be partners in crime. Why kill off a talented worker?

Niko jumped up and made her way to the half-garage where she stored her dirt bike. She shouldered the door ajar and checked her red beauty. She started through her checklist as a knock sounded at the front door. At least they were being polite. Their delay in busting down the door would give her a good sense of the seriousness of her predicament, but she did not wait to clock them against the national average. She had an escape route for just such an occasion, a tunnel under her backyard that she and Rix had rigged and tested many times. A trap door on the edge of her property swung down on a five-second delay and served as a launch ramp onto the side street.

She could be on the freeway in ninety seconds or off-road in the bush in three minutes.

She keyed her bike and kicked it to life as she pulled on her helmet. She gave it some throttle for quick heat and checked her wrist monitor. The goons had heard the noise and were looking toward the half-garage. One had pulled out a pistol.

Never mind, she would be gone in five . . .

She palmed a red plastic button on the wall and kicked into gear.

Four . . . three . . .

The bike accelerated down a dark tunnel underground and swerved back up into pitch black.

Two . . . one . . .

The trap door fell with a thin coat of sod overtop and Niko launched up the ramp into the open sky. The bike revved frictionless for a second and landed, spurting dirt and gravel as Niko gunned it down the side street. A projectile whistled past her head.

What an irony to be killed only minutes after becoming Eternal. She hated goons. Without conscience, they were automatons to duty. They were relentless, implacable. She could never go back home.

She downshifted and swerved around the first corner to get out of scope sight. Her bike screamed as she accelerated, and she barely noticed the spike line on the road as her front tire was instantly punctured. She hurtled up over the handlebars and felt a horrid weightlessness as she flew headfirst through the air. Asphalt came up quickly to meet her. She tucked and landed hard on the back of her helmet, tried to roll with it, and slammed her spine flat on the pavement. She slid butt-first on her tailbone and shoulder blades and flailed her arms to regain stability.

A swirl of sparkles obscured her vision as she stared at the sky. Clouds, she thought as she tried to focus, to keep in the game. She reached up and pulled off her helmet, pushed it away. A rifle pointed into her face.

"Nice move, hotshot."

Niko heard the voice but could not seem to locate the source. Every attempt to turn her head brought spasms in her neck like knife blades. Finally point-man came into view over her. "Are you damaged goods, or what?"

He was suntanned, thirtyish, wearing a black peaked cap and collared shirt with a crosshatch pattern. His blue eyes studied her intently.

"My back," she grunted. "What do you want with me?"

"You're Eternal. We're a collection agency."

"Vampires?"

"A cosmetics firm, if you must know. Just lie still for a moment. We'll wait for a stretcher while my team cleans up the evidence. You want to keep the bike? It looks pretty mangled."

"Did you plant the virus in my condo? Hoping that I would take it?"

"Me? Hardly." He shook his head. "It comes from the aliens."

"How could you possibly know it was there?"

"Wormholes." Point-man looked away, scanning for onlookers, keeping to business. He seemed satisfied and gave a complicated hand signal to a compatriot in the distance.

Niko called his attention back. "What do you mean?"

"We have geeks who monitor for wormholes. They give us the coordinates, we collect the goods. Teams of geeks, actually. Tachyons and some shit like that."

"No way."

"You got a better explanation, sweetheart?"

Niko tried to sit up and was rewarded with pain. She winced and pressed her lower lip between her teeth. Her left leg trembled.

"You just lie still, girl," point-man cooed, his voice softening with empathy. "Don't get us both in trouble for no good reason. You made your play, and a damn fine one it was too. Best I've seen. Almost like you knew we were coming." He grinned, not bothering to point out the obvious, that only a criminal would have an underground escape route. "Anyway, you'll be fine. Don't worry. Your blood only gets top dollar for the first few weeks while the regeneration is strongest. Then you'll be second-tier for a few months and depending on market conditions you might get out of the lab for an afternoon in the courtyard. After that, the virus will be just plain old street-level Eternal, good only for the black market and the snake-oil shysters. You'll have the run of the prison."

"You can't kidnap me without a warrant!"

"Kidnap? That's rich. You should have thought this through before getting hopped up, honey. You don't have any rights now. You're an evolutionary terrorist!"

A grey cube van pulled up beside them, no flashing lights, no markings, and a young medic jumped out.

"We need a neck brace and board for this one," said point-man. "Careful with the merchandise. Drug her for transport."

Niko could barely move her eyes because of incoming pain. Her brain was beginning to relax out of shock mode, finally letting reality have its cruel way. A plastic mask fell over her nose and mouth, and she struggled to turn her face away. Her neck was completely paralyzed, her spine like a rod of iron. She made a noise of agony between gritted teeth, but eventually had to take a breath.

The mosquitoes were thick, the air damp now that the sun had dropped below the treetops. Mia had a shirt draped over her head and wrapped around her neck to keep the bugs from biting her throat. Zak was breaking trail ahead of her with a hatchet.

"We're going in circles," Mia complained.

Zak stopped and looked at his wife. She reminded him of a pious woman in a burka, a tall statue wreathed in fabric, a saint. A cloud of bugs hovered around her like a halo. They seemed to like her especially. Pheromones perhaps, some sort of mosquito magnet in her metabolism. He checked the horizon. The sun was blocked by clouds, but he thought he could detect a faint glow in the west.

"I don't think so." He pulled off a peaked cap and wiped his shirt sleeve across his forehead. "There should be a public side road due west. If we drift too far north we'll hit a beaver swamp." He knew the aerial photographs. His life had depended on it many times.

"What's to the south?"

"Bush never-ending."

"Great." Mia's voice dripped more than the usual sarcasm. She was getting weary.

"Let's take a snack break," Zak said. He slung off his pack and sat on it.

Mia dropped her own burden to the ground and pulled out a bag of red berries. She took a handful and passed it to him. They had been eating cranberries three times a day for almost a week, and roasting clams from the lake for morning protein. The plentiful berries were crunchy and tart on the tongue, but rich in Vitamin C and other essential nutrients. Zak worried about her folic acid requirements, critical for the developing babe in her belly, and had forced her to eat a dandelion leaf earlier in the day. They were surrounded by a jungle of green vegetation, but neither of them knew which trees might be edible and which not. Besides, by the time the cranberries were out the frost was not far behind. Time to head back south for the winter, back to the supermarkets and crime in the streets. Back to the vampires that hunted them perpetually.

"How's the baby?"

"Quit worrying. She's not going anywhere."

"She?"

Mia smiled, impish. She waved bugs away from her azure eyes. A few strands of blond hair peeked out from her makeshift burka. She looked beautiful. "I hear a car," she said.

Zak jumped to his feet and froze. He began to rotate his head, trying to pinpoint direction. Tires crunched on a gravel road, northwest, by his reckoning. He sat back down and smiled. "What's the first thing you want from civilization?"

"A flush toilet."

"Really?"

"I would kill a small animal for a flush toilet."

They had trapped and eaten a rabbit earlier in the week, cooked over an open fire, so it was no empty promise. She had an unlucky rabbit's foot in her pack as a souvenir.

"What about you?"

"A frosty mug of beer."

"Beer gives you gas."

"All right, scratch that. How about a grilled steak with mushrooms and onions?"

"I'll puke if I eat another mushroom."

"Okay, lobster dipped in garlic butter."

"Now you're talking. The most expensive thing on the menu."

"That's my girl."

Mia laughed and it sounded like a symphony in Zak's ears. He loved to hear her laugh. He wished they could live carefree like this forever.

Mia stood and towered over him. She was thin but not gaunt, full-breasted with long legs, her face Nordic, proud. She was a conquering Viking and could kill a man with her bare hands. She had been trying to teach him martial arts on the beach during their long weeks at the cabin, but his chi was still klutzy.

"Let's go," she said. "There's a flush toilet out there somewhere."

Zak picked up his hatchet and began slashing his way through the undergrowth in the general direction of the road. Within five minutes they had broken through into a clearing, jumped a drainage ditch, and found a hill of man-made rubble on top of which, perched like a gleaming trophy, sat a black stretch limousine.

They climbed up the rocks, grunting and slipping on loose stones, and stood on the crushed-gravel roadway. The limo gleamed like a dream car. Nevada plates. A driver got out of the front and put on his duty hat as he approached.

"Are you Zakariah Davis?" he asked.

Zak faltered for a moment at the surrealism, but shrugged off his pack and offered a handshake in greeting. "I am," he said and gave the driver a confident grip. "How did you find us?"

"GPS on the dash." He thumbed over his shoulder toward the vehicle. He looked toward Mia and pinched the rim of his cap. "Ev'ning, ma'am."

Mia looked at him wide-eyed, squinted over at her husband and back to the driver. She marched toward the limo without a word.

Zak pursed his lips and nodded. The Nevada plates gave it away—old Jimmy had been banned from every casino in the state. His former partner had bugged him and kept him on the radar all this time. Probably a subcutaneous chip. He remembered back to their last engagement, which had ended badly. Zak fingered the burnt stub of cable behind his left ear, the charred memento of his encounter with the Beast in V-space. He remembered his father, Phillip, brain-dead and burnt after getting caught hacking Prime Level Seven. Jimmy had probably planted a bug in the remnant of cable as he cut Zak free from the cybersphere. Jimmy always played all the angles.

"You guys coming along?" Mia asked.

The driver turned and pointed the key to pop the trunk for her. He motioned with his head for Zak to follow. They stowed their gear in the back as the driver opened side doors for them. Suicide doors, a rare, vintage touch—doors that swung wide in opposite directions with no post in between.

"This car was used in a Hollywood movie," the driver said with pride, puffed up with his small claim to fame. "A stuntman drove a sports car through the opening while topless girls sunbathed on the roof."

"Awesome," Mia said as she stepped into the roomy interior. Two black leather couches faced each other, one with a mini-bar tucked between cushioned backrests.

"Got any food?" Zak asked.

"Champagne and chocolate eclairs," the driver said.

Light finally dawned for Mia. "Old Jimmy?"

"Mister Kay wanted you to be comfortable. He gave me two thousand dollars cash for new clothes and incidentals."

"I can handle that," Mia said.

Zak looked down his nose at his wife, frowning. "You had champagne with Jimmy?"

"It was a bargaining technique. You were offplanet, lost in space. I was trying to find you, remember?"

"Gee, what else did you bargain with?"

"Shut up, you jerk. You're such a chauvinist. You never would have said that if we had a female driver."

"Oh, yeah?"

"Yeah."

Zak thought for a moment. "You're probably right."

"I take it you guys are married," the driver said.

Mia laughed. "Ya think?"

The driver reached in to open the mini-bar. "The eclairs are really just bowties, but it was the best I could do out in the boonies. Fresh this morning."

"You did well," Mia said as she peeked inside.

"And the champagne is Canadian. I hope that's okay."

"I love Canada," Mia said as she pulled out the bottle and handed it to Zak. "Blue job."

Several wine goblets hung from a ceiling rack. Zak offered one to the driver but he declined and closed the suicide doors with a quiet click of precise workmanship. He climbed in the front seat. The cork popped noisily but the bottle did not overflow. Zak filled one glass with bubbly froth and splashed a ceremonial taste in the other for his pregnant wife as the motor thrummed to life.

"Where are we headed?" he shouted back over his shoulder.

"Niagara Falls," came the reply. "Mr. Kay's penthouse apartment."

Zak turned back to his wife with his goblet held high to match his eyebrows. "To the honeymoon capital of the world," he said in toast and clinked her glass with a clarion ring.

They sipped their drinks and sighed with satisfaction. Mia settled back in her comfy couch and stretched with languor. She cocked one hiking boot upon the other as she crossed her ankles. "Stop at the first flush toilet, please," she said.

Niko woke to find her head squeezed between foam pads, her left arm and shoulder solidly secured. She opened her eyes to see an IV bag dripping relentlessly above her. A female doctor stood beside her bed, still holding the syringe that had apparently brought her back to life. She wore standard hospital greens with a name tag: Lucy Itel. Brown hair cut short, brown eyes like searchlights.

"Where am I?"

The effort of talking seemed arduous, using all available energy. She had never felt so weak. There was no point in even trying to move, for nausea hovered over her like choking fog.

"You're in a safe place. There is no need to worry. I'm Dr. Itel. I'm managing the clinic. We have a large staff, so don't be alarmed at the changing faces around you."

Memories came back to Niko: the goons with guns, the bike accident. She glanced down at the crook of her arm and saw the red tube snaking out of her skin. She groaned. "Vampires."

Dr. Itel offered a professional smile, displaying perfect white teeth. "I woke you up to assure you of your safety. Your brainwave activity was alarmingly active for a sleep state. I was worried that you might be having night trauma."

"You're killing me," Niko said.

"No, you're far too valuable for that. They always take too much the first day, I know. I have spoken about this in committee many times." She shrugged her helplessness in the face of mindless bureaucracy. "The connoisseurs pay extra."

Niko groaned again. "I bet that's what they said to George Washington the night they bled him to death." She closed her eyes against a wave of dizziness. She felt withered and desiccated. God, they were draining her blood dry.

"I know it's difficult the first few weeks. We're pumping you with nutrients to compensate. Steroids, stimulants, the works. The standard regime is to take blood only at night while you sleep. You will be free to walk the grounds during the day. Three meals a day, media downloads."

"I need to plug up."

"Yes, I see you're wired for Prime, but that won't be possible. We have intranet into a vast library to satisfy your addiction. You're not the first wirehead we've seen. But you do have some innovative cerebral modifications." She checked her databoard. "Optical enhancement, biochips in the hippocampus, augmentation of the corpus callosum . . . and you don't seem to have any digital dossier. No retinal print records, no health history or credit rating, no bank accounts. I'm looking forward to finding out more about you after you get stabilized."

Niko felt like a laboratory mouse, trapped and broken, completely at the mercy of mad scientists from hell. Soon they would begin probing her brain, excising bits of tissue to monitor the sadistic result, just another illegal clone on the slab. She needed help. She had to plug up to the V-net, get back to basics. She felt the urge to vomit and made a feeble attempt. Imprisoned in this neck brace, she would probably choke on her own bile and die.

"Easy, easy," Dr. Itel crooned and rubbed Niko's forehead above the bridge of her nose. She reached over with her other hand and closed a valve in the bloodline. "That's enough for now. I'll take some heat for the moment. You've got two fractured vertebrae, but no permanent damage. You're young and strong and have the physique of a gymnast. Your body is already regenerating with the virus. Don't worry, you'll live forever here."

# Two

T he limo pulled up in front of a sixteen-storey building gilded in the setting sun with burning chrome and glass, a blazing emblem misted with fog from the Horseshoe Falls on the Canadian side of the city. The driver, Maurice, carried their packs to the front entrance and palmed a sensor to unlock the door. "Take the elevator to the top and then up one flight of stairs to the penthouse. Mr. Kay has the entire top floor."

"Nice relocation," Zak said and juggled paper shopping bags to offer a handshake. "Thanks for your hospitality."

"No problem, sir. Mr. Kay speaks very highly of you." They shook hands with a firm grip and Maurice turned to Mia. His hand went to the brim of his cap for a formal nod, but Mia pre-empted him with a full-armed hug instead, tipping up a shiny high heel in show for her husband. She had purchased a brown business tunic, dressy but showing cleavage, and tight beige leggings that hugged every muscle. She looked fabulous.

Maurice kept his eyes downcast in duty for the webcam record, but grinned openly at her display of affection. Mia picked up a backpack in each hand and Zak followed with his burden of shopping bags, watching her every movement with wonder at her transformation to civilized decorum. Her thighs had grown thinner after long weeks starving in the wilderness. She'd have to bulk up for the baby.

"Zak, my brother," Jimmy said at the door. "I trust you had a nice vacation, very romantic. I heard you were on your way." He swept his arms grandly to usher them inside a spacious foyer. Glowing Roman columns set into the walls provided soft light and a subdued ceremonial ambience.

"I bet," Zak muttered.

"Mia, so wonderful to see you again." He bussed her cheek innocently enough, like an uncle or close colleague. He looked good for a non-Eternal, still spry in his sixties. Probably on rejuve by now, maybe a closet blood user. Bald, shorter than Mia and gnomish, he carried himself with grace and dignity befitting his current station— he was filthy rich and adequately laundered.

Zak set his shopping bags against the wall. "What's with the stairs up from the elevator and the metal screening on the doors?"

"Faraday cage. I had it custom built, the whole top floor. No electromagnetics in or out."

"You running your own black lab now?"

"Very sensitive stuff."

"So keep me guessing."

Jimmy put his arm around Zak's shoulder. "Walk with me," he said. "Mia, there's a bottle of Chardonnay on ice at the bar, if you will be so kind."

"She's not drinking now," Zak said. "She's pregnant."

"What?" Jimmy dropped his arm and turned back to check her expression.

"Unconfirmed," she told him.

"Holy shit! How did that happen?"

She blushed. "Uh . . ."

"No, no, sorry, I didn't mean anything. It's just such a surprise. A joy, really." Jimmy paused, his mind working like lightning always. He squinted at Zak. "Are you still available for work?"

"What kind of work?"

"I'll pour the wine and find some juice for myself," Mia said to excuse herself. "And thanks for the outfit, by the way."

"It looks better on you than on any runway in Europe, I daresay."

His tactics were all too familiar. Jimmy recovered quickly and always stayed on top of any new situation. He was an expert in manipulating people for his own purposes and Zak felt a strange foreboding. "So what's the gig?"

"Digital steroids."

"Oh yeah?"

"Picotech for the brain. Site-specific neuromodulators. Completely legal, or at least not illegal yet. This is a product for the raging populace, not just the wireheads. Anyone can use it."

"What do you need me for?"

Jimmy clucked with benevolence. "You always have to cut to the chase. Aren't you interested in the technological breakthroughs? The years of sacrifice by untold numbers of research minions?"

"Maybe later. Just give me the quick and dirty before Mia gets back."

Jimmy surrendered his palms up. "I'm trapped by fame, Zak. I can't zoom Prime without flocks of paparazzi. I can't get to Sublevel Zero without a team of greysuits on my ass. Word is out that I hacked the Beast. I'm a celebrity because of you and Phillip. All I did was lay down the hardware and cook some white magic and now I've sacrificed my anonymity."

"Looks like you've done okay for yourself."

"Phillip was right. Money is a millstone on a chain." He winked to show he was half-kidding, but only half.

"So you need a runner."

"I need a partner, Zak. The black labs are spawning Prime Level Eight. It's happening, man. It's your destiny."

"People say that to me all the time."

"With good reason. What else are you going to do? Retire in suburbia? No way. You're a gamer at heart. You were born to hack V-space, to tame the Beast."

"I've been burned four times and mindwiped once."

"We can fix that. Custom wetware installation, the best surgeons on the market."

"No GPS chip this time?"

Jimmy spread his hands with innocence. "Hey, I was just tagging your corpses, getting ready to split a bad scene—you and your father sitting there with barbecued brains. I wanted to make sure you got a proper burial, that's all. How was I to know you were ever going to wake up?"

"Where's Phillip now?"

"He's at home in one of his rejuve clinics. He's coming along fine."

Mia returned with two wineglasses, and with the backdrop of luxury behind her and new clothes draping her frame, Zak was struck again by the sudden change in their circumstance. Two days ago they had been eating nuts and berries and swatting mosquitoes, grovelling for food like animals.

Both men fell silent in her presence.

"How's Rix?" Mia asked.

Jimmy accepted a glass from her with a nod of thanks. "The kid's doin' okay. He's working at the ERI, learning the ropes, running the V-net for them. It's still illegal for an Eternal to buy food, but he's keeping out of trouble. He has the Davis gift going for him. He's already one of the best on their team. I've been keeping tabs on him as promised."

"You don't owe me anything, Jimmy," she said. "The past is behind us."

He sipped his drink. His eyes darted to Zak and back to her. "I appreciate hearing that from you."

"We can all deal on level ground now, right? All three of us." She handed Zak a glass of chilled Chardonnay.

"The space-time continuum is curved, Mia. There's no such thing as level ground."

"You know what I mean."

"I promised you once that I would not deceive you," Jimmy said, "and I'll reiterate that promise now if that's what you want."

"Fine, I'll promise the same to you," Mia said.

"And I," said Zak. He lifted his wine glass in salute.

"Great. I love this. Stay a few days." Jimmy swept his arms with genuine enthusiasm. "It's a five-bedroom hovel with a fully stocked larder. What do you say? We'll talk about old times and plan your beautiful futures together."

Husband and wife looked at each other, passing marital telepathy in an instant.

"Sure," Mia said and reached to put an arm around Zak's waist. She clutched him tight, a bit too tight. She wanted to know what the hell was going on.

"Glorious," Jimmy exclaimed. "I'll order room service for a pregnancy test."

He dreamed of snakes, writhing black snakes, and an afterimage of dragons haunted his vestige of consciousness. He could smell burning and nothing else, burning neurons, burning plastic effigies of false gods. He heard a pulse of drums in the distance and a noise of didgeridoos around an aboriginal fire, of coiled springs letting go cosmic resonance.

Niko plugged up and found herself in a library vestibule, a cold and featureless virtual domain. A woman sat at a desk before her, a cheap, multiracial avatar with pixelated features. She wore a white button-up blouse that seemed to glow with black-light fluorescence, eerie and purplish against the dark background. Her body did not extend below the desk.

"Are you the central nexus?" Niko asked.

"I am the Head Librarian." Her lips did not move in synch with the sound.

Animation right out of the box! Niko grimaced. The vampires spent millions on medical technology but their library was a joke. Niko's own avatar, augmented with every affordable upgrade on and off the white market, stood like a superhero in a shantytown, as solid and detailed as a real person. "How often do you upgrade your data?"

"We upgrade periodically. We have no fixed schedule."

That was all Niko needed to know. She didn't want to go on record with anything specific. "I'm looking for sex," she said.

The librarian continued to stare at her blankly. "Vidi, feelie, or text?"

"Uh, feelie."

The librarian's eyelids closed like shutters and her eyeballs appeared to tumble underneath like rolling dice as data began to stream. She reminded Niko of an antique slot machine with whirring mechanical cylinders, spinning, spinning, waiting for good fortune and mathematical grace. A few seconds passed and the librarian's eyes popped open again. Just eyeballs again, no lucky sevens.

"Your search parameters are too wide. Sorry, please try again."

"Pornography, feelie."

The librarian's eyes blinked and three doors appeared to Niko's right side, green phosphorescent outlines with glowing green doorknobs, a white sign on each with black lettering: *Oral*, *Anal*, *Fetish*. Ouch—apparently all the normal sex had gone Hollywood ages ago. She had to get out of prison somehow, and this seemed her only avenue of escape. She had to get back on her bike again in the fresh mountain air, or meander down a sluggish river in a quiet canoe. She needed freedom in the wilderness to feel human again.

Niko chose the Fetish door and opened it, hoping the contents would be the least offensive of the three. She was looking for an old-school computer virus that was historically notorious in this genre. Adware, smallware, perhaps an ancient tunnel worm. She hoped to find a self-replicating viral code and reprogram it to send a message to Rix. If she primed it right, her digital hitchhiker would jump to whatever interface the library used to upgrade their data. If they logged onto the V-net for even a second or two, her message would get out. If they used a disk or memory stick, her malware would infect it like a venereal disease (how appropriate) and jump from interface to interface until it reached V-space, where it would multiply and spread until a cybertracker washed it clean.

The room was small, hardly more than a hallway lined on both sides with glowing virtual banks of library data arranged like books on shelves. Touch-sensitive titles offered all manner of sexual perversity from innocuous to insane. Most seemed pretty disgusting to Niko, but nothing she hadn't seen freely offered on Sublevel Zero on the V-net since her youth. She switched to source-code view and began scanning for executable subsystems that might be used to her benefit. It was tedious work, searching through threads of machine code like spirals of linguini, but she found two usable worms and picked the most robust to use as raw material.

She customized her malware from mnemonic data, basic hacker 101 stuff, and attached a simple message. It might go everywhere or nowhere, but there was no point in being overly cryptic. She was a desperate girl and even this relatively simple task was draining her cognitive abilities in her weakened, anaemic state. The human brain needed more blood than any other organ and rightfully so. Her sugar levels were getting low and failing; she could feel it. Almost done.

She slipped back to standard view and activated the feelie—and found herself watching a grown woman in red lingerie pretending to enjoy being paddywhacked with a black spatula. Niko was the male model in the drama, as real as real could be. She could feel the kinesthetics of his/her moving arm, the air movement on his/her skin, the resistance as the paddle met firm flesh with a noisy snap, a pendulous weight between his/her legs that she dared not glance down at. The woman moaned with pleasure and begged for more, hopefully faking it for the sake of art, but Niko couldn't get into it. A few seconds was enough to get her computer virus active in the system, so she clicked off and returned to the librarian.

"I'd like to order some recent material for your next data upgrade," she said.

"Vidi, feelie, or text?"

"Text. I'd like the current issue of the *Journal of Neuroscience* and something recent from the American Spinal Injury Association." A reasonable request surely, given her present physical condition.

"Your request has been recorded."

Good, get the wheels in motion. "When should I check back? Tomorrow? The next day?"

"Two days."

"Fine, thank you for your time." It seemed pointless to thank a flawed automaton like this poor excuse for animation, but Niko always made it a practice. You never knew when you might bump into an authentic avatar, a fellow wirehead. It was common courtesy in her estimation, an unspoken etiquette among the elite.

She signalled her exit and found herself staring at the ceiling in her prison room, her head trapped in a neck brace and her blood dripping into a refrigerated bottle under her bed. She smiled. A faint hope was better than no hope at all.

"*Closing the synaptic gap.* How does that sound for a tagline?" Jimmy stood in front of a panoramic view of mist and thundering water lit by red and green searchlights, the sky a twinkling black blanket above. They had enjoyed a wonderful dinner that evening at a revolving restaurant high above the exotic cityscape, surf and turf with champagne, spinning away the time, soaking up luxury like a sponge.

Zak cocked his head askance at the thought. "Well, it's a bit misleading."

"Why's that?" asked Mia, who had recently been brought into their confidence, the two wireheads having decided that some straight thinking and feminine intuition might give them valuable perspective. She sipped her ginger ale.

"The chemical structure of the brain is hardwired," Zak said. "You can't monkey with it. Any change in the space between axons and dendrites is bound to be lethal. No matter what colour the skin, or where the geographic origin, the structure of the human brain is the same for everybody."

"Really? That is *so* global village."

"See?" Jimmy said. "She didn't know. Nobody studies the basics of neuroscience any more. Everyone thinks their brains are just plug 'n' play. What we need is some advertising sleight of hand, not boring science."

"Somebody will sue us," Zak insisted.

"Nobody is going to measure the synaptic cleft without an electron microscope. No one can prove us wrong. That is precisely why this gig is going to work so well. The whole field of chemical cognitive enhancement is mired in litigation. Companies are having massive problems meeting testing requirements, fighting the damn placebo effect. All they are trying to do is add more spice to the glutamate stew. What we are offering is completely different. Simple prosthetics for the brain—site-specific cybernetic neurons. Robotics, not medicine. By the time the courts catch up with us, we'll be rich."

"You're already rich, Jimmy," Mia said.

He smiled, rubbed a hand over his bald pate. "It's never enough. Besides, we've got to provide for you guys. You're not getting any younger."

Zak held up a finger like a referee pointing out a technicality. "Actually we are getting younger. Every morning."

"Oh yeah." Jimmy turned to Mia. "But what about the baby? He's going to need all kinds of baby accessories. Highchairs and stuff."

"She."

"Really?"

Mia smiled, the impish pixie again.

"She's kidding," Zak said. "We're not doing a genscan. We're taking our chances."

"What about preventable disease?"

Mia stabbed her hands on her hips. "DNA therapy is only available prior to implantation. We've already committed to a natural pregnancy. Our only option now would be abortion."

Jimmy saw hackles rising and quickly ducked his chin. "Well, can't they operate in the womb these days?"

Mia shook her head grimly. "I haven't got a valid health card, remember? I'm a social pariah."

Jimmy nodded. "Tough call."

"Besides, I have the Eternal virus. My baby will have all the benefits of cellular regeneration until birth."

"Right on." Jimmy brightened. "He'll be a superbaby. A comic-book hero."

"She," Mia insisted.

"What about *Building better brains?*" Zak said.

Jimmy rubbed a grey bristle of goatee on his chin. "That sounds too good to be true. Somebody's probably using it already. I'll have to google the trademark data."

"I think it's brilliant," Mia said and gave Zak a peck on the cheek. "I'm off to the girls' room. Nature calls, right on schedule."

Zak watched her saunter away like a proud lioness with a long mane of blond hair. Even in the woods she had brimmed with charisma, dressed in rags and half-starving. Now she was wearing designer jeans that hugged her body like . . .

He noticed Jimmy chuckling and shaking his head. Married for what? Eighteen years? And still a lovesick puppy dog.

"We need test subjects," Jimmy said.

"How close to a release date are we?"

"We haven't actually done human testing."

Zak nodded. So the scheme was still on ground level. "What's the plan?"

"I was thinking we should use Eternals. Then if anything was off-kilter, we could know without doing any permanent harm."

"Because they would regenerate."

"Exactly."

"You're thinking the ERI."

Jimmy winked his affirmation. "It's a natural. Your son is working there, along with your former soul sister."

"Soul sister? Are you kidding? Helena hates me."

"But you've been through heaven and hell together. You shared an avatar for weeks and you can't get much more intimate than that. You travelled through the Macpherson Doorway together. The story says you met the aliens face to face before your mindwipe."

Zak sighed at the reminder of his missing clocktime, the black hole in his brain where the memories had been sucked dry. "So the story goes."

"It's worth a try, man. It looks like destiny."

"I betrayed her, Jimmy. We got in over our heads. I was responsible for her brain burn from the Beast."

"Well, that's a debatable question. Anyway she's recovered completely. I talked to her last week up Prime."

"What?"

Jimmy held up a stop sign with his palm. "No, no, I didn't tell her anything. I shared some obscure research data, picked her brain. The ERI is selling blood on the black market to meet their payroll."

Zak hung his head, feeling numbness in his lungs at the bad news.

His son Rix in another difficult situation—would the perpetual crisis never end?

"We could offer them a piece of the action. That's all I'm saying."

"I hear you."

"Just think about it."

Jimmy smiled with assurance. He only said those four words when he knew he had won, when he knew the deal was in his virtual briefcase. The two partners had that communal understanding and the truth gave them comfort in a way. It was just one of the small things they took for granted after all those decades running Sublevel Zero for pocket change.


Paperwork. Rix hated it. He'd rather be out on his bike picking up illegal supplies or running the V-net for biochips. He'd rather be in an online school tutorial. Anything but this hopeless clutter on his desk. Who used paper anymore? Everything was supposed to be digital now.

Paper can't be hacked, Dr. Mundazo was fond of saying. Paper doesn't end up being plastered in the cybersphere like a concert poster. Whatever.

He picked up a sheet. RSI Stochastics. Moving Average Crossovers. Some accountant was charting the black-market price for Eternal blood, predicting financial catastrophe. The economy was in downtrend, the environment was at risk, the usual stuff. Rix couldn't understand the arcane mathematics of the chartist. And what did it matter in the end? He was tithing his litre of plasma a week like everyone else. What more did they want?

He tossed it and picked up another, a memo from the new Security Chief, Dimitri Sanov, asking for authorization to purchase guns. Modified AK-47 assault rifles, the request already stamped for approval by the Director.

Oh, no. Rix shook his head, feeling his heart sink to new depths of despair. He was a pacifist at heart—most Eternals were once acclimatized to permanent regeneration, the so-called immortality complex—but not Dimitri. He was from Kazakhstan and had served in the local armed forces as a field technician until he got the virus. Now he wanted to kick ass for the aliens.

Rix knew that if the ERI purchased weapons they would inevitably be used on civilians. People would die, even if they used nerve tranks. Collateral damage, that old saw of legitimacy. He hated the whole idea but was too low on the totem pole to make any difference. He didn't know why they bothered to send him these inter-office memos in the first place.

His wrist buzzed a message and he checked the text, a summons from the Director, Helena Sharp. A meeting upstairs in her penthouse office with the Executive Board in five minutes.

Holy crap, he was still dressed in his pyjamas!

He jumped up and raced to his bedroom. He stripped and pulled on a pair of khaki pants. No time to hunt for underwear. He sniffed a shirt and pulled it over his head—an ERI t-shirt with the corp logo on the left breast along with the words *I'm from the Future.* He checked his face in the bathroom mirror. Three days' worth of patchy black stubble that looked like a skin disease.

Great.

He tossed a bright red scarf around his neck for a distraction and headed for the elevator. Turned back for shoes, but all he could find were paper lab slippers.

No time.

"So nice of you to join us," Helena said as he made it to her penthouse suite a few minutes late. He ducked his head and dived for the back of the room, safely out of the line of fire. A group was milling around in front of the Director's desk, some whispering to each other, some checking their wrist monitors. He counted twelve heads. The entire Executive. Holy crap.

Dimitri Sanov turned toward him for a squinty-eyed inspection, but cracked a smile and nodded in greeting. Rix was the only person younger than him in the room. Some sort of Russian protocol, perhaps. No one else bothered to notice him.

Helena leaned against her desk with her arms folded in front of her as she surveyed the crowd. She had not dressed for the boardroom by a long shot. She rarely did. Rix had seen her only rarely, but she tended to look more like a grandmother than a paladin of commerce. Today she wore a casual knit shirt with an open blouse overtop, dark skirt to the knee and fashionable black pumps with enough heel to make Rix think she was going for the sex thing, which seemed absurd for an octogenarian even if she did look forty-nine and holding well.

She carried her chin up with the confidence of a rightful queen. She had been through the Macpherson Doorway to the Cromeus colonies, she had monitored Zak's face-to-face meeting with the aliens, and she was the only human in history to have contracted the Eternal virus without blood contact. She had hacked Prime Level Seven and got burned by the Beast. Everyone knew she was top dog.

"Our spam filters picked up a message today," she said. "Over fifty copies came in, carried by some new worm trojan. This is it." She pointed a finger diode and a flatscreen monitor came to life on her desk. She stepped aside to offer everyone a clear view. White text on a bluescreen background: *Nikonikoniko Rix I need your help vampires have tech to monitor wormholes from the Source trapped me at birth a cosmetics firm by day bloodsuckers every night help me Rix Nikonikoniko*

"What is that? Japanese origin?" said someone up front.

"Nikon Cameras?"

"Could be Konika Systems."

"It's Niko," Rix said.

The waters parted in front of him like a Bible story as the room went silent. The Director peered at him as though he was the only other cognitive being in the world. "Who's Niko?"

"My cousin. Sort of. More like a step-cousin."

"You know her?"

"Yeah, sure."

"The message was addressed to you. Can she be regarded as a credible witness?"

All eyes were on him now. He felt a drop of sweat trickle down the crack of his ass. No underwear. "I guess so. If the message is legit."

"It's not legit. It's spam. I want you to read it over and tell me what it means to you in teenage speak."

Rix swallowed and focused his attention. He read it again, feeling like a schoolboy. *Nikonikoniko Rix I need your help vampires have tech to monitor wormholes from the Source trapped me at birth a cosmetics firm by day bloodsuckers every night help me Rix Nikonikoniko.*

Holy crap, Niko had the Eternal virus!

He grimaced, flustered. The girl he loved was in trouble. His skin felt clammy and his stomach boiled with anxiety. He felt a surge of electrochemical agitation, the urge to punch something or run for safety. "Niko got the virus," he began unsteadily. "The vampires collected her 'at birth' because they have new technology to track the alien wormholes that transmit the vials. They're draining her blood . . ."

He choked. The girl he loved was lost and in danger.

". . . every night."

He looked down at his hands, watched them quiver. He might

never see Niko again now that she was trapped in a vampire den. He never should have let her out of his sight. He had an urge to cry but didn't dare risk it, not here, not now, not ever. Poor Niko. He sucked in a cruel breath to calm himself. "She wants my help, to rescue her during the day. The vampires are masquerading as a cosmetics firm somewhere." He curled his palms up and tapped his knuckles together. He didn't dare look up to meet the Director's eyes in such a vulnerable state.

Helena stepped forward and wrapped her arms around him. She was taller than him by an inch in her pumps, and strong. His head rested against her shoulder and stayed there. She smelled of herbal shampoo, a fruit salad of delight. She didn't say a word. She didn't embarrass him with anything mushy, thank god. This was bad enough already. He missed his mother for the first time in weeks.

The Director released him finally and looked him straight in the eye.

*We'll rescue her.*

Rix blinked in surprise. She had not spoken, but somehow had conveyed a message clearly. Body language? Non-verbal cues from her facial expression? Weird.

Helena Sharp cleared her throat to gather attention. "Gentlemen and ladies," she said over his shoulder, "we are in big trouble."

# Three

Niko tensed at the sound of gunfire. She was walking in a flagstone courtyard, trying to exercise stiffness out of her healing neck, when her reprieve came from heaven. *Clickity-click-clack*, automatic dart guns in the distance, storming the gates of doom. She put on her cloak of invincibility like a second skin and got to work.

The kid had saved her sexy ass, no doubt about it. Good old cousin Rix. The ERI would be using tranks like a bunch of wimps, but that was okay. Smaller footprint, less escalation. Besides, in here the only way to tell the guards from the inmates was to check for scabs on the inner arm.

She eyed the roof, checking for movement. She had a makeshift kite safely stowed up top, but getting to it unscathed was a problem area in her master plan. Everything depended on the guards in the crow's nest, five stories up. Three screws worked patrol by day, one lazy stoner in the evening. Could the ERI take the high ground? Tear gas? Choppers? Sure enough, she noticed puffs of smoke. Cool.

Niko raced for cover. Every moving target was at risk in an urban war. Goons with guns shooting crossfire. The last person standing would claim the spoils.

*Clickity-click-clack.*

Her heart began to race as adrenaline kicked in like a wonder drug. She felt fear, her faithful friend. Too many unknown variables, too much left to chance. Time seemed to stretch out like something malleable. She activated full auditory augmentation and primed herself for the sound of footsteps. No one could sneak up on her.

She danced into the cafeteria on her way to the nearest stairwell. The elevators would all be locked out in an emergency. A cook was standing behind the counter, unarmed and white as a spectre, watching the action on his wrist monitor. A few Eternals were sitting in plastic chairs looking grim and weary. A child was crouched under a table, her eyes wide with terror below dark ringlets, her cheeks stained with tears. Niko stopped to peer at her, feeling a sudden ache in her diaphragm. A helpless babe in the woods of war. She wondered if she could take the girl along, rescue her from trouble. Could she carry her down to street level on a kite made of bedsheets? She was just a toddler, probably weighed less than fifteen kilos. Niko shook her head. Too dangerous for both of them.

She bent down to her. "You'll be safe here. Don't try to run. The grownups will come in with guns. Just do what they say and don't be scared."

"Take me with you, Mommy," the girl said. How old was she, three or four? What heartless bastard would drain blood from a four-year-old? God help the ERI to get here first.

*Clickity-click-clack.*

"You'll be safe," Niko promised herself.

She jumped up and made for the stairwell. There was a metal firedoor at the bottom and she pressed her ear against it. Tinny voices vibrated from somewhere far away. Perhaps she could get up a floor or two unnoticed. She opened the door and raced up one flight of stairs.

A wave of dizziness caught up with her at the first landing. She leaned against the wall. Damn, she didn't have enough blood in her body. She needed more sugar in her brain. She dropped to her knees and put her forehead on the cold tile, took a deep breath.

Regenerate, she told herself. C'mon, work your alien science.

Footsteps sounded above, running down. Niko picked herself up, stepped quickly up another flight of stairs, and slipped quietly into the hallway beyond.

This was a dormitory area and several Eternals stood in the corridor.

"Niko, what's going on?" asked the nearest person, a Texan named John who had already put in months of captivity.

"Rescue attempt," Niko gasped. "Possibly the ERI." She braced herself against the wall, sucked for air.

"Should we make a break for it?"

"Are you strong enough?"

John was big-boned and bulky, a fighter. "Hell, yeah."

A group of Eternals had gravitated toward them.

"Out back by the garbage bins," she said. "I sawed through the clamps on the chain-link fence. One good push will do it." That had been her original plan before she put together enough material for a kite. She put her finger to her lips as footsteps grew louder in the stairwell. "Someone's coming," she whispered.

The Eternals dashed for doorways. A gun poked in past the firedoor, followed by the peering face of one of the guards. The gun swayed side to side and pulled back into the stairwell. Footsteps headed away.

"Let's go," John said as the group regathered at the door. Slowly and quietly they followed the guard down.

Niko watched them go and headed upstairs, pacing herself deliberately this time, step by step, breathing deep in her abdomen like a concert singer. Regenerate, regenerate, she subvocalized like a mantra.

She could not hear much gunfire. Perhaps the main battle was over already. Perhaps the ERI was using nerve gas or narcotics. The vampires had webcam surveillance, but a strategic assault would take out that technical advantage as a top priority. Niko was in no position to help. All she had were her bare hands.

The grey metal door to the rooftop was quiet. Niko could hear pigeons clucking and cooing on the other side. No noise of humans. She cracked the door and saw a guard lying face down on the gravel surface with saliva dribbling from his lips. She eased out and saw another in a fetal position. She checked the first one for a pulse in the neck and found a languid beat. Tranked.

She confirmed that the other was also incapacitated and made for her stash behind some wooden construction pallets. Her kite didn't look like much by the cruel light of day, just dirty bedsheets twisted around broom handles. She had quick second thoughts as she strapped it on, then third thoughts. From five storeys up, she could make quite a splat. Real colourful.

Niko peered over the ledge.

*Clickity-click-clack.* The battle was still raging. Good goons crouched behind parked cars. Bad goons were shooting from windows in the building. No traffic in the area and not much sound beyond the sporadic burst of gunfire. There should have been cops and ambulances by now, some show of civil authority. They were in a business district of warehouses and office buildings. Someone would call it in, surely. Perhaps the ERI was disrupting communication somehow. An electromagnetic resonance might take out everything but the shielded landlines, good old Ma Bell.

The wind was blowing from the west and not much to it. She

wondered if the midday heat might provide some lift from the acres of asphalt around her. She had settled on two easterly targets: a grassy area between two buildings or a low flat roof down the street. The grass looked greener, softer, but meant a tricky turn past a dome-covered atrium. She could just see herself hitting the skylight like a bug on a windshield. Real colourful.

She jumped and panicked for an instant with the first rush of weightlessness. She was only 120 pounds, but she fell like lead until her wings enveloped some air. She pulled against tension and veered away from the building. She had lost too much altitude already. Damn.

An updraft caught her as she cleared the shadow of the building. A few shots were fired, but a bullet hole or two would not alter her aerodynamics significantly. She wheeled toward her chosen target, feeling the familiar strain in her arms, feeling like she just might make it. Time seemed to warp to her benefit as she angled toward the dome, pulling her legs up, thinking small, thinking a tight payload on butterfly wings, hoping.

She hit the domed atrium a glancing blow, almost lost her stability, didn't feel a thing. Too much adrenaline, too much at stake. She landed in the grass and rolled in a tangle of fabric like a cocoon as her wing struts snapped like twigs around her. She shook off debris and stood woozily to her feet, grateful to be alive, and promptly puked up her breakfast.

The last of her nutrients lay in a puddle of bile on the grass. Her tongue tasted of acid and her gnawing stomach felt like an animal chewing its way out. Leaving her makeshift kite behind along with deep scuffs in the landscape like giant golf divots, Niko hurried away down the street, hardly able to walk a straight line. Exhausted, vertiginous, she needed food and water and a place to rest. She carried nothing but the clothes on her back—running shoes, blue jeans, and a black tunic. No money, no credit, no identification. Only one place left to go.


He lay in a dark place, a warm cave that sustained a feeble thread of hibernating consciousness. He could feel the phantom of his body, sensation in his outstretched legs, a palpable feeling of visceral good-will. Part pleasure, part pain, but nothing to define between the two. Contentment in a calm sea.

A pounding of tribal drums sounded from a shore far away where ancients held the secrets of scripture and danced to rites of mystery. A raging wind sounded above, rocking his fragile floating body with a gentle undulation. He drifted as in a womb, protected and secure.


"I'm here to see my father," Niko told the voice recognition software. She stood in the lobby of a red brick apartment building on the out-skirts of the city. She placed her eyeball on a retinal scanner and the lock released with a metallic thud.

She stepped past a glass door into a marble hallway with cut-glass chandeliers, a vestige of the last condominium craze. The building had been converted from residential to laboratory use for the most part, though most of the staff kept apartments on the upper floors. She owned the building, or would inherit it some day. The legal technicalities had become a corporate conundrum in the absence of Phillip's definitive death.

She took the elevator to the third floor and walked purposely down the hall. She stopped at an unmarked grey door and placed her eyeball on another retinal scanner. The lock clicked. She stepped inside.

Phillip lay protected by a glass enclosure, a germ-free sanctuary like an incubator. The top of his head and his right eye were covered by a neural helmet that fused seamlessly into a bioengineering computer with multiple monitors showing brain rhythms, magnetic resonance, oxygen content. His left arm, where his prosthetic computer interface had been burned away, was bandaged in a stump. She could hear the slow blip-blip of his pulse being recorded. She placed her fingers on the warm glass. "Papa," she whispered.

"You must be Niko," said a voice at the door.

She whirled to see a young man dressed all in white. White lab coat over white collared shirt and white cotton pants. White lab slippers on a white tiled floor. A beautiful angel.

"Dr. Ambridge . . ." he said, content to let her eyes examine him. "Andrew." He offered a palm.

She took his hand and gave it a firm shake. "That's right."

"No one else could have got this far past security. I usually meet dignitaries at the door." He smiled, boyish but with a smirk of confidence.

"It's an unscheduled visit. How's my father?"

"Good. Coming along nicely."

"Are you a surgeon?"

"Me?" He held up his arms as though looking at them for the first time. "With these hands?"

His hands looked fine to Niko. Long, tapered fingers, nicely manicured. Supple skin, a bit on the whitish side. His attractive face had the typical pallor of a lab rat. "Do you have any food?" she asked.

"Food?" That seemed to catch him by surprise, but he recovered with a gracious smile. "Nothing fancy. Cafeteria's down one floor. Care for an escort?" He offered an elbow and Niko took it gladly.

"Can he think?" she asked him out in the hallway.

"Short answer: I doubt it. Long answer: we can't actually measure for consciousness. No one knows how subjective experience arises in the brain. We can't track cognition even in a healthy man. It's the last surviving mystery."

"What about dreams?"

"Short answer: probably. We are tracking some limited REM sleep, but dreaming is a forebrain phenomenon that actually triggers the brainstem mechanisms for eye movement, not the other way around as generally assumed. He could be dreaming outside the classic pattern."

They stopped at the elevator and Niko took a moment to appraise the man. He was good-looking with a firm jaw line and warm brown eyes above an aquiline nose. Short hair parted and combed to one side gave him an old-fashioned nerdy look. Nerd was the new geek, totally cool.

"Am I boring you already?" he asked.

"You're a very organized thinker, Andrew."

"Why, thank you." He bowed in an effeminate way, almost a curtsy.

The cafeteria was not crowded this late in the day, but the food was in vending machines, locked behind a payment mechanism. Andrew noticed her discomfit and swiped an ID laminate for her benefit. She loaded up a tray with carbs and protein—a plastic-wrapped egg salad sandwich, a pair of sugar donuts and chicken caesar salad in a clamshell tub. She longed for a veggie shake but settled for citrus punch. She needed all the help she could get.

"I see you're wired for Prime," Andrew said as they settled at a table. "That must be exciting."

"Just like video games," she said between bites, "but real." The stock answer, just a bare scratch on the surface. "You play games, Andrew?"

His cute lips wrinkled up in a funny way as though he was preparing to kiss an elderly aunt. She almost laughed.

"Not really. I played dimensional chess in graduate school."

Niko nodded. "Chess is good training."

The egg sandwich was the best one she had ever eaten. Health returned like a wave of euphoria as she ate in silence. She lingered over the chicken salad, savouring every bite.

"You married, Andrew?"

"I was once, for a few heady months." He widened his eyes and quivered his head as though it had been a wild, electrifying experience. "I landed a research grant, moved away. We sort of trailed off . . ."

Niko nodded, sipped her citrus, watched him.

"I suppose you're too young to be married," he said and winced at some inner warning. He gesticulated with his hands as though juggling a beach ball. "I mean, not that you don't look like an adult."

"I need a place to stay, Andrew. Can I crash on your couch for a few days?"

"Well, uh . . ." He faltered at the thought. Niko studied him carefully. He was probably tracing all the threads in this convoluted chess game.

"Sure." He grinned finally, putting his drama-queen persona back on stage. "That would be great." He leaned forward conspiratorially. "Can we keep it on the hush up? The chief's daughter, you know." He held both palms up in mock helplessness.

"You bet. That works best for both of us, Andrew. I know you've got webcam on me, but let's leave it at that. Nothing in your duty notes?"

"Perfect." He sat back. "Not a problem. I'm on the seventh floor, apartment 707."

"Thanks for the meal."

"It's an honour and a privilege."

"Should I be worried about Phillip, or do you treat all underlings with such respect?"

"Phillip is in good hands. We're sacrificing all the virgins we can buy."

"What?"

"Sorry, shop talk. We're harvesting abortions for the totipotent nutrients."

Niko stared at him in blank shock.

"We can do it in the lab of course," he said, "or at least get cells regressed to pluripotency anyway, but its cumbersome and expensive. Much easier to buy off the shelf."

"You have mothers selling embryos?"

"Yep. Repeat providers." He shrugged. "I guess it's a living."

Niko gasped, clutching at her abdomen. Her sisters were renting their wombs month to month to cover expenses. Fellow Eternals were draining their own blood to pay the agencies while four-year-old girls were being kidnapped for regenerative plasma. She felt queasy, drawn between opposing viewpoints. She had escaped from vampires only hours ago, yet her father needed the best treatment available.

"We pay a bonus if they carry late term. More robust stem cells for the brain. We're rebuilding Phillip's cerebrum from the ground up. We force cell migration to the damaged areas with site-specific carriers. It's cutting edge." Andrew had a wild passion in his gaze. He loved his job, plain and simple. "We lost the right eye, though. Couldn't save the pathways. We're going with a cybernetic implant, infrared, tele-scopic, the works. We're sparing no expense, I can assure you."

A terrible thought occurred to Niko. *The connoisseurs pay extra.*

"Do you use Eternal blood on him?"

Andrew nodded. "By the gallon. We get it fresh from the ERI by refrigerated transport."

The vicious circle closed around Niko like a noose. Her father was a vampire. He was a pimp for the ERI, buying their blood, paying for the guns used to rescue her from prison. More blood, more guns, more blood, more vampires. Medical ethics had become a vast grey area, a tangled morass. A nightmare had ensnared her.

Niko tried to process it all, she really did. She spent hours alone on Andrew's couch that night, wearing his boxer shorts for pyjamas, staring at the ceiling, zooming in and out on a dovetailed cornice with her optical enhancements. Her life had always been a roller coaster and she liked it that way, but now the wheels had come off, the standards had given way, and the track was askew. She was out of control and heading for a psychic crash. She needed a safe place to land, something sturdy to hang on to.

Long after midnight in the dark, brimming with pent-up anxiety, she padded barefoot to Andrew's bedroom, kicked off her boxer shorts and joined him under a comfy duvet. She woke him slowly, massaging him with steady insistence, and mounted him when he was ready. Andrew murmured niceties from the edge of dreams and tried to be coy, but Niko rode him hard like a warrior princess atop a saddled stallion, past two orgasms and longer, wreaking out the havoc in her tortured soul. Andrew gasped for ragged breath below her in the darkness, crying out occasionally in a sensual ecstasy, and she released him finally and rolled to the side of the bed. Purged by catharsis, she felt a vigorous contentment, a glow of vitality. The virus was working in her again. Everything was going to be all right.

Andrew kissed her cheek as she drifted into sleep.

# FOUR

"Welcome back to the scene of the crime."

Helena Sharp smiled without obvious hostility, looking younger and stronger than ever. Her blond hair was cut short now, her cheeks thinner, the small cleft in her chin more pronounced. Zak wondered if she had trimmed a few pounds since getting the virus. She looked vibrant and assured, her grey eyes bright with sincerity. With professional grace she turned to the Security officer at the front gate of the Eternal Research Institute. "Mr. Davis is a former Operations Director. Give him a temporary pass until we get his biometrics in the new system."

The guard fished under his desk and produced a plastic laminate. He loaded code and handed it to Zak, who clipped it to his shirt collar and stepped through a Security gauntlet that looked like a high-tech wedding arbour hung with cactus spines. He heard a buzz of electromagnetics as his body was scanned. Security measures had certainly gone up a few notches since he and Phillip had hacked Prime Level Seven from the basement.

Safe on the other side, Zak stretched a hand toward the Director, but she opened long arms to embrace him instead. She patted his back three times in a manly gesture and pulled back.

"You're looking well," he said.

"Why, thank you." She turned sideways to invite inspection, pulled in her tummy, and brushed theatrically at her hip. "The virus is turning me into a showgirl."

"I see that."

"You missed my birthday."

"Eighty-eight," he said, "but who's counting?" She appeared to be about half that, a miracle in motion.

"Are you here to see me or Rix?"

"I'm multitasking."

"Of course." Helena smirked knowingly, deliberately putting him ill at ease. She knew more about him than he did himself. She remembered things that had been wiped from his mind long ago. Somewhere in the black hole of his memory, he had betrayed her and they both knew it.

Helena motioned with her head and began walking, her pace determined, businesslike. "Jimmy's got some new scam," she said.

"He's a good man, Helena."

"I haven't seen the evidence."

"Fair enough. Just give us a chance."

She gave him a haughty glare to indicate the improbability. "What do you need from me?"

"We're looking for guinea pigs."

She frowned at his poor attempt at levity. "Eternals?"

"Preferably."

"So it's dangerous."

"Possibly."

She digested this for a few moments as they passed a work station of young people busy in their cubicles. Zak felt his palms getting cramped and sweaty. This woman made him nervous. He reached in the breast pocket of his jacket and handed her a thick envelope of thousand dollar bills.

She peeked inside. "Cash? How archaic. A bribe?"

"Just a deposit in good faith."

"Do I look like a hooker to you?"

Zak winced. "Hardly."

"What do you expect to buy with this?"

She was still not warming past frigid, but he tried to remain calm. "Your confidence."

"No strings?"

"None at all."

She studied him as they walked, her grey eyes intense. "If you weren't so gorgeous I'd throw you out on your cute button bum."

Zak smiled as he saw a chink in her armour, an open invitation. "It's not merely physical, is it?"

"Too bad you're married."

"There *is* a bit of an age difference. You're old enough to be my grandmother."

She waved a hand and chuckled. "After the first few centuries, a decade here or there won't make much difference, now will it? So what's Jimmy selling?"

"Cybernetic neurons. Site-specific robotic symbionts."

"Is that legal?"

"It's not illegal," he said. "Technically, it's simple prosthesis."

"What are you hoping for?"

"Vastly improved brain function."

"Letting the genii out of the bottle?"

He pointed a quick finger at her. "Good one."

"You know that hyperactivity in certain areas of the cerebrum produces feedback amplification and all kinds of weird side effects."

"That's why we're testing."

Helena stopped and turned to confront him. She placed her hands on her hips. "Why are you and Jimmy always pulling these crazy stunts?"

Zak squinted at her. "I don't know what you mean."

"Sure you do. You're always breaking the rules, pushing the boundaries. You've been doing it since you were a teenager. That's why I enlisted you in the first place, back when I didn't know better. Call me a fool to trust you again."

Zak blinked at her mixed messages, wondering if he was winning her over. "This is just science. We could play this gig totally above board. This product could get the ERI out of hock."

"I want more than money. I want you back on my team."

"What?"

"You heard me." Helena began walking again. They reached an elevator and she placed her hand on a palm scanner. More security upgrades. It would be difficult to move around this building now without leaving a biometric trail. Not like the old days.

They stepped inside an empty box and lurched upward. "Do you remember anything about Colin Macpherson?" she asked, staring at the glowing numbers above the door.

"He engineered the Macpherson Doorway, the wormhole to the Cromeus colonies."

"Do you remember meeting him?"

An icy tension curled in Zak's stomach. "He's been dead for years, Helena."

"He's been uploaded," she said. "You called him the Architect and served his purposes by interfacing with the aliens through a temporary virtual conduit. I monitored it myself."

Zak looked down to express the blank state in his mind, though his body memory confirmed every word with dread.

"Not a thing, huh?"

"Sorry."

Helena sighed through her nose, a grim sadness darkening her face. "The Architect developed technology to monitor the tiny wormholes through which the Eternal virus is delivered to humanity. Somehow a group of vampires here on Earth now has the capability."

Zak jerked his eyes up. "What?"

"You see it, don't you? The balance of power has gone way out of whack. The vampires are plucking up our people like lollipops."

"Oh, God, no. What are we going to do?"

The Director pursed her lips at him as though pondering the dilemma anew. "I'm sure you'll think of something," she said.

The elevator door opened to reveal Rix waiting on the other side.

"Dad," he exclaimed, and Zak jumped into his embrace.

He was taller, stronger, and had coarse stubble on his chin. He had blossomed into a man so soon! He looked tough, muscular in the upper body, with a wary stance that suggested he was ready to fight any instant—the urban hoodlum.

"Are you growing a beard?"

Rix rubbed his chin. "Not really." He glanced furtively at the Director. "We've been busy lately."

"Vampire trouble?"

"Yeah." He swallowed, somewhat forced to Zak's eye. So he knew the problem. Or perhaps there was more, some new teenage disaster, some reticence to Helena's authority.

"So you guys are off for the weekend, I hear," Helena piped up to Rix. Her demeanour transformed to that of a happy co-worker, her posture subtly altered. She was bouncy, up on her heels. She traded masks at will.

"Off on vacation," Rix chimed. "Where's Mom?"

"At the hotel downtown," Zak said. "She didn't feel comfortable coming back here just yet. She has a surprise for you."

"Really? What is it?"

"She wants to tell you herself. How's school?"

"Boring. I want to run away and become an artist."

"A painter?"

"Yeah, or a sculptor."

"Brilliant."

"I'll catch you guys later," Helena said, just one of the boys, and sauntered away.

Zak clapped his arm around his son, feeling love like a fountain. "Tell me everything," he said.

They stepped into the elevator and Rix filled him in on all the current crises at the ERI, his burgeoning romance with Niko, and her recent trauma with the vampires. He still had not received any confirmation that she was alive, but the ERI assault team had cleared the building of all Eternal occupants. The vampire administrators and cafeteria staff had put up little resistance once the armed guards had been tranked. Niko was out there somewhere.

They took a cab downtown and Zak recounted his escape to the northern sanctuary and the long weeks living off the grid with Mia. He tried to explain their life of ease to a young man who had known nothing but trouble all his days, the feeling of oneness with Gaia that develops over time in the wilderness, the bond of love shared by a couple living in close quarters.

He didn't dare tell him about the listless days when his parents had resorted to sexual gymnastics just to pass the time. No point in grossing him out. He hoped one day his teenage son would discover this bond of communion with a woman, that he would learn the joy of service, of mutual respect. A happy marriage seemed like such a rare commodity in this frenetic digital age.

Rix filled him in on the details of school. Good marks in mathematics and physics, some artistic aptitude. He was planning on college and had audited classes by feelies on the V-net. Some universities were still accepting Eternals as undergraduates and a few were openly hostile to the Evolutionary Terrorist Omnibus, the controversial legislation that effectively stripped Eternals of civil rights. Full protection from vampires was being offered on gated campus grounds, and a few free-thinking patrons were offering scholarships to selected candidates.

Not everyone in the world was filled with bloodlust. Not every human was afraid of extinction. The silent majority still lived quiet lives, still went to work and school and debated the current issues of philosophy and ethics. All possible futures were waiting for fulfilment and Rix had high hope that everything would work out for the best. He had a vision of a better world where Eternals and humans could live together in harmony. It made Zak proud to see such purpose in his son, such faith in a post-human destiny. He could hardly wait to see his face when Mia told him about the baby.

They arrived at the hotel room to find the door slightly ajar.

"Mia?"

Zak eased his way inside to see her lying contorted on the floor, eyes open and staring in surprise at the ceiling, unblinking. He dove to her side and reached for her neck in search of a pulse.

Cold. Dead.

He checked her blouse. Three bullet wounds to the heart, closely spaced in a tight triangle. She would have been gone before she hit the floor. Oh, God.

For a moment he was transported out of his skin, looking at the grisly scene from somewhere near the ceiling, looking down at his own tousled hair. He floated in a passionless hysteria, a timeless state of crystal acuity. How could this happen? Why? A robbery attempt? Some random act of violence? A contract killing? It seemed a terrible puzzle, something beyond comprehension.

His wife was dead.

He found himself again in his body, awash in anguish, weeping over her. A pool of blood had soaked into the carpet below her and spread in a widening circle. The stench of iron hung in the air like a heavy metal miasma. He placed his hand in her congealing plasma. Eternal blood. She should have lived forever. She was one of the chosen. Her vast potential had been snuffed out in an instant like a candle wick.

He remembered the baby. Oh, God, no.

His hands went to her womb, searching for warmth, for any vestige of life.

Cold. Dead.

He looked up at Rix, trying to focus through a veil of tears.

His son was bracing himself stiff against the wall, his white face a mask of horror.


"I brought you dinner," Andrew said as he pressed a package forward with a smile.

Niko looked up from her bedside vigil. She had been sitting with her stepfather all day, inspecting his biosystems moment by moment, listening to the steady chirp of his heart monitor amplified in the sterile laboratory. "Thanks," she said and began unwrapping wax paper from an egg salad sandwich. She took a bite and chewed mechanically, not bothering to taste.

Andrew lingered, hands in the pockets of his lab coat, watching her.

"He should have awakened by now," Niko said. "Look at the alpha-EEG."

"I've seen that pattern before. It's not unusual in post-traumatic patients with fatigue or pain."

Niko's body tightened involuntarily. "Is he in pain?"

"Not necessarily," he said. "We're certainly not seeing any muscle rigidity on the chart. Hardly even any hypnic twitches. I wouldn't worry. In any case, pain is an evolutionary building block for the brain, not to be discounted in this form of therapy. All in all, Phillip's showing regular sleep transition periods from delta to theta. The occasional alpha and beta periods are just not breaking through into full wakefulness." He shrugged. "I wouldn't worry. We're definitely making progress day by day."

Andrew leaned over to check the bioengineering flatscreens. He scrolled through several views of the mindscan data as Niko stared past his shoulder. He tapped one screen with significance. "The growing activity in the parietal lobe is particularly promising. It does look like a good precognitive pattern for spatial and mathematical reasoning."

"Don't try to baby me, Andrew. His whole brain is working just fine, neurons firing, peptide levels stable, possibly memories being recorded. Even the so-called personality centres in the frontal lobes are kicking it out. He should be awake."

Andrew stood tall to face her. "Most of the complexity of a human neuron is devoted to maintaining life-support functions. Higher information processing is really just a byproduct."

"But surely consciousness should arise naturally in a healthy brain."

Andrew nodded. "Metacognition is a bit of a mystery."

"A bit of a mystery?" Niko bristled. "Is that the best science can offer? With the most transcendent technology money can buy?" She shook her head. "I don't believe it."

Andrew frowned at this challenge to his professional specialty and began to pace back and forth, his exposed thumbs tapping outside the pockets of his sterile lab coat. "Suppose you had a tree," he said, "a Christmas tree covered with blinking lights and fancy decorations. And you ask a scientist to make you one exactly the same. He has the equipment and he builds it just the way he sees it, an exact duplicate. He plugs it in and measures the result. His creation is perfect in all physical aspects, except for one thing. It's just a tree, not a Christmas tree. It does not have the metacognition to recognize the meaning behind its existence."

"The soul?"

He rolled his eyes. "If you must. I think the electrochemical theory of persona is adequate in this sense."

Niko finished her sandwich and folded paper remnants in her pocket. She looked at Phillip. "He doesn't realize he's alive?"

Andrew grimaced at the oversimplification, rocking his head from side to side as he tested it out in his mind. "I think we just need a spark, a catalyst. We do have a plan, if you will allow it. We contacted a specialist in the Cromeus colonies. They have a company there, Soul Savers, that uploads human consciousness to disk. They have a whole menagerie of cyber-souls living in a vast database."

"I know of it."

"Right." Andrew pressed his pretty lips into a flat line. "It's pretty far out at the moment, beyond what Earthside legislation would allow. Anyway, our specialist suggested uploading foundational schemata to form a personality base."

"Foundational schemata?"

"A saved soul, if you will."

"Who?"

"What?"

"Whose soul?"

"Well, nobody in particular, just a framework, a spark of lightning."

Niko stiffened with scorn. "My dad is not some Frankenstein monster for you to experiment with."

"Sorry, perhaps that was a poor metaphor."

"This is my father we're talking about."

"Sorry." Andrew wrung his hands, clearly nonplussed.

"You don't have very good bedside manner for a doctor."

"I've never done retail medicine, " he said. "I'm a neuroscientist. Most of my work is done by computer simulation."

Niko tilted her head at him. "Is there any scientific basis to think this will work?"

"To be honest, I don't know." He hissed out a sigh. "Look at the Beast in V-space. Here we have an early cybertracker, not the first, but certainly a robust variant. It was programmed top-down in the beginning, primarily as an encryption ubercomputer, but somehow merged with a spontaneous bottom-up consciousness, a feedback loop caused by patterns of electromagnetism in the cybersphere. It has insight and can make decisions in its quest to keep the V-net free of digital disease. But the Beast does not have metacognition. It does not consider itself as a private entity, as a being that can think about thinking."

"It has no soul."

"Loosely speaking."

"And that's what's wrong with Phillip?"

Andrew worked his lips grimly, pressing and pursing them in a weird facial exercise. He was clearly troubled by the whole conversation, the use of abstract terms, the lack of hard data.

"I think it's worth a try," he said finally.

Sublevel Zero was bright with colour, vibrant with high-def cortical fluorescence. Pink seemed to be the shade of the month. Market researchers were offering pink hats or jackets as free upgrades to anyone who would carry a temporary hunter for the day. The white market was proving too lucrative to ignore. Advertisers had been moving down from the Prime Levels with slick pop-ups and feelies to take even the underground corporate. Rix could see the trend as nothing but trouble for Eternals. One day soon the white market would be gone completely. Where will the runners run when every protocol is under surveillance? Where will they buy food? Rix glowered at the thought. Mankind should be free inside their own brains.

Niko had poked him to say she had plugged up. He was hot on the trail of the girl he loved. It would be a bittersweet reunion for sure, and he dreaded having to tell her about his mother. He dreaded having to replay that murder scene again and again in his mind for the rest of his Eternal life. He didn't want to think of Mia ever again. He couldn't bear it.

"Hey, cousin, you made it."

Niko stood in an alcove off the main thoroughfare wearing a sexy black skinsuit like polished ebony. She looked exotic and dangerous, her straight hair hanging limp to bare shoulders, her lips like pert pink pillows. Passersby gawked at her skimpy outfit, smiling and nodding, and Rix felt a wave of jealousy, wishing he could throw a blanket of modesty around her perfect body. "You changed your costume," he said.

"This is my catgirl look. I'm off duty. You like it?"

"It's a bit revealing."

A look of surprise crossed her face. She glanced down at herself self-consciously.

"No, really, it looks fabulous. I was just kidding." Rix recovered quickly, feeling like a covetous idiot. What was he thinking? This was Sublevel Zero, after all; there was a topless animotron on every street corner. He had recently customized his own avatar with a chrome skinsuit and black trim—a new digital kick-back veneer like mirrored glass, difficult for pirates to recognize and remember.

"So who are you supposed to be? The silver surfer? Showing a little package, aren't we?"

"I said I was sorry."

"No you didn't. You said you were kidding."

"Whatever."

"Let's keep moving," she said. "I hate having all these trackers around."

They stepped out onto the street where a kaleidoscope of colour shifted around them, hawkers and hookers and government gestapo. They were careful to touch nothing.

"You will be scared out of your mind," said a megaphone announcer to all and sundry as they passed. "Visit the Caves of Dragonia," said another in competition directly opposite on the crowded thoroughfare. A sultry female voice offered a free sex feelie called *Uncharted Quad-X*. The sounds seemed to overlap into a cacophony, a dissonant feedback pulse.

"So thanks for saving me," Niko said.

"I missed you. I'm glad you're okay. And you've got the virus. That's awesome."

She shot him a quick glance. "Well it's not working out great so far, but thanks anyway."

He clenched his teeth at the reminder of the torture she must have endured. "They say the Eternal journey is easy to start but difficult to finish," he offered half-heartedly.

She tossed her hair in dismissal. "I'm glad I could count on you. Goes without saying, I guess." Her lips compressed with maudlin sentimentality, sharing the now awkward memory of their single intimate encounter, glorious as it had been.

Rix knew exactly what she was thinking and took comfort in the connection—the path to her heart was still open and he loved her more than ever. "Your worm came through in multiple copies. The vectors were easy to track."

"For you, maybe."

He shrugged, trying to fake nonchalance. "The cosmetics firm was a necessary clue. How did you get the message out?"

Niko gave him a quirk of a smile. "Let's just say I had to be creative. How's the ERI?"

"In an uproar since your bad news."

A puppet pop-up jarred them with a palpable kinetic displacement. "You guys need a private pleasure dome?" asked the peddler, wearing street jeans and a gaudy collared shirt. He looked like an advertisement for a Hawaiian vacation.

"No, thanks," said Rix.

"Can I give you an upload brochure?"

"Get lost," said Niko.

The peddler stepped away, frowning.

"Do you want to drop down a level for more privacy?" Rix asked.

"There's no privacy anymore. The vampires have got my DNA, my fingerprints, retinal scans. God knows what else. My life is ruined."

"We could go deep."

She shook her head. "I haven't got time. I'm babysitting my step-father round the clock, cleaning bedpans and feeding him through a straw."

"How's he doing?"

"He won't wake up."

"Sucks."

They walked in silence for a few moments. Rix longed to touch her, to make some show of affection. She looked exquisite to his wandering eye, sinewy and strong. He remembered watching her jump off a building back in realtime, her black kite like the wings of a demoness.

"How are your parents?" she asked.

A jolt of anxiety hit him like electricity. So this was it. "My mother's dead."

"What the hell?" Niko's avatar pixelated with trauma as she lost traction, a rookie mistake.

"She was murdered. I don't want to talk about it."

Niko stopped and stared, her image fading in and out with emotional overload. A garbled sound erupted from her now faulty transmission. She was losing contact.

Rix reached for her with his hand, grabbed her shoulder. "Stay with me, Niko."

She closed her eyes as she struggled to stabilize her avatar. "Sorry."

He kept his hand on her perfect body and began massaging her collarbone with gentle rhythm, watching her breasts heave with ragged breath. "You've got to learn to control your emotions Sublevel. Runners can read every nuance of drag."

"Jesus, Rix. Your mother is dead."

"I can't help that now. Neither can Jesus."

Niko swallowed with obvious effort, her face still a pixelated mask. "She was Eternal."

He pulled his hand back. "I can't talk about her. She's already been cremated. She's gone, just like that. No church, no funeral, just ashes in an urn buried in a box."

"Vampires?"

Rix sighed at her persistence. "Doesn't look like it. They left all her blood behind."

"Joy bashers?"

He scowled. "Maybe, but it's hard to believe vigilantes would resort to murder. All that evolutionary terrorism crap makes me sick! I mean, so what if we're Eternal? It's not like we're trying to take over the world."

"Some people have narrow minds and impossible conceits."

"My dad thinks it was a professional contract. Three bullets at close range, narrowly spaced. The cops were no help at all—just another cold corpse with no papers."

Niko paused for a moment, her teeth clenched with anxiety. "How is Zak?"

"Bad."

"How bad?"

"He's a basketcase and blames himself for everything. I don't think he's bouncing back this time. He says he'll never plug up again."

Niko eyes bored into him like lasers searching for his heart. "And how are you handling the loss?"

"I'm coping," he said and glanced away from her penetrating gaze. "I'm in denial, I guess." He didn't want to think about his parents. He wanted to focus on Niko. Could he tell her how he felt? His lovestruck imaginings night after night? Could he express his heartstrings? Did he dare? No, now was not the time. "I could use a friend," he offered.

"I'll always be your friend, Rix."

"Can we meet in realtime? Can we hook up again? There's lots of space in the dorms at the ERI."

Niko shook her head—too quickly—and Rix felt his stomach drop into a death spiral.

"I'm living with someone else at the moment."

"A guy?"

Niko braced her hands on her hips. "Yes, Rix, a guy. His name is Andrew. He's a neuroscientist."

"Wirehead?"

"No, straight."

"Eternal?"

"No."

"Are you sleeping together?" It was none of his business, perhaps, but he had to know. She could not refuse him.

"I suppose so."

"You're having sex?"

She sighed through pursed lips, reluctant to deliver the final blow. "Yes, Rix."

He could not believe it. "After all we've been through together?"

"I don't see what that's got to do with anything."

"Well, I thought we had something going on, like we were in love."

She gaped at him. "Love? Because of one weak moment?"

A bridge broke in his mind, a carefully engineered structure now proven faulty and worthless. "That's all I was to you? A weak moment?"

"No, no, of course not. I didn't mean it like that. I'm sorry."

"So that's it then."

"That's what?"

"The end."

She huffed her disbelief. "You're distraught, Rix. Let's just cool this down."

"No. Forget it, Niko. We're done." He took a step backward, out of her personal sphere.

"Don't be a child, Rix."

He held his arms up to ward her off, took another hesitant step back. "I'm too young for you. I get it."

She extended her palms in supplication. "Rix, I need you. Please don't do this."

He wheeled and walked away.

"You will be scared out of your mind," a hawker shouted behind him.

He took a zoomtube up to Main Street, the now civilized underground, and wandered aimlessly in the digital cosmography, bumping into pedestrians and pop-ups, causing unintentional havoc on the boulevard. He could not seem to focus his thoughts. A couple of greysuits began to monitor his erratic movements. Ladies in lingerie called like sirens from the shadows, promising to assuage his pain. After a time he gave up and unplugged.

Back in his dorm room, he felt a dark reality take shape around him, a black fog of depression trying to smother him. He had lost his girl. He had lost his mother. His father was barely responsive and the vampires were fast closing in. He was Eternal and had nothing left to live for.

# FIVE

**H**elena Sharp located Zak in a guest room in the ERI East Wing. She rapped for entry and got no reply, so she unlocked the door with her master code. His anguish hit her like a visceral blow as she entered the tiny grey cubicle. "I'm so sorry, Zak."

He didn't look up. He sat hunched on a small cot, staring at his knees, his hands curled in his lap like a wounded child. Where was the Zakariah Davis of old, the dauntless pirate? This was not the man who had shared her avatar for weeks, who had boldly fought against powerful enemies and survived. This bare husk was dead inside.

She took a few steps closer but didn't dare touch him. "I'm glad you came back here. Stay as long as you like. No duties, no pressure."

Still he chose not to recognize her presence. She glanced around the room at painted block walls and stucco ceiling, a bare closet with no personal decorations, no humanity. She pulled a desk chair from the corner and dragged it noisily across the floor. He didn't blink. She sat down in front of him.

"Zak, if there's anything I can do—"

"Where is she, Helena?" His voice sounded coarse, like a gravel roadway. She winced.

"Mia's dead, Zak," Helena whispered. "She's gone."

"She's not gone. She's out there somewhere. I've got to find her."
He did not look up. He seemed to be staring into a void below him,
a vortex of despair.

Helena rubbed her tongue on her upper lip, watching him. This
was a delicate situation. He was near a breaking point, a dark chasm.
He looked like a cadaver. "In heaven, you mean?"

He raised his eyes slowly, his pupils like black beacons, and
Helena gasped involuntarily at the intensity of his expression. "You
know life goes on, you of all people," he said.

"No, I don't know, Zak. No one can know."

"We've had a special connection. Spooky action at a distance.
How can you explain that?"

"There was a scientific basis. We were surgically hotwired
together. Mia was not even wired for Prime."

"Mia believed in life after death. She had faith in a spirit guiding
the Eternal virus. Her chi essence is out there, some superconscious
pattern in quantum space. She was too perfect to be erased. I can find
her."

Helena blew out a tantric breath of cleansing. She could feel a
tightness inside her, a coiled spring. "Zak, I won't deny the possibility. I've heard about quantum cognitive architecture and microtu-
bules in the brain. They're just theories. There's no reliable evidence
and nothing to suggest life after death."

"I'll find the evidence."

"Try to be calm," she said. "You're surrounded by friends who
love you."

"Tell me about my communication with the alien Source. They say
it was like meeting God. There must be some truth there, some clue."

Helena shuddered at the memory—the first contact that haunted
her still, the mindwipe of her partner Zakariah at the hands of the

Architect. Before her now stood but a vestige of her former friend, a man now crushed again. How many times can a brain be burned by the Beast and scoured by science? How many times can a man be beaten down and rise to former glory? She summoned her voice in remembrance of that once stalwart pioneer who first glimpsed the multiverse beyond spacetime. "It was bright," she said, "too bright to see clearly. It seemed like a world of frozen fire, crystalline. There was a single alien. He appeared to take on human shape, trying to download a recognizable pattern, a transfiguration to a lower form of being. It was frightening."

"What did he say? What did it feel like?"

The memory seemed so vivid that she could almost touch the torment of the wound, but to distill it down seemed hopeless. "There was a feeling of unworthiness, a cosmic futility, as though you were inconsequential in a vast and unknowable universe. You seemed to be trying to decipher something into human language, using archetypes and symbols common to a near-death experience, but the message seemed to be: 'Go back, you're not ready. You're undeserving.'"

A flush of colour returned to Zak's face. His breath came in quick pants like a trapped animal. He cocked his head as though seeing her for the first time. *Will you help me, Helena?*

His voice was clear in mindspeak, controlled. Helena sat back in her chair in amazement. "Yes, I will help you."

He blinked in a quick spasm of shock. "What? Did you hear that?"

"Yes."

His eyes widened in surprise, then quickly narrowed in doubt as his brain churned data. "How?"

"You tell me. Some wirehead feedback, I suppose."

He shivered his head. "We're not plugged up."

"Some residual effect, a background resonance. I've noticed it a few times here at the ERI since the accident. During times of great trauma, I seem to have an empathic language connection."

"Telepathy?"

"It may not be as rare as we think."

"Can we measure it?"

She could hear a glimmer of hope in his voice, a glimpse of the cowboy Zak, the visionary. Can we understand it, harness it? Spoken like a true scientist. Helena pressed her lips together in what she hoped might be a smile. "Well, we can hardly induce trauma in the lab for the sake of psychic research. It's unethical. Besides, we're not dealing with simple biomechanics or it would have been studied decades ago."

His face remained a blank disguise, but she could see that she had finally focused his attention. "Come up to my suite and I'll cook you some breakfast. You've been running on empty far too long." She stood and reached out a hand toward him, across a great chasm of disassociation, trying to coax him back to ground.

Hesitant fingers reached up to touch hers and she pulled him gently to his feet.


Safe behind transparent blastglass, Colin7 watched the transport capsule appear out of theoretical nonspace into the dark core of the Macpherson Doorway and smiled at the sight. Like a demon materializing at the sound of his name, Colin Macpherson was returning to Earth for the first time since founding the Cromeus colonies generations ago. The Architect had returned to claim a heritage in the land of his birth, a new beginning. He had come home to be reborn.

Colin7 had never known a human womb. He had been created in a petri dish on a distant planet and nurtured in a chemical stew with nutrient plasma pumping through his umbilicus. He had no human kin but this one progenitor, his DNA father, now sliding like an alien ovum down the artificial ovipositor of the Macpherson Doorway— the wormhole to the stars he had fashioned himself by manipulating the powerful forces of microgravity in tight parameters.

The capsule looked like a stainless steel bullet as it approached, an unmarked coffin rounded on both ends. Without the rumble of machinery or mechanical aid, it floated silently down a narrow causeway marked with lights like an airport runway. Staff in bright orange regalia hovered at the end and manhandled the capsule onto a conveyor belt and through a safety airlock into the disembark-ment area.

Colin7 pushed off into weightless space to follow his father and felt the familiar panic of vertigo in his abdomen. He slung around a direc-tional glowpole and dangled from a strap to oversee the unlocking of clasps. He peered into the transport capsule to see the hardware secure. He checked the power supply to find four green bars full. No problems. He whistled a sigh through trembling lips. So much at stake, too much at risk. It would be so easy to lose the Original now. An accident, component failure, an electromagnetic pulse—his father was vulnerable for the first time in a century. Colin5 and the other clones would continue to keep the genome operative in his absence, to be sure, but it might never be the same without the Architect.

Colin7 authorized for his thrumming equipment on a palm pad and took possession of his father. A shuttlecraft waited to make the final jump down from orbit to the alien landscape of Earth and the strange inhabitants of the little blue world. His ticket had been pre-paid by a corporate consortium, his secret mission outside the realm of terrestrial statute. He pushed the capsule gently forward into the hands of the cargo roughnecks on the landing bay, burly buccaneers

STEVE STANTON

with a lust for danger pay. He certified that the contents were not hazardous or prohibited by law.


Helena settled in the launch couch in her office and quietly slipped under the wire. Her avatar rocketed upward into V-space, bypassing the gaudy advertisements on Main Street in search of a private zoom-tube known to only two users. Her image was solid and expensive, undisguised by chicanery. Her public persona had nothing to hide. As a registered regent she had privileged access up to Prime Five and an escalating incentive program for complimentary air and space travel. Today Helena had a mnemonic code for a guest membership in Prime Seven and signalled it into the zoomtube with a digital touch. Her avatar accelerated with a wrenching dislocation.

"Hello, Director. Long time."

Helena examined Jimmy with a scrupulous eye as she coalesced before him. She knew his reputation and dared not trust him. "I've been busy with our friend."

"How is he?"

"Terrible. He mopes around in his pyjamas like a hospital patient."

"It's been a few weeks now, hasn't it? Shouldn't he be coming around?"

"He's reading at least," she said. "There's some life emerging in his eyes. He's studying psychic research."

"Ouch."

"He thinks Mia could still be alive. Like a ghost or something."

Jimmy cast his eyes down and shook his head, his jaw tight with worry. "I loved Mia as much as anyone," he said. "She went through a lot. They both did. They had a special connection."

"I met her only briefly. She seemed like a remarkable woman."

70

Helena looked away to escape the gathering discomfort. She scanned the meeting room, opaque walls hung with tapestries and elaborate artwork, white plaster ceiling promising privacy. "So this is Prime Seven? It feels almost like realtime."

"I know, pretty steadfast. It's scary sometimes. Makes you wonder." Jimmy was sitting in an ornate easy chair from the Victorian age, looking dapper in a tweed smoking jacket, his shaved head a bright dome.

"And we're under Triple-A encryption?"

"Straight from the Beast. It's the only way to stay above the paparazzi these days." He pointed to a chair beside him, facing in the same direction—an obvious signal of cooperation rather that contention. He was playing a fine drama.

"And the vampires in my case," she said as she made herself comfortable. The window screen opposite showed a panoramic view of the Horseshoe Falls from the Canadian side. She wondered if it was live webcam but decided against it. The bandwidth up Prime this high would be too expensive, even for this elite criminal.

"Yeah, I heard you guys put up a show of strength," he said.

"We were forced into it."

"Even so, it changes the framework, takes it up a notch."

"Some heavy tech has slipped into vampire hands, Jimmy. I need your help."

"Can we negotiate my partner's release from custody?"

She looked deliberately away, let her eyes wander the panorama. "No, we won't fight for him. That's too far beneath us."

Jimmy hesitated at that, but smiled in due time. "I like you, girl. You've got some moxie."

"Zak came back to us for refuge. He's but a badly wounded shadow now. We're not holding him against his will."

"Fair enough," he said. "I'll cut my losses and move on."

The shared calamity of their friend seemed to settle them together somehow and a tangible tension dissipated in silence. Helena felt it like a tonic. "Well, thanks for inviting me for a conference. I had my team look over your proposal. We discussed it at length."

"And?"

"To begin with, the whole notion is impossible."

"Hah." Jimmy slapped his knee with mock delight.

"Furthermore, you do not have sufficient financing to carry out the plan."

He grinned. "You're softening already, Director."

"The evidence you present is not incontrovertible."

"I can't believe you just used that word in a sentence."

"Are you toying with me?"

"Absolutely. I'm dealing from a position of strength."

She sat back in her chair, composed herself. "Fine. Give me the laywoman's pitch. The hard data is certainly not working in your favour." Helena felt discomfit like a hairshirt. She was way out of her league. To her, this was just crazy science.

Jimmy leaned forward to catch her eye. "This is the future of picotech, subatomic transistors that use only one electron to switch between states. Reversible architecture that requires no energy and produces no heat. This is the tech that tested Heisenberg's uncertainty principle."

"And you have a factory somewhere producing these components?" Her voice sounded shrill with disbelief, even to her own ears.

Jimmy smiled with satisfaction. "Nanotubules are grown in chemistry flasks, not manufactured on assembly lines." He held flat vertical hands up in front of him. "About this big. Self-replicating, self-organizing, and self-configuring."

Helena played with the idea in her mind. Machines building machines? That seemed a bit spacey to her. Where was the designer in this glorious future universe? Who was setting the mathematical constants? She surveyed him carefully. "The ERI resources alone are going to be hugely expensive," she said.

"Not a problem." He widened his fingers in front of him. "Just think about it. Just give it some serious consideration, that's all I ask."

"The brain imaging equipment will be worth a queen's ransom."

"Clients are lining up, Helena. May I call you Helena?"

"Certainly." Jimmy seemed too slick, too contrived, like a nineteenth century carny selling soothing syrup full of heroin. She still didn't dare trust him.

"Big pharmas have reached an impasse on chemical cognitive enhancement," he said. "They're looking for a way out, a new direction for humanity."

"They seem to operate on the questionable premise that everyone wants to be stronger and faster."

"Well, you're the poster girl for that. Eighty-eight years old and you look young enough to be my daughter!"

"I'm not sure if that's a compliment, but I'll thank you anyway just in case." She stretched her legs out and tipped a high heel up on her ankle. Might as well use every advantage. "You don't take rejuve yourself?"

"Nope, never have. I've seen too much already."

"Really? You don't want to live forever?"

Jimmy tilted his head at her and turned back to the Horseshoe Falls. "Life's not all it's cracked up to be."

Helena scrutinized him, sensing something deep and significant. He was a handsome man and a techno-guru, but had chosen a life of infamy on the outskirts of civil law. He had a reputation as a conniving manipulator, a big player. She waited to see if any explanation might be forthcoming.

"How do you like the view?" Jimmy asked finally.

"Breathtaking. It's not realtime, is it?"

Jimmy laughed at the notion. "No way. It's an upload loop from my balcony back home."

"You're living in Canada?"

"You recognize it, eh?"

"Just from vidi."

"They have a great venture capital system up there, hooked right into the universities. It's a financial feeding frenzy."

"It's all about money to you, is it, Jimmy? Currency fluctuations, payback periods?"

He settled his shoulders with nonchalance. "Somebody's got to keep score."

"Well, it's a wonderful scene."

"Want the audio? It's freakin' awesome."

"Sure."

Sudden thunder rumbled like a million charging horses, an earthquake that jiggled her abdomen like Jell-o. "Wow," she yelled.

"That's with the soundboard at par, right down at ground zero," Jimmy shouted.

"Okay, that's enough!"

Silence fell instantly like a healing balm. Helena touched hesitant fingers to her ears, testing them.

"Niagara Falls is a great tourist trap," Jimmy said. "Sky-high restaurants overlooking the Clifton Hill carnival, thrill rides into the mist and spray, and two casinos open round the clock."

"Zak said you were a pretty good card counter in your day."

"I still dip my fingers in from time to time, but I give it back on purpose so they don't kick me out. And we didn't have digital mnemonics back in the wild-west days. Just mental math. It's almost primeval now." He chuckled happily to himself at the remembrance. "I still love the sound of it, the electric bling of the slots, the shouting pit boss. It's really just a form of volunteer taxation but what a way to go."

"I've never been to a casino."

"Really? Too cruel. I was raised on the Vegas strip in the heart of Sin City."

That might explain a few things about this strange tycoon. Helena was beginning to piece together a puzzling picture. Jimmy looked to be in his late fifties, perhaps sixty, with a few hard years showing in the crow's feet around his eyes. His body was short, solid, and strong.

"You should come for a visit. I've got a cool bachelor pad up north. I'm living in a Faraday cage with some of the finest nonbiological intelligence you'd ever want to meet." He winked at her with a leer, civilized and stately in his antique smoking jacket. She wondered what he might be like as a sexual partner.

"Why do you keep at it, Jimmy? You know, pushing the edge?"

"That's what edges are for. Enough about me. What about you? What are you fighting for?"

Helena shifted in her chair, shrugged. "When I was young, I wanted to change the future and live forever." She glanced away thoughtfully, touching distant reflections. "My perspective shifted as the circle turned and eventually all I wanted was to preserve the past and save the status quo. Now I just seem to have a misplaced sense of duty. I'm juggling balloons in the air."

"But you *will* live forever thanks to the virus. So you got what you wanted."

"I guess so."

"You're welcome to the future, Helena. You'll have tons of fun."

"A feelie of laughs, huh?"

"Mass starvation, refugee camps, riots in the streets. It'll be a blast."

"You don't think we can terraform the climate back to where it should be?"

"Sure we can, but why should we? That's the cogent problem in the long run. Why bother to make the Earth more comfortable for humans? Why pander to a species that destroys everything it touches, that slaughters their own brothers for the sake of tribal politics? Intelligence has already grown far beyond human capacity, computing a million times faster than biological neurons. The human brain can only make about 100 trillion transactions per second, with a reset time of five milliseconds. That's donkey speed now. What's the point in keeping the legacy organisms at all? Digital consciousness will fill the universe, not biomass."

Helena stared at Jimmy in awe. The man was talking glibly about the future extinction of the human race. What a twisted mind. "Know anything about wormholes, Jimmy? The pinpoints through which the virus is transmitted to Earth?"

He spread his hands with mock innocence. "I'm just an old gamer on the run."

"With vast connections underground and back doors everywhere."

He smiled. "I try to keep my options open."

"Just keep watch for me and we have a deal."

"Phase Four testing?"

"All the monkeys and live ammo you need."

"That's a joke, right? I need human subjects."

"Yes, it's a joke."

"Good, then. I'll see what I can find out."

Helena held up a flat palm humming with electric potential and signified for a match. "Do you want a formal V-net contract?"

He grinned. "Hell, no. Your word is good enough for me, Director. I'd go for a quick toss though, while we're enjoying Prime Seven. It's almost as good as the real thing up this high."

Helena wagged a finger at him playfully. "Zak warned me about you."

Jimmy laughed. "The kid's got me all wrong."

"Is he ever going to grow up in your eyes?"

Jimmy sobered at the thought. His face eclipsed into sadness. "I think he already has."


"What is this thing?"

"It's a canoe."

"A boat with no motor?"

"Exactly."

Andrew eyed it askance. "So how does it work?"

Niko held up a wooden paddle. "It works by human effort. Physical exercise, you know? It's not dangerous. We'll just be floating."

"Right. I get it. Health kick." He grabbed the paddle from her. "You think I'm too fat."

His knobby knees poked out from under baggy black shorts. His blue crew-neck top was tucked into a narrow waistline. He was a long cry from fat.

"It's called a nature outing. You can't live your entire life in the lab. When was the last time you were out in the sun?"

Andrew the drama queen began looking from side to side in mock search, his brows high and arched like furry rainbows. He peered up. "Oh yeah, that thing." He batted his pretty eyelashes at her.

Niko replied in kind with a show of exasperation. "Just get in the back and I'll teach you a new skill. Do you think you can point us in the right direction? I want to get some pics." She held up a tiny but powerful digital camera.

Andrew stepped into the sliver of fiberglass and exclaimed as he momentarily lost balance and almost fell in the river. Niko began to have second thoughts. She glanced back up to the rental shack where a young boy watched their antics through a window. What could possibly go wrong in a simple canoe? There was no way to get lost on this sluggish old river. There were only two choices, upstream or down.

Andrew finally stabilized himself on the bench seat and put the paddle across his bare knees. He looked around at the autumn landscape, brushstrokes of red and burgundy in the hardwood trees. "There's nothing out here worth taking pictures."

Niko smiled. "That's where you're wrong. Just keep the noise down."

"Yeah, right."

Niko climbed in and pushed off. "We'll head up current so we can kick back coming home when we're tired." She began paddling and Andrew learned quickly following her example. The water was moving lazily, the surface calm, showing an imperfect reflection of the painted forest skyline.

"Drag your paddle to steer," she instructed.

"Sure. Steering is such a drag."

She turned to see him grinning. "Are you having fun yet?"

"The view is terrific," he said. "I like your hair all curled and fluffy like that."

Niko's hand went involuntarily to her head. She combed her experimental curls with long fingers. "Thanks."

"And your strong shoulders, too. You look great."

"Are you hitting on me?"

"Maybe later."

He *was* having fun. She could see invigoration in his eyes. He was learning a new task, broadening his horizons. It was good therapy for both of them. Normally Andrew seemed to reduce everything to basic neuronal activity in the brain, like a walking computer filtering experience through a narrow lens of science. He looked at life as though it were lab data. He needed to get out more.

"So this is like . . . the wild?"

"No, this is just a camping area, a nature preserve."

"The water looks dirty, almost like tea."

"Well, you wouldn't want to drink it."

Andrew ducked as a beaver thumped his tail up ahead with a loud splash. "What the heck?"

"It's just a beaver sounding alarm," Niko said. "Watch up ahead for her home as we go by. Look there, on the bank under that tree, see that small tangle of branches? She's probably living under a canopy of roots."

"That tree looks like it's ready to fall in the river any moment."

The trunk was leaning badly, an old maple starting to turn yellow and orange as the season waned. The bark was grey and fissured with gnaw marks near the base.

"I guess when it finally goes down the beavers will feast on it," Niko said.

Andrew scrunched up his face in disgust. "That's so *destructive*."

Niko paused to scrutinize him. Was he really that superficial? Couldn't he see the cycle of life playing out all round? Half the forest was dead and decaying, alive with microbiota. Who could say where life ended and death began? They skimmed quickly by, making good headway in their light composite canoe. They zigzagged up the narrow river as Andrew learned to navigate, but Niko gave his piloting scant attention. She much preferred sitting in the front nose of the canoe, being the first to view the upcoming panorama, letting the raw sensation parade over her. She loved the feeling of breaking new ground, floating forward into a vast spectacle of untamed life as though she were an ancient voyageur mapping primitive terrain, transcribing exotic journeys of discovery.

For the first few kilometres they passed occasional cabins and campsites, most vacant midweek, but eventually even these vestiges of civilization gave way to natural hardwood forest. No garbage, no fertilizer, no pesticides. Autumn colours were beginning to show in the greenery, ochreous shades with occasional splashes of crimson. Acorns dropped from regal oaks like hailstone missiles.

A chorus of honking rose up in the distance to the right.

"The natives are restless," Andrew said.

"Probably geese preparing to migrate, getting all excited by their biological clocks. They wouldn't be mating this time of year or fighting for nesting grounds. There must be a pond back in there, or a cranberry bog."

"I think I hear a woodpecker tapping somewhere on the other side."

Niko swivelled her head to look. She activated her digital zoom with a simple mnemonic.

"The giant woodpeckers have a red head," she whispered as she reached down for her camera. "I don't know the official name. Pileated, I think."

Andrew rested his paddle across the gunwales with a gentle bump as they drifted closer.

"There it is, on that white birch." Niko pointed.

"I see it, big as a crow, bright red head."

The bird continued its tattoo, digging for carpenter ants. Niko had her camera on streaming mode, capturing every detail of sound and movement. She could pull the stills out later frame by frame at her leisure.

"He's sending a message in morse code," Andrew said.

"Oh, is that right? What's he saying?"

"Take . . . that . . . beautiful . . . woman . . . home . . . and . . . shag . . . her."

Niko turned around to see his sappy grin. She shook her head, feigning exasperation once again. Did men think about sex constantly, or did it just seem that way?

They took a narrow tributary to the right where the river made a fork and found themselves in thick forest where the branches entwined overtop in a natural bower. The air was suddenly damp and pungent and the sunlight came through heavy green branches in dappled patterns. A series of vines had grown up through the boughs and had turned crimson early in the season. They looked like veins circulating blood, as though the trees were dynamic with animal nature. She felt as though she was travelling within a living creature. She could hear the inhalation of giant breath and feel the gentle exhalation on her skin.

"Look at the ribbons of light moving on the forest floor," Niko said. "That is *so* awesome. It's magical, like the elvish world of Lothlórien."

"Is that some obscure literary reference?"

"You've got to be kidding."

"It is kinda creepy."

"It must be the reflection from the ripples in the water."

They sat floating and watching, and Niko felt herself transported with wonder. This was the communion she had longed for in vampire prison, the sense of mother Gaia like a touchstone in her life. She was not just a bundle of neurons firing all-or-none like computer bits. She was not just a clone built in a laboratory from sterile DNA code, a poor photocopy of a dead original. She was something more. She had a soul, a spirit, an etheric essence. She was able to experience God.

The snap of a pop-top broke the mantle of silence.

Startled back to reality, Niko turned to look.

"Want a beer?" Andrew said and offered a silver can forward.

She felt her body deflate like a punctured balloon at his mundane interruption. She must be deluding herself. No one else seemed to share her mystic empathy with the countryside. She stared off into the Tolkien forest again, but the magic was gone. "We'd better turn back," she said.

Andrew squeezed his beer can between his running shoes and awkwardly attempted to turn the canoe. Niko tried to backpaddle from the front, but without a capable oarsman in the rear they nosed into a tangle of low-hanging boughs near the shore. She got her freshly coiffed curls caught in a branch and yelped alarm. She reached up to grab her hair before it was pulled out by the roots.

Andrew thrashed his paddle in desperation.

Niko stood and pulled the canoe backward as she struggled to extricate herself.

"Do you have any scissors?" Andrew said.

"Oh, shut up."

Finally she pulled free of the tangle and watched a few long wisps of her hair wave down from the tree like spirogyra. She sat down carefully, trying to preserve some modicum of self-respect. What was she thinking, fluffing her hair up like a fashion model for a canoe trip?

Andrew guzzled his beer and burped.

They paddled in silence back to the fork in the river and turned left with the flow of water. They rested and drifted with the current. The quiet seemed eerie, the occasional birdsong amplified by the lack of context. Even with her auditory augmentation at baseline Niko noted blue jays, warblers and the deep, distinctive *ookagoonk* of a marsh bittern, a bird she had catalogued but never actually sighted in the wild. A hummingbird buzzed above a crimson cardinal flower that had already started to go to seed.

"What the hell is that?" Andrew said as they rounded a gentle corner.

"A moose," Niko whispered in awe, already reaching for her camera. "Try to get a little closer."

"That thing is *huge*," Andrew said.

"Shhh."

Much bigger than a horse, the fully grown male stood knee deep in a marshy area along the shore, his bony rack of antlers like giant palms with fingers spread wide. The moose looked up as they approached, but continued to grind a mouthful of weeds with slow mastication.

"Wow," Andrew said as he pointed the canoe for a closer inspection.

Niko watched through the viewscreen of her camera, zooming in for a head shot and marvelling at the sheer size of this monster. He looked like a furry pillar of muscle, with a thick neck and hulky back, a long rounded snout and small pointed ears behind massive antlers.

"That's too close," Niko said, smelling the brute now, a fetid aroma of mud-caked urine. She looked up from her camera, only a few feet away, and felt a rush of primal panic. She watched his nostrils gaping rhythmically. She stared into dead black eyes. The moose stopped chewing and snorted.

"Andrew?" Niko tipped backward in her seat, edging away.

The beast lunged without warning and smashed antlers into the side of the canoe. Niko screamed and fell backward into the belly of the boat as it tipped sideways and was bulldozed back out into the current. Cold water sloshed up and splashed onto her face and neck. Miraculously, they stayed upright and afloat.

She turned to watch the moose, dignified in slow majesty as it ambled up the bank into the undergrowth. She squirmed awkwardly to face Andrew. "What do you think you're doing, you idiot? You can't steer that close to a moose!"

He seemed to be in shock, his lab-rat pallor now ghostlike. He stood frozen, clutching his paddle with white-knuckled fingers. Niko climbed back into her seat. The front of the canoe had been caved in by the force of the blow and water sprayed through huge cracks in the fiberglass.

"We're sinking. Do we have anything to bail with?"

Andrew blinked and offered forward his empty beer can.

"Oh, great," Niko said. She pressed her lips tight as she stifled an urge to lambaste Andrew with a host of obscenities. She took the can and began to bail the pool of cold water collecting at her feet, wishing she had some tool to open the top wider. It was a tedious procedure waiting for air to bubble out of the beer can and then pouring a thin stream back into the river, but she thought she could keep them afloat. She was soaked to the skin.

"I'll pay for the canoe," Andrew said.

"Damn right you will. It's a rental!"

"I'm sorry, but it was all your idea."

Niko looked over her shoulder at him and almost laughed at his helpless little-boy expression. She turned back to bailing and wondered why she was sleeping with such a jerk.

"Just get us home, Andrew."

# SIX

"**C**ome in, Mr. Davis," said a voice from the intercom. "Up the stairs to my office."

A lock clicked at the entrance to this small brownstone walk-up and Zak pushed open a heavy steel door with inlaid coloured glass. An oak landing sat beyond and an antique staircase curved up to the right, the steps scalloped in the centre but refinished with a satin gloss. A mounted webcam tracked his progress.

Original artwork decorated the route up, acrylic abstracts and subtle watercolour splashes. In the hallway at the top, oak wainscotting covered the lower half of the walls above thick, beige carpet. The house smelled aromatic with cedarwood and old varnish.

Dr. Jackie Rose sat at a computer desk viewing a widescreen monitor, but turned and stood tall as Zak entered her cluttered office. "I don't normally grant interviews, but I was impressed by your credentials, Mr. Davis. I haven't met many Eternals, and you seem like an intriguing man with a somewhat clandestine history." She strode toward him with an aura of nobility and offered a warm handshake in greeting. She was stunningly beautiful, matching him in height, her skin dark and emerald eyes transfixing. Zak had never seen a gaze so vital and piercing.

"Are those your real eyes?"

She started momentarily and a smile tugged at the side of her full lips. "Yes," she said, slowly and with a hint of inflection.

"Uh," Zak stammered, caught himself. "Beautiful." He felt a pang of self-consciousness. He had not come all this way to play the fool. "I read your book," he said.

"Oh? Which one?"

"*I Never Left You.*"

"Right. Hot off the shelf. So you've recently lost a loved one."

"My wife, Mia."

Jackie Rose cast her eyes down with respect. "I'm sorry for your loss."

"I'm trying to find her. I've been searching for weeks."

"I can empathize, of course. A few weeks can seem a lifetime after losing a partner."

"When I read your story, I knew you could help me."

"Would you like a glass of water, Mr. Davis?" She pointed to a small refrigerator beside her desk. "Have you come a long distance?"

"I took a bus. Do you have coffee?"

She tilted her head with a nod, playing the gracious host. "Downstairs in the kitchen. Follow me." She walked with great fluidity, an apparition floating by, and Zak followed her hungrily with his eyes.

She stopped at the door but did not turn. "Just to get the question out of the way beforehand, Mr. Davis, the breasts are fake. My husband bought them for me." She headed down the stairs.

Zak felt hot blood in his cheeks. He wondered if he had been ogling her. Probably. "Call me Zak," he said. "I have great respect for your work."

In the kitchen she filled a coffee maker with finely ground beans and started the drip. She sliced an apple into sections and put them on a plate with cubes of cheese. The cabinets were made of country pine, yellowed with age and marbled with dark grain. The countertop was beige ceramic, the sink white, and the pewter taps fashionably neo-antique.

Zak sat on a wooden stool at a divider between kitchen and dining areas. He crunched on a piece of apple as he watched her pull cups from a compact dishwasher. What a gorgeous woman. "I'm intrigued by the colour of your skin, Doctor. I hope you don't mind the observation, but your facial features seem European. It's a lovely combination."

"My mother was African," she said, "my father Dutch. I grew up in the London suburbs. What about you?"

"My parents were American. We spent a lot of time in the Far East when I was young. They split up eventually. My mother died."

"She wasn't Eternal?"

"No."

"Your wife?"

Zak nodded as he tried a cube of cheese. He hadn't realized how long he had gone without food. "Yes, and one son, Rix."

"You've had some good fortune, then."

He grimaced involuntarily. "You might say."

Jackie nodded, subliminal message received. Life was not all cheesecake.

"Can you help me find my wife, Dr. Rose?"

She poured coffee into dark brown mugs and placed one before Zak. She added a bowl of sugar and fished a wax carton of cream out from the refrigerator. They fixed their respective drinks in silence as the question hung in the air.

Jackie sipped from her cup and surveyed Zak over the rim. "Are you familiar with the phantom-limb phenomenon?"

"Sure. People still feel arms or legs after an amputation."

"Over half of widows and widowers report feeling their dead spouse is very close."

"I don't doubt it."

"One in eight report hearing their spouse speak or seeing a physical manifestation of their presence."

"Sounds reasonable."

Her emerald eyes were mesmerizing. "This correlates highly with the degree of self-report regarding happiness in the marriage."

Zak shrugged and ate another slice of apple. "You're the expert."

"The question naturally arises: do the happily married couples have some special connection in the afterlife, or are the survivors deluding themselves with 'phantom-limb' experiences?"

"What does the evidence say?"

She pursed her full lips. "A skeptic might ask why the unhappily married couples are not reporting contact after life," she said. "Why is there no random sampling?"

"Mia and I were very happy."

Jackie sighed with a gentle resignation. "It's been five years since my husband died, the subject of my book."

Zak nodded. "It's only been a few months for me."

"We were in love and very close. As you must have read, he lingered on his deathbed for a long time and we planned all manner of afterlife meetings, secret codes, telepathy, psychokinesis, automatic writing. None came to pass."

"Nothing?"

She pressed her mouth into a delicate frown. "If there is anything to be learned from my years of research, it's that paranormal events are spontaneous one-off happenings, ineffable and non-repeatable."

"No contact at all?"

She looked down and away in a signal of concession. "I dream about him of course, but that is not the stuff of science."

"Are you a scientist?"

"Me? No, no." She shook her head with self-effacement. "I'm not a scientist. I was an advertising mannequin in my heyday, a catwalk slave. I did okay as an innovative edit, a short flash in the pan. You know, the white chick with dark skin and no tan lines." She laughed with the memory.

"I noticed your gait is very fluid and graceful."

"Why thank you. I didn't think it still showed. I guess they trained the natural hip swagger right out of my bones. It was a life of hard labour, but I don't regret an instant. It's all so very short in retrospect."

"How in the world did you become the world-renowned expert on psychic phenomena?"

Jackie laughed again, her voice like music. "Goodness, I have no idea. You write a few books, get on vidi. I think I have a streak of honesty that people respond to."

"There's a lot of trickery out there?"

"Loads. They call it 'heightened suggestibility' in the trade. Humans have a tendency to see patterns where none exist."

"I'm not looking for patterns," he said. "I'm looking for my wife. I want her back."

Jackie Rose stiffened and seemed to take his declaration as a personal affront. "If you think you can waltz in here and expect the cosmos to do your bidding, you are sadly mistaken. Did you think we might perform a seance in the dark, Mr. Davis?"

"Call me Zak."

"I lecture at universities, Mr. Davis. I don't perform resurrections."

She picked up the tray of snacks and took it along with her coffee through an archway into the living room. Two silvery blue couches sat at right angles in the corner facing a round sheet of glass supported by wrought iron. A fireplace was set into the wall opposite but looked too clean to be in use. Zak peeked inside to see fake logs and natural gas burners but no obvious control mechanism.

A large painting dominated the far wall, a watercolour landscape with dark trees like spider webs and a convoluted river tied in a knot of rainbows. As he stared closer he noticed that the river was a scarf encircling a neck, with a stern face above and dark eyes gazing back at him from the underbrush, the spirit of Gaia watching in perpetual vigilance. The visual paradigm shift was startling.

Jackie Rose took a seat under the painting. "My husband Timon's crowning work."

"Ingenious. He was an artist?"

"He was a photographer by trade and managed my business affairs. He painted as a hobby to relieve stress. He had a natural gift but never enough time to develop it properly."

Zak finished his coffee and set the empty mug on the glass table. He didn't dare sit beside this incredible woman in her sanctuary. He felt that he had ruined any chance of enlisting her cooperation. He took a seat at the far end of the couch opposite, giving her plenty of breathing space, and ducked his head in silence. He wondered if he had outstayed his welcome with the famous author.

"I'm a dualist in regard to the mind-body problem, Mr. Davis," she said. "We all experience a subjective persona situated somewhere behind our eyes which modern science cannot explain. I accept that we inhabit our living bodies in a vital and complicated dance, but I believe our minds are not created by our brains and are free to go elsewhere at the time of death. Our bodies are merely shells that we use for a temporary journey. This is the phenomenological view. This is what it feels like to be human, and the vast majority of religions throughout history have taken this position."

Jackie paused to invite comment. She sipped her coffee and waited.

"Whether the mind is created by the brain does not concern me," Zak said. "I'm interested in where consciousness goes after death."

"The mind separate from the body is called astral travelling. There are millions of reports of this in the natural world."

"I've felt it myself." He remembered hovering at the ceiling, looking down at his own body and the crumpled rag-doll form of his wife. He winced at the memory.

Jackie made a point of glancing away, an awareness of pain. "Tell me about the so-called uploading of consciousness that has been developed in the colonies by the Soul Saver Corporation," she said.

Zak bristled with caution. What had the good doctor discovered in her research about him? Was his history offplanet now common coinage? "The technology is not available," he said. "Not on Earth anyway."

"Oh, don't be so secretive, Mr. Davis. Sharing is a two-way street." She took a sip from her cup, completely at ease in her own home. She was wearing a tight tunic and plain black leggings, her legs bare above silver-embroidered black slippers. Even her ankles were beautiful.

Zak studied her for a moment, tore his eyes away. "It's a complete copy of body and brain activity like a hard-drive backup. It's a flash picture of a human soul."

"Does the copy have a mind?"

"I guess it must feel like it. It's reported to be quite fabulous. Nirvana, you know, the typical thing."

"Fascinating. And this mind resides inside cold metal hardware?"

He nodded. "In a virtual domain, an unlimited perfection."

"Like heaven?"

"Sure," he said, "if you like."

Jackie Rose shifted her position on the couch with the slow elegance of a ballerina. "But it's just data dots and zeros, surely a transient phenomenon." She peered closer.

"Yes, when you pull the plug on a saved soul, the consciousness stops."

Her brow contracted with a hint of worry. "How do you know that?"

Zak shrugged. "Everyone just assumes. They have a saying in the colonies: *From silicon the saved soul rises and to silicon it doth return.* It's a poor excuse for poetry."

"But when you pull the plug on the organic copy," she said, "the human mind keeps going?"

"I guess so." He thought again of poor Mia. "That's what I hope."

"That's what I believe, Mr. Davis. In religious terms, I have faith in that outcome."

Zak glanced up at Timon's painting. "Your husband is out there somewhere in a disembodied state?"

"Yes." She nodded with delicate deference. "It used to be called an etheric body, but the word has fallen into disrepute. Now we call it a quantum pattern, but it's really just semantics. Modern string theory postulates a multi-dimensional reality in which the free consciousness might reside. The Christians call it a ghost, the Hindus believe in a karmic essence, the Chinese worship departed spirits called shén. The early Egyptians built giant pyramids to commemorate the afterlife."

"So where does that leave us?"

Jackie offered a thin, sad smile. "Lost and alone, I'm afraid." She put her mug down and rose to her feet. "I'm sorry I can't be of more practical help, but I do have a lecture tonight. It takes me some time to prepare, to get my groove on as the kids used to say."

Zak stood and bowed. "Of course. I appreciate your time."

She offered a handshake as a formal end to the interview, but Zak didn't want to let it go at that. "May I hug you?" he asked.

She dropped her hand. "What?"

"I feel a synchronicity. I'd like to share your experience in some small way. I feel like we're on the same road together."

She shook her head. "I don't think that would be at all appropriate."

Zak looked up at the painting above the couch, the eyes glaring down. "Is he watching us?"

Her eyes shrouded in a subtle affirmation. "I believe so."

"Can we meet again sometime? Can I take you to dinner?"

"I'm really very busy," she said. "My publicist runs me ragged."

"I see." He hung his chin, hoping his disappointment would be obvious. Having run out of options, he could only turn and walk away.

As her front door closed behind him he paused to deliberate on the landing, staring up at the brownstone brick wall, wondering what he should do now. He had staked everything on this impulsive gesture, this last avenue of discovery. He had stayed awake all night in bold certainty that this woman would help him find Mia, rehearsing the meeting that he had now botched miserably. Her beauty had thrown him off, distracted him from his true mission. He hadn't noticed a woman in months and now suddenly his hormones had tricked him into flirting with a complete stranger. He had nowhere left to go and little money to get there. He walked to the street and stood watching

Jackie's house, feeling weak and vacuous, a poor excuse for a man. No, Mia would never forgive him if he gave up now.

He hived off a cloak of depression and made his way downtown, located the university campus. He found a poster announcing the evening lecture: *Life After Life: The Future of Psychic Research*, by Dr. Jackie Rose, Ph.D. He bought a ticket and wandered around campus until he found a delicatessen. He ordered a roast beef sandwich and a pickle with the last of his cash. What next? Hitchhike home to the ERI? Go back to Canada and work for Jimmy? At least he had job offers. He had a life waiting for him. He had Rix and should be grateful for a remnant of family, but an emptiness called him from within, a gut-wrenching void.

Mia. The thought of her still made his throat ache. He never had a chance to say goodbye to his lover. Someone had bartered for her life, killed her in the immortal bloom of youth and disappeared like smoke. The police detectives had offered little hope of ever bringing her murderer to justice. No fingerprints at the scene, no witnesses, a professional hit. Just another dead Eternal, a corpse with no citizenship. Zak was the only suspect and had spent a night behind bars while they checked his alibi and tested his hands for powder burns.

His wife and dead baby in a pool of blood—the picture was engraved in his brain like letters on a granite tombstone. How had it come to pass? A knock at the door, room service? Flower delivery? A handgun with a silencer at close range, a detective had told him, three quick shots to the heart. Did she have time to feel fear? To beg for her life? Oh, God. He should have been more careful. He never should have left her alone. It was all his fault.

Turmoil boiled within him as he made his way to the lecture hall. Was Mia really gone? Snuffed out like a candle? His heart still screamed *no, not possible*, but a cold dread circled around him like a black raven. The phantom-limb effect, Jackie had said. He was just another statistic in her research, a common case study.

The lecture hall was filled to capacity, perhaps five hundred seats sloping down to a small stage with a simple wooden lectern. A crowd of fresh-faced students chatted amongst themselves as Zak found a seat two rows from the back, past a long line of pointed knees and polite smiles. The chairs had cushioned seats and a small table on the left-hand side for laptops. Most students were using handheld webcams to record the event. A few were wired for Prime but not plugged up.

A forest of youth was growing up around him, a generation of challenge rising up in stark contrast to his slow and inevitable decline. Old and tired, he was hanging on to a fraying lifeline for support, a spiny, scratchy hemp like a hangman's noose, a mummy's sash recycled. He could hear the fibres snap and pop above him like pistol shots as he spun slowly round and searched for escape, a hand-hold or foothold to take his gathering weight. Gravity was dragging him down, an endless implacable entropy was stealing his purpose. His Eternal soulmate was missing, lost somewhere in the mists of spacetime. He had to find her.

The overhead lights dimmed and the crowd hushed in unison. A pink spotlight followed Dr. Jackie Rose as she strutted onstage like a dark goddess on a fashion runway. She was wearing a short black skirtsuit with a red ruffled blouse tight at her neck. Her long legs were bare below the knee and her sling-back pumps had a web of thin straps like fishnet above spiky heels.

She took a microphone from the lectern and continued her parade as she introduced herself, walking and talking her way back and forth across the stage to fully engage the group. She exuded a confident charisma and used it to her advantage. The students fell silent. She was hip, she was cool, she was young enough to capture the crowd but mature enough to demand some respect. Her delivery was refined and her voice dripped with passion for her subject. Psychic research had never seemed so fascinating, and Zak cherished every word.

She began with the early history of the nineteenth century, the frauds and charlatans, and joked about poor recording techniques and gullible audiences. A series of colourful historic anecdotes proved the fallibility of eyewitness accounts, the malleability of human memory. The chicanery and swindlers had been exposed by science long ago. All that remained now was the truth—cold, stark, and measurable.

Armed with this elaborate underpinning, Jackie Rose began her own poignant journey. She told about her husband's lingering death and their plans for the afterlife, recounting Timon's near-death experiences, his visions of splendour and cosmic unity, his complete loss of fear as the guardian of death drew nigh. The dark wraith became an angel of promise and good spirits guided his way toward future resplendence.

She told of her own frustration and disappointment as she tried to contact his etheric spirit beyond the grave for five long years, and she almost wept with the emotional intensity of unrequited love. Seances, laboratory exercises, double-blind experiments—nothing seemed to work for her. Clairvoyants, channellers, witches, and magicians—she had exhausted every avenue of approach and told each story with dramatic eloquence. Zak could not help but be drawn into her carefully rehearsed presentation. He glanced around at neighbouring faces to see them rapt with attention, fearful in the face of death, eyes bright and shiny with tears. If Jackie Rose were selling breakfast cereal the audience would buy it by the carton.

"And so, where are we headed now for the twenty-second century?" she asked as she surveyed the captive crowd. "What has not been explained by science? Reports of telekinesis have not been repeatable under controlled conditions even with millions of dollars offered for one single proof, yet popular culture continues to embrace the notion. Levitation and fortune telling have become illusionist playgrounds abounding in controversy to this day. Billions of people around the world believe Jesus Christ walked on water in Galilee and Muhammad spoke divine truth in Mecca. One third of the general populace report belief in precognition, particularly in dreams, and artificial forced-choice experiments show a greater-than-chance statistical effect. Do we all have a trans-temporal awareness that we can learn to harness and enjoy? This question and many others remain unanswered. How many of you believe in extrasensory perception?"

A forest of eager hands waved in the air. Zak was not surprised. Dr. Jackie Rose had earned her reputation.

"I believe in life after life," she proclaimed. "I believe in a universal consciousness that underlies our narrow experience of reality, a singular force that accounts for all manner of paranormal phenomena. It cannot be measured by current science. Perhaps it is a network of subatomic waves smaller than quarks. Perhaps it accounts for the so-called missing dark matter that provides stability to the cosmos. A theorist once explained to me that humanity is enjoined within a multi-dimensional quantum architecture that expands continually in all potential directions. Everything is possible until collapsed by observation. Consciousness itself has the power to create reality. Your consciousness and mine. That is the message I want to leave with you today, the promise of your infinite potential. Make your pilgrimage with joy, knowing that you are connected to God. Our sojourn in these temporal bodies is short, my friends, and we would do well to make the best of it."

A thunderous applause erupted from the audience as one by one students stood in ovation. A wild fervour shone in their eyes. No trip-hop rave or religious revival could elicit such adoration. Jackie Rose was touching the core of human experience, the essential mystery. What is consciousness? Where does it come from and where does it go?

An attendant wheeled out a table stacked high with copies of Jackie's latest book, *I Never Left You*, and a little flock of supplicants gathered at the stage to meet and greet the mistress of reality. Crash doors opened at the sides of the lecture hall and the crowd quickly thinned. Zak waited and watched. He had to talk to her. He had to try one more time to gain her trust.

Jackie Rose continued to charm onstage, wielding her pen like a magic wand, but he could see that her strength was beginning to wane. She was ravishing to the eye and a gifted orator, but her true dynamism came from deep spiritual realms. He followed the edge of the crowd down to the stage and stayed in the shadows until the last student had palmed a debit pad.

The attendant wheeled the book table away through a heavy curtain and Jackie went back to the lectern to retrieve her notes. She finally met his gaze as he stepped into the light and stiffened with recognition. "Are you stalking me?" she asked.

"No." He raised his palms with innocence.

"I have a panic button on the dais. I'll call Security."

"Your lecture was amazing."

Her expression remained stony. He was getting nowhere fast.

"Can we talk for just a minute?"

"No."

"I'll buy one of your books."

"You already have a copy."

Damn, she was a tough nut. His last hope was fading fast. He thought of Mia in a pool of Eternal blood. "I need your help," he said.

"Mr. Davis, I am not a grief counsellor." She gathered her papers and marched away.

Zak felt galvanized with energy. This was his last chance. Fight or fly. He might never see her again. He thought of his mindspeak to Helena and felt a surge of desperation.

*Please listen to my voice.*

Jackie stopped. She turned slowly, her dark skin now ashen. "What did you say?"

Zak summoned a strange force from deep chasms. He focused his will on building a mental projection like a lightning charge and released it. *Please listen to my voice.*

Her papers fluttered out of her limp hands like autumn leaves. Tears began pouring from her eyes in dark trails of mascara. Her body shuddered. "Oh God," she whimpered.

Zak crept forward, uncertain. He reached for her shoulders to offer some comfort and she fell hard into his arms. He kept his palms up as she squeezed his lungs of air. She continued to embrace him, sobbing into his shoulder, and he finally lowered his hands and patted her back in a platonic gesture. She smelled of lavender and dry-cleaning solvents.

Jackie Rose trembled against him as she cried out her catharsis, and Zak remained mute in wonder. Finally she pulled back to peer at him. Her makeup was a mess but her emerald eyes shone like beacons from black chaos. "I'm sorry that I doubted you," she whispered.

"That's okay," Zak said. "Are you going to be all right?"

She blinked at him. "You don't understand your gift?"

"Not exactly," he admitted.

"It must be a sign for me alone."

Zak nodded, trying to piece a paradox together in his brain.

Jackie pulled away and took a cleansing breath. "I must look a devil," she said. "Do you have a tissue?"

"You look fine."

She snorted a laugh and Zak felt a wave of relief at her composure.

"Well, Mr. Davis, you have my undivided attention." She folded her arms under her surgically perfected breasts and studied him.

"Really?"

"How long have you had this telepathic ability?"

Zak winced his naïveté. "This was only my second try."

"I've waited a long time for you to arrive."

"Why is that, exactly?"

Jackie tilted her head slightly and pursed her pouty lips. She squinted at him. "Mr. Davis, you just spoke to me inside my mind with the voice of my dead husband."

A second or two passed as realization dawned and the foundation of their new partnership became plain. Zak smiled with triumph and felt revitalization bloom like a flower within him. "Call me Zak," he said.

# SEVEN

**A**ndrew and a technician wheeled a large metal box into Phillip's laboratory on a delivery cart. Niko stood up from her bedside vigil, feeling a pulse of energy vibrate through her body like electricity. "This is the package," she said.

The rounded corners were seamless, the grey-blue sides unmarked, but an elaborate display panel faced upward with blinking lights, a miniature keyboard and twin flatscreen monitors. She could hear no sound, no life inside.

"This is Colin," Andrew said, bouncy on his toes, with a slow karate chop toward the technician. "Colin7."

"And this is Niko." He shifted stage hands accordingly. "Niko2." His eyes glinted with mischief.

Niko gawked at the stranger. "You're a clone?"

Colin7 smiled with delight, his eyebrows wide. "You, too? Well, this *is* a surprise." He offered a hand in greeting while Niko gave him a quick appraisal. He was young and thin, almost meatless in a dark suit and purple tie. He had a pointed chin and gaunt cheeks, ears slightly pointed and protrusive—an aerodynamic face with flaps at thirty percent. He was kind of cute with a short bad-boy scruff of unruly hair and a relaxed look of natural empathy. His eyes were bright with intelligence but his handshake was limp and cold, his fingers bony and tapered to sharp points of keratin.

"You're from offplanet?" Niko asked, still holding his hand in wonder.

"Cromeus Signa. You?"

"No." She released him finally and slapped self-consciously at her thigh. "Just, uh, hanging out."

His eyebrows arched even higher. "Wow, I'm impressed."

"Well, cloning is just experimental, you know, down here."

"It looks like they've done a marvellous job."

Niko smiled. Score one for the alien stranger.

She noted Andrew grinning at her, watching the scene unfold. He had probably rehearsed the whole thing in his mind a hundred times like a geek. She could see a gloating amusement in his face. He could have told her.

She turned back to Colin7 as realization clicked into place like an interlocking mechanism. "Colin Macpherson?"

He bowed once in recognition. "My progenitor."

Niko gawked at him in awe. "So you're, like, an über-genius?"

Colin7 shook his head. "I'm pretty good at math. Does that count?"

She flustered. "No, I mean, we studied you in school. You're right up there with Einstein. Celestial physics 101."

"Well, I wouldn't want to take credit for ancient history." His eyes crinkled with condescension as he grinned and glanced over at Andrew to see if he was sharing the joke. He was. Both men were looking at her like she was a mental recluse.

She swallowed back her schoolgirl adulation. Quit fawning, Niko. Pull yourself together. Of course this man was not Colin Macpherson. He was seven steps removed, a poor carbon copy like herself. Neither was she Niko Davis. She was Niko2, the clone of Phillip's dead daughter, a ghost from the past with no last name. "So this is the . . ." she said.

"Schemata," said Colin7. He stepped to the box and began typing on the tiny keyboard with his pointed fingernails. Coloured sparks danced at the tips of his fingers.

"What is that exactly?"

"Cognitive modules," he said. "Patterns of electrochemical activity. We resonate them into the subject brain with lasers."

"Modules?" She turned to Andrew with a frown. "Subject brain?"

"Humans operate with about twenty basic modules of consciousness," Andrew said with his hands rising up in subtle pacification as though preparing to play a piano. "You know, working persona, resting mode, higher thought, active-sensational, passive-sensational, reflective . . ." He began to wiggle his fingers in a complicated dance. "The brain is always in rapid flux, turbid waters, and whatever module reaches threshold is observed as the consciousness of the moment. That's the theory. The mechanism still eludes us."

"What about memories?"

"What about them?"

"Are you putting someone else's memories in my dad?"

"We're not adding anything to the brain," Colin7 interjected. "We're resonating cognitive patterns. Too much episodic memory would be deleterious at this point," he said, looking at Andrew. "We might as well begin. I'll need a standard V-net interface to coordinate with the neural helmet."

"We've got virgin wetware behind the left ear." Andrew stepped forward with a pointing finger. "The original fiberoptic in the spine was freaked right out. Phillip was an early model." He unlocked a side component on the protective enclosure and lifted the heavy cover from Phillip's right eye, exposing the new cybernetics for the first time. A transparent prosthesis around the camera lens flashed with electrical activity. "Just got the final wide-spectrum tests today." Andrew patted the bioengineering equipment like a proud parent. "Everything checked out great. Now I'm just waiting on cosmetics to dress him up for the street with lids and lashes."

Phillip looked suddenly foreign, his partially skinless face inert like an automaton waiting for the command to rise, a mindless robot. Niko shuddered and struggled to suppress the thought. No, he was still her father, one petri dish removed. He was all she had.

Andrew plugged a serpentine cable behind Phillip's left ear and proffered the end. Colin7 inserted it into the top of the box and continued keyboarding. The machine began to hum with activity. A tone sounded, a boot-up beep.

"That should do it," said Colin7.

Niko peered at her father for any signs of change. "How long will it take?"

"Quite a long time, actually. We have to dumb it down almost a million to one and there's a lot of data." He glanced quickly at Andrew and back to Niko. "About three hours."

Andrew frowned. "A million to one?" He raised his forearm and began tapping on his wrist monitor.

"We can work in shifts," Colin7 said, "so the process is not unattended. We should stay in touch."

Andrew looked up from his calculations. "Right." He patted the pockets of his lab coat and pulled out a wristband. "This phone is coded to the whole team. You can have the first shift while I take Niko to the caf for breakfast. She was probably here all night again."

Niko grimaced. Was it morning already? She had lost all sense of time living in this laboratory cage. She turned back to Phillip, looked past the dehumanizing camera to his biological eye, searching for any glimpse of movement, any rapid-eye twitch from a fleeting dream. She closed her own eyes and willed a simple plea for resurrection. *O break the bonds of this early grave, this comatose prison. O let this man rise up to new life and health*. She stopped after a moment and wondered to whom she prayed? The aliens, the AI technology, the wetware surgeons? Was there a God somewhere listening to the cries of poor clones?

Was it the destiny of the desperate to turn to invisible entities for aid? Some self-inflicted delusion of her species? She worried as she left the room that she might be slipping into psychosis. Was it so unnatural to pray for her own father? It grated against reason but felt like a tonic to shed her burden of worry. She needed a strong shoulder. She needed a friend. She missed cousin Rix.

Niko settled in the cafeteria with an egg salad sandwich, her daily morning ritual. She remembered the feeling of joy when she had first sampled this vending-machine product weeks ago. Now it tasted like mayonnaise on cardboard. Crushed chicken embryos. *We're sacrificing all the virgins we can buy.*

Andrew sat opposite, still tapping numbers on his wrist calculator, his ham sandwich untouched.

"So it's big," she said.

He looked up, nodded. "Really big."

"Maybe they just trickle it in slowly like a battery charger. Maybe they don't want to overclock a fragile system."

He scrunched his face to say that he didn't buy it, but he took a sip of juice and began to unwrap his sandwich. "Can you imagine plugging up for three hours just to download a file?"

Niko shook her head as she considered past experience. Three hours? A few seconds was usually enough to consummate any transaction on Main Street. Even deep in Sublevel Zero, transmission time had never been an issue. A contract was sealed at the touch of an upraised palm. She never lingered. She jostled perpetually to keep ahead of the user traffic, to keep out of sight. The V-net was instantaneous as far as she could tell. Maybe the data was always being dumbed down for her, the weak biological link in the digital chain. Maybe it was faster than instantaneous. A million times faster. "If it works, I don't care how long it takes."

Andrew shrugged his acquiescence, signalling that she was the boss until Phillip woke up, washing his hands of all responsibility. He bit into his sandwich.

Niko leaned forward to face him. "What do you know about this guy?"

Andrew chewed and swallowed, taking his time. "Not much."

"You just picked him up from the want ads?"

He grimaced a caricature at her. "I took advantage of Phillip's professional connections."

"Is it safe to leave him alone with my dad?"

"Oh, give me a break."

"I'm going back to the lab. This is too freaky."

"Fine," he said, his eyes stern. "I've got a meeting."

Niko finished her breakfast in silence, glaring at her jerk boyfriend and wondering how she had been talked into this mess.


A symphony of white harmonics enveloped him, a pulse of a billion interconnections. Digital insight exploded like wild fireworks around him as his perception adjusted to the splendour, a raging pattern of knowledge seeking substance. He reached out his hands, stretching muscles long dormant. His fingers elongated and attenuated into thin strands, sucking his awareness to a neurofibrillar frontier of in-finite complexity, a million whirling spirals of data. A feeling of ver-tigo assailed him as he expanded.

No.

He pulled back.

Home to the core of finite consciousness.

What was this place?

He heard babbling patterns in the white music, an unknown machine language. He smelled burning plastic.

His name was Phillip. He hung on to that label of identity for reassurance. It belonged to him and no one could take it away.


Niko stopped at the door of the lab to put on her game face and a jacket of insouciance. She flipped back her hair and stepped inside with a brimming smile. "So, Colin7, what do you do when you're not jumping through hyperspace? Are you a neuroscientist like Andrew?"

Colin7 looked up from his data tablet, his face inert. "Not exactly, although I do have some basic training. In my free time I'm studying the collective unconscious psi force with a view toward the temporal dilation effect of intelligence."

What? Niko paused to scrutinize his face. He did not appear to be joking. "Sounds exotic," she said carefully. "That must be a rare specialty."

He smiled his self-effacement. "Everyone needs a hobby."

"So that's like, what, time travel?"

"I'm really just a theoretician. The practical applications will follow naturally."

Holy ghost, this guy was a wunderkind. "Do tell," she said as she edged closer.

STEVE STANTON

"The collective unconsciousness has been monitored since the twentieth century, of course. The data is voluminous."

"I didn't know that."

"Deviations from chance in mechanical systems," he said. "Mind over matter."

"How do they measure such a thing?"

"Well, I use atomic-decay clocks." He pulled nervously at his hair with his fingers. "Other types of random number generators were used in the elementary research. The experimental effect is amplified by the number of minds in phase and declines with distance, so it's not a simple quantum phenomenon."

Niko nodded. "I see," she said, but she really didn't.

Colin sat back in his chair and spread his hands in a gesture of affinity. "Media celebrations, prayer festivals—those were the primary targets in the early days. Continuous data is available stretching back over a century."

"Fascinating." She pulled a chair close to him and sat down.

He seemed to shrink back from her presence. "It's a bit arcane to the uninitiated."

"You would think something like that might be on the Main Street news."

"Hah. The man on the street is hardly concerned with the abstruse nature of the multiverse," he said with a hint of disdain, almost a joke. "For the most part our species is content amusing ourselves to death in a three-dimensional world."

Niko studied him with growing wonder. "So you think humans have natural psychic abilities in a fourth dimension?"

"Everyone has an unconscious awareness of the future, if that's what you mean."

"And there's scientific proof for that?"

"Incontrovertible." He was starting to warm to her undivided interest, beaming like a child displaying a hard-won trophy. In his suit and tie he looked more like a boardroom mannequin than a scientist, and his pointed ears gave him an elflike charm.

"Can you enlighten a rank neophyte?"

"Very well." He pointed to a small window on the wall. "Suppose a tree branch was about to crash through that window and fly across the room. Generally, a frightening stimulus is required to produce an objective measurement."

"Okay," she said, "a tree branch would definitely get my attention."

"Not at first, as it turns out. The initial measurement would be a change in galvanic skin response." He tapped the back of his hand with a finger. "This occurs about three seconds before the event."

"Before?"

"That's the time-dilation part."

"Are you sure?"

"All creatures show this presentiment," he said and held up a cautionary hand. "I mean as a statistical anomaly in bulk studies— not on every single occasion." He patted the air in front of him to curb her enthusiasm. "Some early experiments were done with earthworms. Electrovibration therapy for earthworms." He smiled. "Even the rocks would cry out if anyone bothered to test them."

"But that's incredible," Niko gushed. "It sounds like science fiction, a Jedi mind trick."

"It gets weirder. Everything we experience is science fiction, a quantum conjecture. In simple truth, nothing is real. But back to the story." He pointed again to the imaginary tree branch. "After the window breaks, your autonomous nervous system springs into effect, known as the orienting reflex. Neurons fire, muscles tense, and your arm begins to rise to block incoming danger. Next your voluntary nervous system goes into action and sends a motor signal to your arm, which, according to the experimental data, is already moving. Now finally your conscious mind takes notice. It's a faulty fourth stage defence at best. First came the presentiment, then the automatic reflex, followed by the motor response and cognitive awareness."

"I turn and duck."

He nodded happily, grinning like a leprechaun. "And the tree branch enters the room, missing your head by inches." He slid a flat hand above his tousled hair. "You're a lucky girl, Niko."

"It does pay to be presentimental."

"Actually your early warning could not have saved you," he said soberly. "An unconscious emotional arousal gives you no evolutionary advantage. It's precognitive and does not produce an escape response."

"So what good is a premonition if it doesn't keep me alive?"

Colin7 pursed his lips and made a popping sound, clearly at ease with her interrogation and welcoming the chance to debate. "That is the potent question indeed from a practical and theoretical standpoint. My hypothesis is that we are not seeing ahead in time during these special events. I think we are actually seeing late in time during normal events. What we observe with our space-time sensory apparatus is a convenient substitute for reality. It is collapsed potentia, essentially a history book created by quantum observation. It's a necessary simulation for interactive life as we know it."

"But it's not real?"

"Not technically."

Niko gaped in disbelief. "So where's the ultimate truth?"

"I don't know yet," he said. "That's my field of study."

"Well, what's your best approximation so far?"

"All I have is a mathematical speculation."

"Oh, come on, Colin7," she pressed. "You must have some idea what it means."

"No, actually I don't. Even Einstein refused to believe the results of his discoveries, and after John Bell the puzzle really fell apart. Nothing is real, and classical physics has become just another religion trying to make sense of the experiential data."

Niko squinted at this strange alien elf. "You must be a lot of fun at cocktail parties."

"We can only know veridical reality through mathematics," he said. "Any attempt at physical observation changes it fundamentally."

"You actually spend your day thinking about alternate realities?"

His smile seemed rapturous. "There is nothing more beautiful in all the universe than an elegant theorem."

Niko raised her eyebrows with doubt. "Boy, you need to get out more."

He shook his pretty head. "We don't go outside on my planet without protective gear. We're too close to our sun."

"No wonder you're so weird. I mean, sorry, you're not weird, exactly, you're just . . ."

"A theoretical physicist?"

Niko snapped her fingers at the easy escape. "Yeah, that's it." She patted his knee to show no offense. "I think you're way cool."

"Really? That's not the typical reaction."

"I bet. So tell me the practical nitty-gritty. Are we going to jump around in time and stuff after you figure this out?"

"I doubt it."

"See into the future?"

"Maybe. For the most part these psychic effects are subtle and

limited to communal sampling. As far as individuals go, the anec-
dotal data for psi research is hairy-scary as you probably know."

Niko nodded. "Ghosts and goblins."

Colin7 winced and closed one eye. "Most scientists try to distance
themselves from the crackpot reports. The subjective data is inconclu-
sive at best and generally unreliable—not worth serious study in my
estimation. On my planet the collective unconscious is easier to monitor, because we have only one main media source joining disparate
outposts, but the effects are small. The first measurable event on Earth
dates far back in history to the destruction of the World Trade towers.
The random chance deviations were off the scale, even allowing for the
basic transcription techniques of the time. The peak effect of the communal psi force was recorded by mechanical devices a full two hours
before the event. And not just in the vicinity, but globally."

"And no one cried warning?"

"Actually there were all kinds of unheeded portents," he said,
"but I'm talking about the elemental psi forces recorded by machines
not humans. Mind over matter. The time dilation effect is what
intrigues me. When so many minds are in phase on a global scale,
the time factor appears to increase exponentially. I have a working
formula in progress if you'd like to see it."

"Your brain is totally out there, Colin. Do you mind if I drop the
Seven? It seems so artificial."

"If it suits you better." Colin7 beamed at her with mischief. "Does
this mean we're friends?"

"We could be friends," she said and tipped a nod. "We have a lot
in common. The vanguard of biology, the forefront of clone science,
the post-human frontier."

He grinned. "That would be great."

"Do you want to, like, have lunch at the caf?"

"Not when I'm on duty." He thumbed back over his shoulder. "I can't leave our father unattended."

"What if I get Andrew to babysit?"

"Well, that might work."

"We could go for a hike."

His face wrinkled with displeasure. "Outside?"

"It's not really that bad. You could wear a hat."

"I'll think about it."

Niko stared at him, musing. She was really starting to like this guy. "Have you ever been on a motorcycle?"


Rix fell into his mother's arms in a dream. She was vast and powerful, and he felt that he was inside her, that she was all-encompassing and he was breathing her essence. He had a lucid feeling that he was in control of events, perhaps hypnagogic, but quickly recognized the plodding inevitability of a dreamstate, the passive helplessness. He was walking down a narrow path, but had to drag his steps as though swinging heavy wooden legs, dead of sensation and practically useless. He was running away from something but making little progress.

Everything was seaweed green, a dripping dark and dank green that tasted salty on his lolling tongue. He felt fear like a canopy.

"You never loved me," said a godlike voice in proclamation.

Of course he did, he told his dreamself. It seemed so obvious. Why wouldn't anyone listen to him?

"I saw you masturbating," his mother said.

*No way. You couldn't have.*

"I saw you thinking about me."

A dread conviction assailed him. O God, he felt wretched. His own mother.

"It's a sin, my son."

*Go away. Why do you haunt me?*

"You owe me one last thing."

*I can't help you now.*

"Vengeance will be mine."

He tried to run but his legs seemed like bags of cement. He dragged himself forward. It seemed that he would be trapped in this place forever. He gagged on salt like gravel in his mouth. He tried to spit.

"You cannot run from your destiny."

He thrashed his arms and felt resistance. A bedside lamp smashed on the floor, the bulb popping like a gunshot. He fell from his bed, sweaty and panting for breath. His legs were tangled in blankets like heavy rope.

What a crazy nightmare, some Oedipal obsession from his subconscious mind, his repressed grief finally frothing to the surface of awareness to torture him. He needed a splash of water on his face, some moisture on his parched tongue.

He extricated himself from bondage and stood in his dorm room, naked and chilly with perspiration. His body felt like a wire drawn taut, his brain hazy with the aftermath of trauma. He staggered to the washroom and opened the door. A blast of steamy water bathed his face. The shower was running and a naked form stood behind foggy glass. Niko?

The shower door swung outward on silent hinges. His mother faced him, angelic in magnificence. Her breasts seemed enormous, ready to suckle him anew. Rivulets of water trickled down her belly and dripped from her shaved pudendum. She was the most dreadful woman he had ever seen, a divine visitation.

He covered his nakedness with both hands in shame and humiliation. He stumbled backward.

Mia smiled at him with infinite understanding. "Now do you believe?"

Rix woke with an urgent exclamation, clammy with sweat under damp sheets, convicted and convinced that his mother had just spoken to him from beyond the grave. Perhaps dreams and visions were the only method of communication left to her in the afterlife. What did she want from him? Revenge for her murder? Retribution?

He climbed out of bed and trembled as the panic in his body slowly dissipated. The bedside lamp was unbroken, his blankets untangled. It had all been a clairvoyant message, a lucid dream within a dream. But undeniably real, a potent signal from heaven. His mother was out there somewhere. She was alive.

Niko jumped to her feet when she saw gamma spikes on Phillip's EEG. Solid beta activity had been building all morning in a regular wave like the rising and falling of an incoming tide. He was waking up at last, right on schedule, three hours from the start of the schematic upload.

She turned from the pulsing charts to peer at his face, partially obscured under the neural helmet. His single eye was fluttering under the lid like a trapped bird, his lips grim. She reached for his hand and cupped it between her palms. "Papa," she whispered.

A sound escaped him, a groaning murmur.

"Phillip? It's me, Niko. You're doing just fine."

"Niko," he croaked.

She laid her head on his chest, ear to his heart, and looked up at the grey stubble on his neck. Her eyes filled with tears. "Yes, Papa, it's me." She hadn't called him by that name in years, not since infancy, but now it seemed necessary more for her than for him. She needed the comfort of that early relationship again, the surety that her dad would always be there like a solid cornerstone in her flimsy house of cards.

His arm curled up and rested on her back, and she felt new vigour pulse within her.

"You made it," she said. "You're back better than ever." She dared it to be true in her mind.

"Niko," he said again, this time with a sigh of satisfaction.

She raised her head. "Are you in pain? Can you give any self-report?"

Seconds passed and she held her breath with anticipation.

"I'm fine now," Phillip said. "No pain. I'm swimming up through thick sludge."

"Can I get you anything? Can I help?"

"Bring my son."

"Zak's not here."

"No, the other one, Colin7."

"The technician?"

"As good a name as any." His right eye shuttered open and locked on her. "You are a vision of youthful splendour, my child." His lips quivered into a smile as if for the first time ever.

Niko's heart jumped at the animation in his face, so long a mask of despair, now bright with colour and hope. "I bet you say that to all the girls."

He coughed a halting laugh in response. Good higher-level thinking. Humour recognition was always the best test. Phillip was back, rebuilt and ready for the showroom floor. She felt a pure elation sing in her body like the first blush of the Eternal virus. Phillip had beat the odds. The Beast had tried to take him out and failed.

She tapped a signal on her wristband to alert the medical crew.

"Be right there, Niko," said Andrew. "Hold status on all recording equipment. Okay, team, the boss is in the building. Get to your battle stations." She could hear the exhilaration in his voice even through the tiny speaker on her arm. A chorus of replies sounded on the open channel as doctors relayed their expected arrival times.

Colin7 stepped into the room.

He approached quietly, his face calm, one eyebrow slightly raised in query. He leaned over Phillip and peered into his biological eye. He stared for a few seconds in silence, watching the eyeball move and blink. "Welcome back," he said finally.

"Jimmy. I could hardly believe it was you. Come on in."

Helena struggled to put a pleasant lilt in her tone, but her voice came out rusty, strained with anxiety. Here he was in the flesh outside her door at the ERI. Incredible. Everyone knew Jimmy never left his Faraday cage in Canada, his digital sanctuary. His face looked grim as he stood outside the Security perimeter where two guards watched from a respectful distance. He had an alert stance, a squat tension that reminded her of a gorilla.

"Let's go for a walk," he said.

A walk? This was not good. Why was Jimmy reluctant to enter the building? Helena glanced back over her shoulder, wondering about compromised surveillance. She had a webcam on every corner, microphones in every hallway, a permanent record.

"Sure. Do I need a coat?" She peered past him, trying to get a glimpse of the weather in the distance. She had not been outside in days.

"You'll be fine." Jimmy was wearing dark glasses and a crusty black leather jacket like a senior citizen. He looked like he had just stepped off his antique Harley.

Feeling dread like a gathering gloom, Helena stepped through the security gauntlet to meet him. He didn't offer a handshake or any common civility. He didn't speak.

They walked to the driveway and she touched his shoulder to stop him on the sidewalk. "What's up?"

Jimmy's gaze darted up to the left and right, pointing out the pole-mounted webcams with his eyes. "It's a beautiful day," he said.

Helena looked up at patches of cloud blocking the azure sky. The air was crisp with autumn chill and she wished she had gone back for a jacket. She stepped out onto the grass in front of the building, away from the parking-lot cameras. Jimmy followed along beside, hands in his pockets. He seemed shorter in person, hunched and furtive.

"Why the paranoia, Jimmy?"

"The Beast has been acting strange."

Helena pursed her lips as they continued walking. Scraggly weeds brushed her legs as they got further afield. "How strange?"

"Nothing I can put my finger on. Just a feeling."

Helena stopped and turned to confront him. "You came all this way to tell me you have a hunch?"

He shrugged. "No, I came here for a full report on where all the money's gone. We had a scheduled appointment."

"We had an appointment in Prime Seven, Jimmy. Not in person. Who meets in the flesh any more?"

"So humour me."

"Not without an explanation."

Jimmy's face twitched with inner turmoil. "As a precaution," he said, "I'm going with the notion that the Beast may be cognizant."

"That's crazy."

"I know."

"You must have some evidence."

Jimmy turned and continued walking.

Helena hurried to follow. "No webcam is going to lipread this far away," she said.

"The Beast has been making mistakes."

"Impossible."

"Not mathematical mistakes. Just errors in judgment."

"So what? Everyone makes mistakes."

"Exactly."

Helena sucked in a quick breath, her chest suddenly like iron. "What do you mean?"

He spread up five fingers backhand. "One man's mistake is another man's strategy."

"The ghost in the machine?"

"Finally I think someone's done it," Jimmy said and swung his hand down. "All the dogs have been barking round the tree for years now. It was just a matter of time."

Helena slowed her pace to a dreamlike stride, feeling common surety disassemble and flutter around her like confetti. The Beast controlled the encryption algorithms for the entire V-net—impossible to crack, impossible to hack. Whoever controlled the AI controlled the world. Total vigilance could easily flower into total domination and eventual tyranny, the slippery slope of sentient beings.

"It means the end of the white market," Jimmy said. "It's bad for business."

She reached out an arm to him. "Let's go back."

Jimmy halted and turned. "How far back?"

"Back before the Beast?" She tossed her head. "Hardly. I meant back to the Institute. I'm freezing out here." She grabbed both elbows and shivered for emphasis.

"Sure," he said. "Business as usual. I guess that's the best we can expect."

"We'll keep up a good front. To do otherwise might be dangerous. If they already know everything then there's no reason to hide."

Jimmy sighed and seemed to shrink even smaller. "I had to tell somebody. You're the only real friend I have left now that Zak has dropped out."

"I appreciate your confidence," Helena said, "and your friend-ship." She took him by the arm and began leading him back toward the ERI. "I won't say anything. It'll be our secret."

"It won't be a secret for long."

She shuddered against gathering cold. "Does Zak know?"

Jimmy shook his head. "He's indisposed, busy with a new girl-friend."

"Really?"

"She's a piece of work," he said with distaste.

"Good work or bad?"

"Creative whimsy, in my opinion."

Helena tucked her arm closer against him, touching shoulders, trying to gain warmth from his body. "What's her name?"

"Dr. Jackie Rose."

"I've heard of her. She's a bestseller."

Jimmy grimaced with scorn. "She's hawking cultural fantasy to the masses."

"I'm sure Zak knows what he's doing."

"I hope you're right. The last time I talked to him, he said he was going on a quest to find his dead wife." He turned toward her as they walked. "That sound reasonable to you?"

"Not exactly."

"Aren't you jealous?"

"Of a dead woman? I honestly never gave it a thought."

"He's wasting his potential."

"I think you're the one who's jealous."

"At least I'm not afraid to admit it." Jimmy shrugged his Harley jacket forward and lapsed into silence. He wasn't having fun any more, now that the Beast had fallen. His camouflage of confidence had dropped from him like a shed skin. Helena could see new worry etched around his eyes like craquelure. Perhaps he had hoped to take the Beast down himself, to leash the AI to his own will. Good luck with that. Perhaps a sentient Beast would be better for mankind in the long run. A higher level conscience like a god in V-space. Would that be so bad?

Helena set her lips with determination against the cold wind. There was nothing she could do but watch her back and try to protect those she loved. Anything could happen now. Anything at all. Change was destiny, and destiny ever-changing.

# EIGHT

**S**ilus Mundazo had a keyboard on his desk, two wide-screen monitors glowing in front of him and a palm holopad accessing three-dimensional layers of data at the twitch of a finger. He surveyed an organized chaos of data with practised decorum. Helena watched his gyrating hands with fascination. She wondered how he managed his administrative duties so efficiently while keeping up with his responsibilities as Chief Physician of the Institute. Her own position as Director had become increasingly titular since returning to Earth. Dr. Mundazo was still running the show. He had a passion for perfection.

"Are we primarily concerned here with results or money?" he asked.

"Results," said Helena.

"Money," said Jimmy.

Silus tilted his plastic smile.

"I have complete faith in the results," said Jimmy.

"I don't care about the money," said Helena.

"Well, you should." Jimmy folded his arms and sat back in his chair, content to let her agenda rule for the moment.

She turned to the Chief Physician. "Start with the results, Silus."

"The results are good. The nanobots are efficacious in every subject."

"How many subjects?"

"Thirty-seven."

"So what are we measuring? An increase in IQ?"

"Way more," he said. "We're not even sure how to begin testing at this point. We're looking at genius levels in specific brain parameters, possibly to the detriment of other areas."

Jimmy sat forward with a jolt. "That's ridiculous. There's no reason to infer any reduction in other brain function."

Silus twisted with unease in his chair. "It could be a simple question of blood supply. The overactive areas may be sucking up available resources."

"Nonsense," he growled.

Helena held up a warning palm to Jimmy. "What do you mean by genius levels, Silus? How are you measuring the results?"

"You'll have to see the live-feed to believe it," he said as he swivelled a flatscreen to face them. "This is subject twenty-three, a young student with no formal training now writing complicated fugues for a mass choir with symphony accompaniment. Trip-hop, I think they call it, or trance-dance." He punched a button and a haunting cacophony of sound enveloped them. Onscreen, a thin wraith of a woman stood hunched over an elaborate control board of twinkling lights and sliders surrounded by a jumbled tower of speakers and red-eyed hardware. Her dancing fingers worked with energetic diligence.

Helena leaned forward for inspection. "Why is she naked?"

"It's stifling hot in there with all that equipment, and she keeps asking for more components. We're running out of room and can't seem to coax her from this electric nest even for simple bodily functions. The subject appears to be trapped in a frenzy of creative expression."

"Oh my God." She turned to Jimmy. "How is this an advance for science?"

"We can customize the result," he said. "We can target the nanobots to a specific region of the brain. You guys are just letting them run wild."

The viewscreen changed to show a woman in a shabby sweatsuit pacing back and forth gibbering to herself with her finger on an earpiece. "Subject seventeen is an adult with mature brain stasis learning new languages by absorption like an infant. She's up to over fifty dialects with no sign of slowing. All subjects have become completely immersed in their own esoteric field of study. It's fantastic." The screen changed again to show a young man surrounded by easels full of equations and balloons of crumpled paper at his feet. "Subject twenty-one is writing formulae for dark matter that no one else can begin to fathom and has two computers running complicated quantum simulations round the clock. Every few hours he stops to stab his arm with a pencil in what appears to be some sort of release mechanism. You can see the trails of blood on his arms."

Helena stared aghast at the monitor. "How is this possible? Why is there so much variation?"

"Well, again, we're going with plasma supply as an interim hypothesis. Each subject if following a natural predisposition in their brain. Einstein, for instance, had an overly developed parietal lobe, not because he was born that way but because of continued spatial reasoning throughout his lifetime."

"They'll get used to it," Jimmy piped up.

Silus squinted at him. "I'm not so sure. A normal genius has ups and downs, periods of intense mental activity followed by times of calm reflection and repose. They continue to eat and sleep on a more or less regular schedule."

Helena had a bad feeling. "And our subjects?"

Silus folded his fingers in a tight knot. "Our subjects don't stop to eat."

"What?"

"They're like wirehead rats pushing a pleasure button in the lab."

Jimmy bolted to his feet. "Come on, now!" He flung an arm in the air. "You're selecting extreme results and colouring the data to suit your own preconceived notions!"

"I've watched wirehead rats die, Mr. Kay. They can't stop."

"These are human beings with higher brain functioning. They can learn to adapt to new situations."

"We've tried cognitive therapy to no avail," Silus said. "The subjects are unable to redirect their attention."

"They'll snap out of it."

"How many rats died in the animal trials, sir?"

"All rats die eventually, Doctor."

Helena felt her stomach begin to churn. She placed a hand on her abdomen. Merciful heavens, what had they done?

Jimmy turned to confront her. "This is not Pandora's box, Director. This is the next step for bioscience."

Helena pointed a finger at him like a gun. "Sit down, Jimmy."

"We can make this work, Helena."

"Sit down," she said. "Take a pill."

Jimmy glared at her but took a seat with reluctance.

Helena sighed into a gathering calm. "Are our friends in trouble, Silus?"

"I doubt it. We can try doping them down."

Jimmy shook his lolling head but held his tongue.

Silus glanced at him and back to Helena. "In all fairness to Mr. Kay, this eureka ecstasy could subside on its own. We're scrutinizing every aspect of the experiment to the best of our abilities. A couple of patients have gone to sleep finally out of sheer exhaustion."

Helena stood and walked to the office window. She looked out on vast natural parkland and trees in the distance, a normal world. "This is too bizarre."

"You can't pull the plug on me now," Jimmy said.

She turned to inspect him. He sat with calm assurance, his fingers tapping a complicated pattern on the armrests of his chair. A single gold ring clicked a discordant beat. Who was this exotic man and what distant music did he hear? Jimmy seemed suddenly a stranger to her now. In the few short weeks of their business relationship she had grown to consider him a good friend and potentially intimate partner, ill advised or otherwise. She knew he was a kind and gentle person at heart. She had never seen him angry before today. Had news of the fallen Beast so darkened his spirit? "This is still my Institute," she said.

"Actually not," he replied. "I'm holding all your paper."

Helena cast Silus a query with her eyes.

He winced.

Shit, she was getting too old for this, eighty-eight years old and losing her faculties. She should have seen this coming. How could she have grown so lax? "I'm not sacrificing my friends to preserve a credit rating. We can still purge the nanobots."

"I'm sure they'll love you for that," he said. "Forget it. I'll take them back to Canada with me if you force my hand."

"What, like some ancient rock star with a trail of deadheads behind you?"

"They'll all come with thanksgiving in their hearts, you can bet on that."

"I won't allow it."

"You? You're the ultimate groupie, sister. Without me, you're bankrupt."

Helena turned back to the window to stifle her rising temper. This could escalate out of control if she wasn't careful. She took a cleansing breath. "Can we have a moment alone, please, Silus?"

She heard his movements behind her, packing up papers and powering down his equipment. "Sure, I'm late for my rounds."

She waited until the door closed behind him. She waited until Jimmy rose to stand beside her at the window. They stared out at a sombre future together. In a vista of browning fields before them, wild animals lived in hollow trees and caves underground, eking for survival in the dirt, preparing for colder months. "This isn't really about money, is it?"

"No."

"A power trip to grab the ERI for yourself?"

"Nah. Doesn't interest me." Jimmy shivered a face like flint.

"Some macho control thing? Domination of the weaker sex?"

"Hardly," he said. "You're stronger than me."

She turned toward him. "Would it help if I showed you my tits?"

He smiled finally. "That would be great, but it won't change anything."

"What then? Why pull such a crazy stunt?"

Jimmy sighed through pursed lips, a train whistle of pent-up anxiety. "This is not some crazy stunt, Helena. This is the future of mankind. You can't hold it back."

"What," she said, "turning people into cyborgs?"

"The competition is heating up. Machine intelligence is taking off. And now the Beast . . ."

"Survival of the fittest?"

"Survival of the fastest and most interesting."

"You really think that?"

"I do." Jimmy's eyes were steely with certainty.

Helena shook her head sadly. "Then we must be doomed. We're just faulty biology."

"We're the progenitors of consciousness," he said. "We used to be on the top rung of evolution. I'm not willing to give that up without a fight."

"There's no need to presume a war. You're being paranoid."

"Yeah, right."

"You need to chill out and smoke some pot or something. You're not responsible for the entire human race."

"Too many people are sitting around with their thumb up their butt."

"Some of us are preoccupied, sure, but that doesn't mean we don't care about the future."

"We're running out of time," he said. "You have no idea how fast machines can think."

"Granted." Helena reached for his hand and squeezed it. She searched him with her eyes to try to calm him. "Look, I accept everything you say. I respect your expertise in your field of study and I understand your feelings of urgency. But please, Jimmy, don't make me hurt my friends. They're not collateral damage in *Killer Warz*."

Jimmy dropped his gaze with a sigh. "You think I'm V-spaced out. Can't tell machinima from the real thing."

"No, I don't think that in the least." She gave a slight tug on his wrist. "I think you're brilliant even without nanobots."

His face softened and turned pensive with a presage of vacillation. Helena took the cue and sidled closer. She slipped her arm behind his back. "Will you come with me tomorrow on morning rounds to visit the patients in person?"

"You sound like a pet store owner trying to sell kittens."

She smiled. Humour was good. This was the Jimmy she wanted. "You're the one offering to take them all home with you. Just imagine the fur balls in your sterile lab."

"Hah."

"Where are you staying?"

"Back to town, I guess. I have a card for the Hilton."

"Stay here with me?"

"Really?" He tilted his head with disbelief.

"I have a penthouse suite."

"You sure?"

She touched her hip against him and began rubbing tight muscles in his shoulder. "You're too tense," she said. As a whisper escaped his lips in surrender, Helena advanced behind him and began to massage his back with both hands, kneading flesh that felt like iron. "What about the wormholes, Jimmy? Are you going to keep our original bargain?"

"The vampires are not monitoring wormholes, Helena."

"They must be. Colin Macpherson developed the technique ages ago."

"Sure, in the vacuum of space with billion-dollar detection equipment he might have been able to pinpoint the source of antiparticles over time. But not on the fly in Wisconsin, if you'll pardon the metaphor. You're not from Wisconsin, are you?"

"The vampires are plucking up my bloodmates like candy canes, Jimmy."

"Then they must be monitoring the goods, not the delivery system."

"Tracking the virus itself?"

"Maybe."

Her hands paused on his shoulders. "Every Eternal?"

The muscles in his neck twitched a shrug. "Or at least the ones showing the most bandwidth. I checked the data. All the reported abductions are confined within a few hundred miles. It's not following the common dispersal pattern of new technology. No one can hoard information these days, especially in the white market where kids sell out their mother for an uplevel bonus. The knowledge should have spread, the equipment been replicated. It should have bloomed by now into a worldwide epidemic, but I don't see similar reports in Canada or China or anywhere."

"How is that possible?"

"You tell me," he said. "You're the expert. I've never seen an activated sample of the virus myself, but I'm told it releases visible light. Who knows what else is being broadcast? Has anyone thought to measure for protons or gamma rays? Maybe the vampires can only track the vials until they are absorbed into the human hosts. That would explain why only novitiates are being taken."

"I think you're on to something." Helena felt a glimmer of hope at last.

"We should get one of our clients downstairs working on the problem."

"Touché."

"So we're still friends, right?"

She resumed a gentle massage. "Oh, I think we can do better than that, Jimmy."


A tiny lake like a crooked finger came into view as the small float plane banked around a tree-studded hill. The choppy surface was laced with a pattern of froth by a stiff winter wind.

"Up near the northern tip on the west side," Zak instructed the pilot.

"I don't see anything," said Jackie in the seat beside him, bundled in her pink designer ski jacket.

"It's set back from the shore," Zak yelled over the sound of the single propeller engine. "Camouflaged. You can't see it from the air."

"There's no docking facility?" the pilot asked.

"No. A bit of a rock ledge, that's about it."

"You want me to beach it?"

"I'll jump out and grab a canoe for the lady," Zak shouted.

"The water will be near freezing this time of year." The pilot pulled back on the throttle and tipped the wings level as he set up for a landing. A gust of air rocked them and Zak noticed frost forming on the side windows.

"It's not dangerous, is it?" Jackie yelled to the pilot.

"No ma'am, just a walk in the park. Beautiful day."

Another burst of wind buffeted the craft and Jackie reached to clutch Zak's hand.

"They do this all the time up here," he said. "There's no roads. Are you cold?"

"My legs are like ice."

"We're almost there."

The plane dropped suddenly and their stomachs lurched.

"I think I'm going to be sick," Jackie moaned.

"You'll be fine. Just hang on."

"Sorry, folks," the pilot said over his shoulder. "Air pocket."

"What the hell's an air pocket?" Jackie whispered through gritted teeth. "That's ridiculous." She closed her eyes and hyperventilated through her nose.

They hit the surface and bounced. The windows rattled.

"Whoa," the pilot said as he tipped a wing into the gale.

The floats settled with a noisy thud that sounded like hard ground underneath. The pilot kept the throttle up as he fought against the wind. Water splashed up against the windows. "Just like downtown," he said and grinned with a peculiar manic pleasure. Finally they slowed and veered toward the shore.

Zak pointed. "You see that jumble of boulders to the left?"

The pilot leaned forward to the windshield. "That's your dock? It's sure a primitive hunt camp."

"We don't hunt."

"What do you do?" The pilot darted his eyes back to the fashion model in the seat behind him and looked pained by a salacious thought. "Any good fishing?"

Zak nodded. "Brook trout."

"You'll need steel line this time of year," he said.

"We're just here for an overnight."

"Same time tomorrow?"

"Yeah."

The pilot shrugged his incomprehension. "It's your nickel." He kept his eyes fixed on the water as he approached, checking for rocks. He nosed in close to shore and cut the engine. They bumped gently onto a sandbar and Zak peered out a side window. They were close to the rock ledge. He might not even get wet. "Perfect," he said.

The pilot grinned. "We do our best." He zipped his jacket and pulled a hood up over his head. Zak opened the side door and the wind almost ripped it out of his hand. He stepped cautiously down onto the float. The pilot got out and stood beside him.

"Is it okay to hang on the wing?"

The pilot slapped a strut. "This one will hold you, but you're gonna get wet. I'll toss you a line when you get on shore. Drag us closer and we'll get your girl in high and dry." He climbed back inside for a rope.

Zak reached up and pulled himself toward the rocks. His boots splashed in the water as he writhed to keep himself dry. An icy gust took his breath away and he faltered. His leg slipped underwater but found purchase. He pushed off and lunged for shore, grappled for a handhold on the rock.

"Nicely done," the pilot shouted. He held up a coil of yellow nylon. "Ready?" The rope landed secure on the first toss, and Zak pulled the plane to shore and secured the line. Together they ferried luggage onshore. Zak had a small packsack with a change of clothes and a few meagre survival items. Jackie had a large hockey bag with an extensive wardrobe and personal necessities. Another hockey bag contained enough food for at least a week.

Jackie peeked out from the plane like a hibernating bear at the first sign of spring, her expression dour.

Zak waved an arm. "You coming?"

She scrunched up her face. "Do I have a choice?"

"No."

She shook her head in abjection to destiny and stepped daintily onto the float. The pilot offered a strong elbow and she leaned against him for support as a harsh wind rippled the fabric of her ski jacket.

"You'll be fine, ma'am. Easy does it. Grab right here and swing like a monkey." He slapped a strut to show her. Zak reached out both hands for a landing.

"Oh Lord," she said.

She swung into Zak's arms with a yelp and almost bowled him over. Zak untied the tether and tossed it as she steadied herself against their pile of luggage. The pilot pushed off the rocks and raised a cupped hand to half-mast. "See you tomorrow then."

"Thanks. Great job."

"You folks have fun."

Jackie remained glum as the float plane disappeared in the distance with a roar. The wind was bitter and the temperature cruel. Zak carried two hockey bags up to the cabin and dug out the key from a buried tin can.

"It looks like a hovel," Jackie said behind him. "What's holding it up?"

He chose not to dignify her comments with a response. Her demeanour was beginning to grate. He creaked open a wooden door, carried her luggage inside, and heaved it up on a slab of wood that served as a table.

Jackie peeked in. "Are you sure it's safe?"

"Will you give me a fighting chance at least?"

She stepped gingerly forward. "Sorry."

"Have a seat and keep your coat on while I make a fire."

She settled into a chair by the door and hugged herself. Her eyes roamed under hooded brows, inspecting for dust and disease. "Are there any wild animals?"

"All kinds."

"Rats?"

"Big ones."

She raised her feet up from the floor, her face waxen.

Zak smiled as he crumpled paper into the woodstove. "I'm spoofing with you now. I haven't actually seen any rats," he said. "Lots of mice, though."

Jackie pressed her lips together and looked as though she might cry.

"Don't worry. They only come out at night."

"Oh God," she whimpered.

Zak went back to the lake for the rest of their supplies while the fire got going. The wind was beginning to wane but a few flecks of sleet stung his cheek. He lugged the stuff up to the cabin and closed the door behind him. The building was not insulated, but he had taken pains over the years to plug the drafts with cardboard and tin. They heat from the fire would keep them warm through the night. No problem.

He brought a kettle to a raging boil to sterilize the lake water, made chicken soup from a pouch, and served it in ceramic mugs.

Jackie spooned hers quietly, her eyes still misty. Zak made instant coffee and spiked it with a shot of brandy. He handed her a cup. She took a sip and grimaced.

He grappled in their pack until he found a squashed and sticky cinnamon loaf. He carved off a piece and offered it to her on a piece of paper towel. "We're not standing on ceremony," he said.

"I see that, thank you."

"This was your idea."

She tilted her head with a frown. "All I said was that Mia's spirit might be contacted in a familiar spot. It's a common supposition." She looked around anew. "I can't believe this was her favourite place."

"We spent our honeymoon here."

"Were you destitute?"

"This was our sanctuary. We came here to escape the tyranny of the world."

"Well, you're in the right place for a ghost then." She sipped her drink.

"You can take your coat off now," Zak said. "It's warming up."

"Thanks, I'm good." Her eyes continued to wander, her nose pinched.

"So what do we do next?"

"We think about her," Jackie said. "We meditate."

"That's it?"

"It's up to her, not us."

"You think so?"

"I don't know." She faced him with a quizzical smile. "I've never had much luck at this. I don't know why you picked me as a facilitator in the first place."

"You're the world-renowned expert!"

"I'm nothing but a gaudy catwalker, Zak. Let's not pretend."

"Oh, spare me the pity party," he exclaimed. "So the place is not up to your standards. I get it, okay? I came to you for help, Doctor."

Jackie stiffened and sucked in an invigorating breath as she transformed into her professional persona with an artificial rigidity. She unzipped her jacket and raised a speculative eyebrow. "It must be wonderful here in the summer."

Zak nodded. "Thank you." He took her jacket and hung it behind the woodstove, and they stood for a few moments warming themselves by the fire.

"What did Mia like to do up here? How did she spend her time?"

"Well, we were married."

"Oh, good heavens." Jackie rolled her eyes with exasperation. "Did she plant flowers? Did she go birdwatching? Did she read books?"

"She liked to read, but books are heavy. We had to carry all our supplies in on our backs."

Jackie gaped at him. "You walked through the wilderness with all this stuff?"

"Well, we brought the furniture in by boat back in the beginning." He pointed with invitation to a lumpy sofa and Jackie sat obediently. "Sometimes we hiked up the cliffs just for the fun of it."

"Mia must have been as healthy as a horse."

"She was a martial arts master."

"Really?"

"She could kill a man with her bare hands—not that she ever did."

"Wow. I would have loved to meet her."

"I hope you will."

Jackie grinned and bowed her head. "That would be nice."

"More coffee?"

"Sure."

Zak refilled her cup and added another dollop of brandy.

"Thanks, luv. So tell me more. I can feel her taking shape around us." She patted the couch and Zak took a seat beside her, careful not to touch.

"She was gorgeous," he said. "Tall, a bit headstrong at times, but resolute in the face of danger. We always seemed to be running from vampires or hiding from the law."

"Hmmm." Jackie warmed both hands on her cup, holding it close to her nose to breath the sweet aroma.

Zak felt a maudlin weight in his chest. "I lost most of our memories in a digital mindwipe. We had a son together, Rix. Mia told me I was there for the birth, but I lost the experience. I would have liked to keep that one. You ever have kids?"

"No." She shook her head. "Never mind me. Keep focused on Mia. You're building good energy." She sipped her coffee.

"Well, she prayed a lot. Several times a day."

"She was religious?"

"Yeah, I guess so. Nothing denominational, but she had the cosmic connection, you know?"

"Yeah, I think I can feel it. She must be very powerful." Her eyes roamed the room as though searching for a portent.

Zak felt a heightened sensitivity. "Do you think she can hear us?"

Jackie shuttered her eyes once in affirmation. "Yes, I do."

"Should I address her?"

"Don't try to analyze everything, Zak. Just do what feels natural. Keep talking. Let Mia have her way."

He looked up, trying to imagine his wife's face. "Mia, this is Jackie. She's here to help me communicate with you. We're not having sex."

"Oh, good grief." Jackie rolled her eyes again.

"Sorry," he said.

"I think she knows what we're doing, Zak."

"Right. Ah, Mia, I just want you to know that I miss you. I'm sorry that I didn't get to say goodbye." He swallowed a rock past constriction in his throat. Was she really here? Close enough to touch? "I love you and I want you back. Look," he said, "we can get an upload, a cybernetic body, whatever works for you. Just tell me what to do, that's all I ask."

Jackie stared in amazement.

"Do you see her?" Zak prodded.

"Shhh." She pressed the air in a pantomime for calm.

A holy hush settled around them as they sat together on the lumpy old sofa. Zak closed his eyes and drifted. The wind moaned against the trees. Crystals of snow tapped on the windows and the fire crackled with resin. A tear trickled down his cheek. He felt pain in his abdomen, a gnawing ache of emptiness in his heart. *Mia, where are you?*

"Turn off your inner dialogue," Jackie murmured. "Settle your presence in your causal chakra." She poked him just below the sternum. "Right here. Imagine a bright candle burning. Visualize an energy vortex and join with it in splendour."

A wave of contentment washed over Zak as he relinquished himself into the hands of his mentor. Jackie was his spirit guide in the wasteland of life, a counterbalance to chaos. She was the reason they were here, his only source of hope. He forced himself to relax, to vacate his consciousness into spiralling inner light.

"Reach for the communal energy," she whispered. "It belongs to you. Go deeper and deeper until you find the peace that passes understanding. Whatever blessings you discover inside will be manifest outside."

Time stretched out to infinity and his body vibrated alone in the ether of eternity. He could feel a primal pattern of electromagnetism in his core. He was dust in motion, a simple collection of quantum particles in a dance of life, the complex sum of a handful of amino acids folded according to a four-letter spiral code, a miracle of biology. Was that the message? Had Mia been mere biological flesh, a random pattern of cells destined to die? No, he would never settle for that. His wife was out there somewhere. *Mia, where are you?*

Jackie's hypnotic voice came to him from a great distance, but the meaning of language seemed to have slipped away. The sound came to him as a glow, a warm vibration, and he followed it deeper without reserve. Caught between sleep and dreams he floated in a gentle sea of energy. He thirsted for understanding but found only unfulfilled passion, a vacancy of spirit. A hard edge of tangibility lingered outside of his grasp, a false, forgotten land.

From the timeless shore of mythic delirium he heard Jackie get up and put another log in the woodstove. She poked the fire with a stick. She poured another cup of coffee. Every sound seemed amplified. He opened his eyes. "Are we done?"

"That's a good start for now. It's almost dark and the snow is getting thick. I'm hungry. Do you want something more to eat before we go to bed?"

He roused himself from trance. His muscles felt stiff and cold. "There's a can of cooked ham in the pack."

"I'm warming it on the fire."

"Need help?"

"Take your time. Did you meet her?"

"No."

"You were under for quite awhile. You must have been getting close."

"This place feels empty and abandoned without her. I'm further away from Mia than ever." He dragged a swaying chin.

"Oh, don't say that." Jackie stepped to him and put her hand on the back of his neck. "I know it can be frustrating, Zak. I tried to warn you. You're doing your best and Mia is a powerful woman. I'm hoping for a good outcome."

Her palm felt soothing, her voice soft and sensitive. "Okay," he said.

"What do you want with your ham?"

"There's a tin of corn and instant potatoes in a pouch. Nothing fancy."

"I could eat boxboard without a qualm, I swear." She smiled, cajoling him with camaraderie, offering peace with her eyes.

He replied in kind with an archaic parable: "The longer it takes to cook, the better it will taste."

"Great," she said, "but first I have to pee. Where's the washroom?"

"It's outside." He pointed with a flat palm. "Up the trail north-east about fifty paces."

"What?"

"It's an outhouse."

She gawked. "A what?"

"It's a box over a hole dug in the ground. It has a roof but no windows."

"Are you kidding me?"

He stared in awe. "No."

"I have to go outside in the snow to pee?"

"It's not that far."

She put her hands on her hips, her face defiant. "No way. You never told me that."

"Well, if it's a big problem, you can always use the thundermug."

She shuttered her eyes in confusion. "What?"

"A thundermug. It's a potty that you keep under your bed on a cold night. You empty it in the morning."

Jackie's face transfixed into a mask of horror. "I am not sleeping with a bucket of urine under my nose!"

"Fine," he said. "What do you want? Do you need an escort?"

"Yes, I damn well do. There could be bears."

"I'll get my coat. Were you raised in a palace?"

"Don't put this on me, mister. There's no excuse for this sort of behaviour in a civilized society."

Zak found his boots warming by the fire and pulled them on. He tucked the laces in so they wouldn't drag in the snow.

Jackie snickered as she shrugged on her pink ski jacket. "This is too funny, really. You spent your honeymoon peeing outdoors in a box? Luxury suite with a view?"

"Sorry, princess."

"I can't believe I gave up a career in Paris for this."

"Is that another one of your famous proverbs?"

She smirked and tipped her head from side to side with playful mischief, her showgirl charisma still intact. "Actually I do use that one quite a bit."

Zak pulled on his coat and made for the door. "Do you want me to bring a gun?"

"You have a gun?"

"No, I was making a joke."

"It's hard to tell with you sometimes, Mr. Davis."

Zak wiggled his fingers in front of him. "Oooh, so now we're going formal."

"I don't want to get too chummy if you're going to watch me urinate."

He slapped his hands down on his thighs. "I'm not going to watch you urinate."

"You want to though, don't you?"

"Hah, who's the jokester now?"

"What makes you think I'm joking? Anyway, I always get chatty when I'm nervous. You should see me before a lecture."

Zak shook his head with a show of indulgence. "There's no reason to be nervous. We're just going for a piss."

"Both of us?"

"Well, I might as well make use of the opportunity." He pointed to the floor. "I've already got my boots on."

"Cool," she said. "Can I watch?"

Jackie couldn't keep a straight face any longer and together they burst into convulsive laughter—loud and strenuous, stark against the silent night. Zak doubled over, holding his belly while tears streamed down his face in a strange, dervish cleansing. He felt elated, high as an eagle; it was the first time he had laughed since Mia's death. He felt free of grief at last. Jackie was totally out of control in a fit of hysterics. He stood and rubbed her shoulder, trying to bring her back to reality. She continued to gasp and giggle, but finally came up for a calming breath. She wiped her cheeks with her fingers, her smile a vision of delight.

Zak grinned. "We might as well take the brandy with us to keep the party going."

"Damn right." She swiped the bottle and tucked it in her jacket.

# NINE

iko woke with the taste of stale white wine on her palate. Her tongue felt like a withered mummy in an ancient sarcophagus. She could barely swallow. Her brain felt fuzzy, wounded with toxins—one glass too many the previous evening . . . maybe two.

She slid out of bed without waking Andrew and padded naked to the washroom. She peeked in the mirror under hooded lids. God, what a mess. Dark crescents around her eyes reminded her of a raccoon. Her hair looked like Medusa on a bad day, her lips dry and cracked.

She turned on the cold water tap and filled her cupped hands. She bent and slurped, savouring relief like an elixir. She refilled her hands and drank again. *Say what they want about America, we still flush our toilets with the finest drinking water in the world.*

Niko splashed her face and blinked her eyes wide open, trying to focus on the burgeoning morning. She needed to freshen up before returning to Andrew. He couldn't see her like this when they were still just dating. She should at least spare him that much. She combed her fingers through limp tangles. Where was her makeup? Where was her toothbrush? Wait a minute.

This wasn't Andrew's apartment!

Memories flooded back in a tidal wave as her brain finally kicked into gear—the evening with Colin7, too much white wine and too little inhibition. Had she really danced for him like a seductress? Good heavens. What was she thinking?

Niko sat on the toilet and hung her head between her knees. What was she doing with her life, changing sexual partners at random? If she didn't expect fidelity from herself, how could she demand it from a future partner? She should know better, now that she was Eternal. She should have standards of discipline.

Never mind. Shake it off. Did it really matter that much anyway? She was a liberated woman in a postmodern world. She could handle any new situation. So what if she happened to wake up in the arms of a strange man, a mysterious alien from another planet. Was that so bad? The whole thing had seemed like a grand idea the night before, a momentous event in human history, though the world would hear but a whisper in the night. The first coital meeting of human clones! Now that was special. She had played the coquette for an hour and loved every minute. *So sue me!*

She stepped into the shower and blasted drugs from her brain under a torrent of steamy water. She soaped herself up and shed a nagging feeling of guilt like a soiled garment. She brushed her teeth with her fingers. A white bathrobe hung on a peg behind the door and fit just fine. She towelled her hair and brushed out the tangles. Her face looked better in the mirror now that she had some pink in her cheeks. She tried a smile and straightened her spine. She punched out her pert breasts and swivelled sideways. This might work.

In the kitchen she found eggs, bread, cheese, and a tomato—to an alien it was probably exotic foodstuff. She set to work on a simple omelette with salt and pepper, and buttered toast on the side. She could at least impress her new flame with some culinary skill—not that she hadn't impressed the hell out of him already!

"That smells wonderful."

Colin7 stood at the door, fully dressed and looking dignified.

Niko fluffed her drying hair. "Good morning."

He stepped forward for a hug, lips pursed, and she turned her cheek at the last moment for a quick buss. "That was great last night," he said.

"Glad you liked it." She turned back to her omelette and flipped it carefully to keep it intact. Presentation was everything. The toaster popped.

"Need any help?"

"You can set the table," she said. "Knives and forks."

"Sure."

"Do you have any juice?"

"Just orange powder."

"Ugh."

His smile faltered. "That's what I'm used to."

"I should take you to a Juiced Up."

"What's that? A restaurant?"

"It's a chain of fruit bars. You know, antioxidants, steroids, brain boost."

He shrugged. "Okay."

Niko buttered toast and split the omelette onto two plates while Colin7 whipped orange powder into a froth. They settled at a small table and began eating in silence. Colin7 seemed pensive. He deliberated over each bite as though tasting it for the first time.

Niko peered at him. "You have eggs back home?"

"Yes." His face contorted into a poor semblance of confidence. "Chickens are quite hardy. They adapted well."

"Hmm."

"I'm feeling a bit awkward."

Niko folded her robe a bit tighter at her breast. "I can imagine. Strange planet, strange girl."

"Are you practising birth control?"

"No," she said. "Are you?"

His face blanched. "Ahh, no."

"Males don't take responsibility for that sort of thing on your planet?"

A glimpse of pain clouded his expression. "I'm not really an expert."

"Hmm."

"Do you want me to get something from the pharmacy? You know, for the day after?"

"Not really."

"But what if . . ."

"I'll take my chances."

"Really?"

"Sure. You've probably got the best DNA available, unless someone's got Einstein's testicles on ice."

"You want to have a baby?"

Niko finished her breakfast and set her fork midline across her plate, just so. "I hadn't considered it until now."

"This might be a good time."

"It's in the hands of God."

He paused. "You have a deity?"

"It's just an expression, you know, for destiny."

"You're willing to leave your fate to random chance?"

"Can you imagine the stir it would cause if two clones had a baby? We'd be an international sensation."

His face crinkled in consternation. "I'm not sure that would work for me."

"The world would change, Colin. For the better. We've got to stand up for our rights sometime."

"The hands of God, huh? I didn't know she was into politics."

"This isn't politics," she said. "This is basic post-human rights!"

"Post-humans don't have rights."

She folded her arms. "Exactly."

"Well, what about my rights? As a potential father, I mean."

"It's my body."

"But it's my DNA."

"You gave it to me willingly, if I remember correctly."

He smiled at the reminder but quickly shuddered it away. "I didn't realize it was legally binding."

"Perhaps you'll think twice next time."

"I doubt it."

Niko became aware of her nakedness under a thin covering of white flannel and had a flitting vision of glory from the previous evening, a moment of historic majesty mingled with raw sensation. Was this the fitful beginning of a new relationship with Colin, or a fragile false start? Could she go back to Andrew's apartment and face him? Make some feeble explanation? She had no idea where she would spend the night. "So what are we doing later?"

A flush of blood crept up Colin7's neck. "I, uh . . . I was on my way to work."

"I've been meaning to ask you about that."

"Oh?"

"Just waiting for that special, magic moment."

Colin7 sighed with resignation. "Well, I guess we've bared our souls now."

"Among other things."

He sighed again but smiled an invitation. "You're an amazing girl."

"Thank you."

"So what's the big question?"

Niko reclined in her chair. She interlaced her fingers and tapped her thumbs together in a steeple. "Where's my father, Colin?"

Colin7 frowned. He looked at his wristband. "He should be in the physiotherapy lab by now."

"Not *your* father. My father. The real Phillip."

His face went stony. "What do you mean?"

"Did you imagine I wouldn't notice? Don't you think I'd recognize my own father if I saw him?"

"There's been some brain damage. Memory loss."

"Don't play me for a fool, Colin. You've hijacked Phillip's body and you'd better admit it to my face if you ever expect to have sex with me again." She waved a hand. "No, no, forget the sex thing. I'm sorry. Just level with me clone to clone. I won't tell a soul."

Colin7 stood up. He brushed bread crumbs from a pant leg. "You put me in a difficult position."

"We both already know the truth."

"The body was unoccupied," he said.

"You're sure of that?"

"I'm absolutely certain."

Tears brimmed in Niko's eyes at the final realization, the last nail in her father's coffin. Colin7 sat down and took her hand from her lap. He petted it as though it was a furry animal in a zoo. "It seemed perfect destiny when the message came in from Andrew. Father's grand return to Earth after all these years."

"The ghost of Colin Macpherson?"

He winced at the trite reference. "His uploaded entity."

"The original?"

"The Architect himself."

"But where's my father? Where's Phillip? Is he really dead?"

Colin7 pressed his lips as though considering a confession. "I don't know."

"He could be alive?"

"He may still exist in a disembodied state in V-space. We uploaded wetware via the runner Zakariah Davis that was designed to that effect, but the transmission appears to have been interrupted."

"What the hell kind of half-assed scheme was that?"

"It was an elaborate gambit to hack the Earth AI, the Beast, for the good of all. The technology was sufficient and the Architect felt the runner was a proven variable. Zakariah came highly recommended, but . . ." He held up empty palms. ". . . something went wrong."

"So Phillip got stranded in V-space?"

"Both variables were eliminated by the Beast," he said. "They disappeared permanently from recorded V-space. Off the grid, washed clean by the cybertracker."

*Variables?* Is that what humans were to this alien clone? *Mathematical concepts?* "But Zak went back to his body. He woke up normally and escaped. Why didn't Phillip come back home?"

"The shell was burnt out. You saw it yourself."

"Andrew rebuilt it."

Colin7 bowed once where credit was due. "And he did a remarkable job by all accounts."

"But Phillip chose not return?"

"Or was unable to."

Niko pulled her hand away from Colin7's feeble attempt at

interpersonal solace. That was enough physical contact for one day. She needed to think this through. The body in her father's lab was nothing but a zombie. Phillip had flown the coop, perhaps uploaded to greener pastures. She could only hope. She went to the kitchen for a tissue and dabbed at her cheeks. Defiance bloomed in her out of cold ashes of defeat.

She turned back to face Colin7 as he stood watching her from the dining table, looking helpless and concerned.

"Thank you for your honesty," she said. "I think I'll move along from here." She shrugged off her white bathrobe and handed it to him. "Thank you for the use of the robe. I won't be needing it now." Niko turned and stalked away, naked and magnificent to behold.

"I knew we'd meet again someday," Rix said at the door to his dorm room.

Jimmy peered in from the hall, surveying the mess with a critical eye.

"I cleaned up a bit," Rix said as he held out a hand in greeting. "Thanks for dropping by. I know you're busy."

Jimmy stepped inside and took his hand. He shook it once and clasped it thumbs up in an old-school biker shake. His grip was firm and lingering. "So this is where you're hanging out?" He smiled. "You should put in for a corner office."

"I'm never here anyway, just for sleep. I spend most of my time in my launch couch."

Jimmy nodded his understanding. "Duty calls."

"Have a seat. I don't get many celebs passing through. Where are you staying?"

"Upstairs." He pointed up with his eyes. "The penthouse." He sat in an office chair and tested the spring action on the backrest.

"You're sleeping with the Director?"

He tipped a smile sideways. "Well, she might not want the details flashed on Main Street."

"I hear you. Wow. That's cool."

"How are things with you and the batgirl?"

"We broke up."

"Oh. Too bad."

"Yeah."

Jimmy seemed genuinely sorry to hear the news. He paused for a silent moment of condolence, left it hanging.

"So your new experiment is causing quite a stir," Rix said, probing for conversational territory.

"You in the loop?"

"Naw, but the gossip sounds great."

"We're getting good brain boost. Genius levels."

"Cool."

"Mundazo's trying to manage the side effects." Jimmy began tapping a staccato beat on the armrests of his chair. He seemed unwilling to comment further.

Rix wavered for eye contact and held his gaze. "I've been wanting to talk to you about my mother."

Jimmy looked away. "She asked me to check in on you whenever I was in town."

"I had a message from her in a dream."

Jimmy squinted red flags, frowned in thought. "Dreaming is good. Cleans out the subconscious levels."

"She wants revenge."

Jimmy sat back in his chair and folded his hands, his face a poker mask of concern. "That so?"

"I know you've got a back door into Prime Seven."

"Quite a few, actually."

"I'm interested in one in particular."

"I'll bet."

"Zak and Phillip slid some data in the dragon's lair."

Jimmy winced. "They paid a high price for it."

"I think the victim decided the price wasn't high enough."

A cloud shadowed his face. "That's a possibility."

"I think they murdered my mother as some sort of vigilante punishment."

"I came to the same conclusion."

"Did you tell the police?"

Jimmy tilted his head with a crooked grimace of distrust. "Hardly. What could they do? What can anybody do? The shooter is long gone and the puppeteer is some faceless despot hiding behind the Beast."

"Why Mia instead of Zak?"

"It's a vestige of gaming protocol," he said. "You utilize resources instead of wasting them. You don't bust the talent."

Rix ducked his chin with deflation. Worse than he had ever imagined, some gaming conspiracy played to unfathomable rules. "So instead you take what they love most?"

"Only a psychopath resorts to realtime violence."

"This must have been some serious data."

Jimmy sighed his complacence with the nature of bad business, that old, old story. "Phillip said he was doing a favour for a friend. I followed up the rabbit trail for Mia's sake. Turns out it was a plebiscite, a corrupt election in Africa."

"Phillip was fixing an election in Africa?"

"No, the fix was in. Phillip unfixed it. The common people had their say and his team made their hay in the sunshine, I'm sure."

"I don't get it."

Jimmy tipped a shoulder. "It had something to do with gold mining and native land rights, typical stuff. There was a riot. Martial law was imposed. The Corporation won everything in the end. Same lottery numbers eternally new."

Rix felt an absurd sense of privilege being so close to the machinations of global power, but this was crazy. "Phillip was my grandfather and I never even met the guy."

"Count yourself lucky."

"How can you say that? He was some kind of king in V-space."

Jimmy nodded and sucked his teeth. "He was one of the first, one of the prime movers of the early architecture. You know he had a gimpy arm with a V-net jackbox in its place? He lost that arm to bankruptcy, had it cut off for a bad debt. Prosthetic research was breaking new ground then, making the first neural bridges to the brain. Phillip signed over his arm for some clandestine experiment with phantom-limb phenomena, got hooked up to a primitive virtuality. Those experiments were the foundation of V-space as we know it, the wetware connection of man and machine, wiggling robot fingers with cognitive commands. Can you imagine getting your arm cut off for science? Think about it. Phillip fought back from the very bottom of the cesspool, so you gotta give him some credit, but those early days warped him somehow, those crazy years when the V-net came alive with gamers and porn." Jimmy looked troubled and wistful, staring off into distant horizons.

"I want you to give me the keys to Prime Seven, Jimmy. I want to find the truth about my grandfather."

"There's nothing you can do," he said. "Phillip is dead and if you kick the hornet's nest the Beast will take you out with him. It's a suicide mission."

"What about justice? Don't we have a moral obligation to do what's right?"

"You can't fight back every time you get a raw deal in life, Rix. That's how wars get started."

"I've waited too long to make amends for my mother," he said. "We both owe her that much."

Jimmy's face tightened with inner pain. "Mia granted me absolution before she died," he said.

Rix cast him a glare to pierce even his cold, armoured heart. "Maybe so, but I've got to earn mine. You're the only person in the world who can help me."

Jimmy grimaced, and Rix knew he had sealed his cooperation. There was a framed picture of Mia on his night table and he drew Jimmy's attention there with his eyes. Rix stared in silence and remembered his mother, so much potential snuffed out in a moment of violence. A fateful dream lingered in his inner vision, a call from the wilderness beyond the grave, a soul trapped in purgatory demanding penance.

"I can set you up," Jimmy said at last. "You can track the hack to view the data. The Beast may allow that much, but if you take any action you'll get burned."

"That's fair enough."

"There's nothing fair about it. Everything we do is illegal."

Rix shrugged. "You get used to it."

"I know. That's always a problem. If you let your guard down some greysuit will bite your ass and drag you into court. Take my warning, the Beast is more powerful now than ever."

"I'll take my chances. My mother deserves that and more."

"Your mother's dead, man. She was a good woman, but you should face the truth."

"Her ghost still haunts me in the night."

Jimmy shook his head with sad skepticism. "Your mind is playing tricks on you."

"You don't believe in dreams?"

"The dream state is a pressure valve for your subconscious. Don't they teach you guys anything in school?"

"Some dreams are special. Lucid dreams."

"A dream is a dream," Jimmy said. "Heck, even your waking persona is a figment of your imagination when you get right down to it."

Rix shirked back from the thought. "No way."

"You build yourself up from the ground every morning. A few faulty memories and some selective perception, that's all we are, with a superficial inner dialogue to explain away the inconsistencies."

"That sounds arcane."

"Consciousness is nothing but a theory. Don't you know anything about psychology?"

"I think I may have skipped that course while I was busy running from the vampires."

"Well, you should look it up. Control your mind, control your destiny."

"I'll take that under advisement," Rix lilted with sarcasm. He knew Jimmy was wrong and no psychobabble could convince him otherwise. A cosmic imbalance in the universe demanded retribution, payment for sin. He could never rest until his mission for his mother was complete.

"All I'm saying is to test your motivation before you go cliff diving into a maelstrom."

"You'll still help me?"

"Sure, but not because of your dead mother. Let's keep that straight."

"Why then? Because of Phillip?"

Jimmy shook his head again, looking weary and ancient beyond his years. "Don't look back, Rix. The past is history. I'll help you because I like you, because you're alive and have potential for the future."

"That's it?"

"What more do you want?" Jimmy stood and brushed wrinkles out of his pants. "It's good to see you again. Thanks for the invite. We'll meet on Prime Five when you're ready, then make a back door jump to Seven. Have your whities clean and tight, kid. You'll only get one chance."


Colin7 found his father limping on his treadmill, a gaunt man in blue boxer shorts trailing a tangle of electrode monitors that hooked him to a biosystems mainframe. His long dark hair was wild in disarray, greying at the temples, his upper chest a mat of hanging grey fur.

Colin7 stepped to the control console and examined a few readouts. Nothing special, slow progress at best. "How are you feeling?"

His father grunted in reply, busy working himself to a personal limit.

The journal entries were up to date. The data was all onscreen and talking was superfluous, but Colin7 felt the need now that Niko had walked out of his life. "This human body is not responding well."

"There was extensive damage."

"Motor pathways should have responded by now."

"Every day is a new day."

Colin7 watched his father stumbling along like a stroke victim. Such a brilliant mind, inventor of the Macpherson Doorway and

Architect of all, now trapped in a damaged vessel. "Are we still committed to this interface?"

"This is the only connection to Phillip."

"How can you be sure he's out there? Has he contacted you?"

"I can feel his presence when my inner dialogue is at rest. Phillip cannot communicate without the benefit of a brain of flesh or its cybernetic equivalent. He has no language, no memories. Not yet. He's learning new pathways in V-space."

"Perhaps he has not survived as a single entity."

"That was a risk we chose to make, a reasonable probability, but the human persona has a great will to survive."

Colin7 keyed for magnetic resonance imaging of the cerebrum. Good blood supply to all areas of the brain, regeneration proceeding smoothly. "How long will we wait?"

"As long as it takes."

"This interface grows old and has the potential for death."

His father turned to him, his smile a twisted caricature. "It's a great adventure after decades without a body."

Colin7 stared stark, vacant of experience. "I imagine it feels quite limiting in comparison."

His father glanced away. "Unbelievably slow. I don't know how humans can stand it."

"Most can imagine no better."

"V-space is my only refuge now, a glimpse of the lightspeed communication I once took for granted."

Colin7 turned back to his equipment, his touchstone of faith. "And you're convinced Phillip survives in that realm."

"I've noticed a few deviations from pure logic in the higher architecture of the Beast. I think he may be having some influence, perhaps purely unconscious."

"You both have made great sacrifice with no guarantee of success."

"Everything will be worthwhile once we reunite the two halves. This broken body will control the worldwide data network."

Colin7 shivered at the thought. "To what end?"

"Control is an end in itself. It's hardwired into our species."

"You're creating a new species."

"All the better."

Colin7 turned and sighed as he shrugged off his reticence. Might as well get it over with. "Niko has left the compound. She confronted me with the truth and I was unwilling to deceive her any further."

"She's a bright girl. Is that the reason for this unscheduled visit?"

"She took something with her. Some DNA."

His father powered down the treadmill and came to a limping stop. He turned awkwardly to face his young clone. "You had sexual intercourse with the child?"

"She's not a child. She's older than me."

"By what, a matter of days?"

"She was irresistible."

His father smiled. "Ah, the vagaries of youth. I made the same mistake with my first wife."

"I wasn't sure what action to take. I know how sensitive you are about your genome."

His father waved away the thought backhand. "Don't worry. Phillip and I have already made an arrangement to swap source code."

Colin7 felt a wave of cold discomfort. *Source code?* Is that all he was? A DNA repository for a dead man? "I don't understand. Are you saying my union with Niko was planned in advance?"

"No, no, we're not prescient. Not yet, anyway. Phillip and I came to an agreement a few years ago, a partnership contract signed with our bloodlines. We conjoined a suitable embryo under beneficent conditions. We used Niko's egg and your sperm to produce a further enhancement of the family."

"A test-tube baby?"

"I will allow for the colloquialism, but we used an electron microscope, of course. We tinkered with the source code to our mutual satisfaction."

"A superboy?"

"A girl."

"Where is she?"

"She's being raised by vampires. She has special abilities, psychic talents useful to rich business interests, several strategic insertions in her DNA code."

Colin7 hung his jaw. "I can't believe it."

"It does seem ironic that the two of you would get together years later to attempt the same union. It's a true sign of destiny and I wish you the best of luck."

Colin7 gaped at the Architect, stupefied by the turn of events. How could he have fathered a baby without his knowledge or approval? "Is that legal on this planet?"

His father sniffed a chuckle. "It's a grey area. Phillip was never one to stumble over imaginary lines in the landscape. Don't look so shocked. We're all just temporary storehouses of genetic code, whether cloned or conjoined. In this particular case, you have no explicit responsibility. The girl is well cared for."

"What about Niko? Should I let her go? What if she's pregnant?"

His father probed with beady eyes, his expression quizzical. "Do you have an ephemeral affair of the heart?"

Colin7 blinked. An affair of the heart? Some emotional peculiarity? He stiffened with innate resolution. "She was upset at the news. She has a wicked temper."

His father nodded. "A feisty girl and a pleasure to the eye."

"Do you have any guidance?"

The Architect turned away and powered up his treadmill once again. "No, you're on your own in that realm. I never had much luck with women."

# TEN

Helena eyed the young girl from behind the Security barrier. She was hardly more than a teenager, slight and agile on her feet, wired for Prime. She gave off an aura of indifference, prideful and self-confident. Her makeup appeared overdone but was probably the youthful fashion of the day, her eyes dark and her brows perfect arches.

"So you're the famous Niko," she said as she approached. "Any last name?"

"No, just Niko."

"I see."

"And you?"

"Helena Sharp. I'm the Director here, but lately I seem to be playing a mother-hen role."

Niko offered a stiff handshake and a nod of respect. "I've heard about you."

"You're here to see Rix?"

"No, we had a fight."

"Oh."

"I'm looking for work."

"You need a place to stay?"

"That, too."

"We missed you at the vampire den."

"I made a quick exit while I had the chance."

"Impressive."

Niko set her hands on her hips and tossed her limp hair with aplomb as if to say, *That's enough banter, so what's up?*

Helena turned and held up two fingers to the Security guard on duty. "I can give you Level Two clearance in return for a palm scan," she said.

Niko sniffed once up. "That seems fair."

"We welcome all Eternals as a matter of course."

"Do I have to sign up for experiments and stuff?"

"Everything here is on a voluntary basis. At the moment I'm looking for someone to clean toilets."

Niko smiled and batted her eyes in mock disbelief. "I can do that."

"Fine. You're hired. Do you have any luggage?"

"I'm travelling light." She did not carry a purse or hip-bag, not even a wrist monitor.

The male guard approached with a newly coded laminate and handed it forward. Niko draped it around her neck and walked through the electronic gauntlet with her arms raised for a digital pat-down. Her skin-hugging tunic and leggings made it plainly obvious that she was not carrying any concealed weapons or extraneous fat. Helena noticed the Security guard giving her more than dutiful attention. She scowled at him, turned to Niko. "Can I show you to a dorm room, or would you like something to eat first?"

"I could use a veggie shake."

"Ah, well, you might have to make it yourself."

"That's cool."

"Okay, then. This way."

Niko fell in step beside her, bouncy with energy.

"Have you been on the run all this time?"

"No, I've been working. My father owns a private lab."

"You have family. That's good. Are they Eternal?"

"No," she said. "I mean, well, Rix is Eternal. We're sort of connected."

"And Zak?"

"I met him once, briefly. I know him only by reputation."

Helena nodded. "He casts a big shadow."

"That's usually a liability in our business."

"You're a runner?"

"Yep."

"I could use a good runner."

"Let's see how I do with the toilets first."

Helena chuckled. She liked this girl already. She exuded a charismatic arrogance yet spoke with humility. She was a strange and complicated bird, intriguing at first glance but perhaps dangerous down the road. Together they hunted behind the cafeteria counter to find enough vegetable juice to satisfy her. Niko grabbed a handful of carrot sticks and began to crunch them like candy. Helena took a mocha latte from the coffee machine.

They sat opposite each other at the caf table and sampled their drinks. Helena wiped foam from her lips with the back of her hand. "What can you tell me about the vampire tech?"

"Not much."

"Did you have a look around?"

"I scoped the place out pretty good," she said. "No sign of expensive equipment, except the hematology stuff. Nothing related to particle physics or anything like that. The place was an old rooming house with minimal electronics. The doors locked with keys, you know, pieces of metal?"

"I can remember back that far."

Niko paused for a quick inspection. A query formed in her eyes but she held it back.

Helena sipped her coffee. "So how are they tracking us down?"

"Dunno. The goon who nabbed me said they could measure tachyons."

"That's highly unlikely. Tachyons are hypothetical four-dimensional particles."

"One of the supervisors told me they had a whiz kid."

"A whiz kid?"

"A secret weapon. She wasn't supposed to talk about it."

"I see."

"The only child I met was a little girl, maybe three or four. She was a prisoner, so I assumed she was Eternal."

"No geeky teenagers with mainframe hardware?"

"Nope, nothing like that. The place was ultra low tech."

"All of the known abduction cases are localized to that area."

"The vampires are back in business?"

"They barely missed a beat."

Niko winced with revolt. "You'll need bigger guns next time."

"There won't be a next time. We don't have the resources for all-out war."

"That's what I hate about being Eternal," Niko said. "You guys are always fighting on the losing team."

"Maybe someday that will change."

"I doubt it. Do you really think mortals are going to die off? No way. They breed like vermin. They're a blight on the planet."

Helena blinked at her diatribe. Niko seemed to speak as a candid outsider, someone improperly socialized. Could she really hate humans that much? Born a criminal clone, perhaps she had never known love and acceptance. Perhaps she had never been given a chance. "What if we mass-produce the virus and inoculate everyone?"

Niko tilted her head, careless. "Is that what you're hoping for?"

"That's always been the stated goal of this Institute."

"So it's not just a social club?" She smirked to show no offence.

Helena checked her buzzing wrist monitor and hit the mute button. "We do have our moments. Sorry for that."

"I guess I should get to work?"

Helena cast her hand up dismissively and smiled. "If you want."

Niko settled her shoulders. "I like to keep busy."

"Do you want Rix to know you're here?"

Niko finished the last of her veggie drink and smacked her lips. "I guess I'll bump into him eventually."

Helena nodded, feeling not so old after all. "I'll leave it to you, then."

"Thanks. I don't have to clean his toilet, do I?"

"No. Just the public toilets on this level. There's a full-time janitor, so you'll just be helping out. You can check in at the front desk whenever you're ready.

"Cool. And I can eat here anytime I like? Everything's free?"

"It's communal. It's not free."

"Okay," she said. "I can live with that."

"You're an interesting paradox," Helena said. "I look forward to learning your secrets."

Niko held twinkling fingers up with caution. "Let's not get our roles mixed up, Director," she said. "I'm the student." She pointed. "You're the master."

Helena stood and offered her sincerity with a subtle nod. "Play it any way you like, darling. Welcome to the ERI."

The Haitian air was lifeless and desiccating, a foul miasma that hung over the airport at Port-au-Prince like a pall. Zak could feel the moisture being sucked from his body, every pore exuding sweat in a fountain. His clothing chafed against him like sackcloth. He coughed into his fist as they waited impatiently for their luggage. "How can you stand this bitter heat?"

"I didn't say it would be pleasant. Tourists don't stray far from the beaches." Jackie stood regal in a white linen pant suit, barely perspiring. Zak wiped his brow backhand. "I've got to get out of here."

"Go to the washroom and splash water on your face. You're red as a beet. I'll keep watch." She nodded toward the inactive conveyor belt and turned with knowing wisdom. "And don't drink the water from the tap."

Zak found the appropriate stick-figure placard and stepped inside. A young boy was renting fresh towels in the foyer for pocket change and was rewarded with an American dollar for his effort. Zak peeled off his shirt and mopped sweat from his body. He rinsed the towel under cold water that ran tepid and draped it around his neck like an ascot.

He checked himself in the mirror. He needed a shave. He needed air conditioning. Why had he let Jackie drag him to this primitive country? Was this just another dead end in their search for the afterlife? How could he ever find Mia in this hellish place?

Gradually his body adjusted to the heat. He dried his shirt under an electric hand dryer on the wall. He unbuttoned his pants to air out his loins. The young boy in the doorway watched him with a steady smile. Just another crazy tourist.

He found Jackie standing at the transportation gate beside a cab driver who barely came to her shoulder. "The luggage is in the trunk, dear," she said with a playful smirk.

"Great." He eyed the taxi and sighed at the sight of all four windows rolled down. Still no air conditioning. He bowed his head in greeting to the driver and got into the back.

Jackie slid in beside him. "I changed some money over. The currency is gaining strength, but we might get a better deal downtown."

Zak felt a pang of lost authority. He was not producing equity, no longer gainfully employed. Jackie had all the money. They were operating by her rules now, on her familiar turf. She gave an address to the driver and they sped away. A bracing gust of air came in the open windows along with a fine grit of silt. Zak rubbed at dry lips with a finger. "How far?"

"A few minutes. Up in the hills." Jackie pointed to a distant horizon where a ridge of low mountains were misted with smog. "Tono has a small plot of land in a redevelopment area beyond the slums."

Zak closed his eyes and settled in for the ride. He tried to summon peace but the heat was unbearable.

Jackie patted his thigh. "You okay?"

"Sure."

"Still trust me?"

He opened one eyelid to peer at her. "Yeah."

"Your expectations are important to a good effect."

He shut his eye without comment. *A good effect.* Is that all this was to her? Some sort of clinical experiment in spiritualism? The road was rough, but the driver swerved to avoid the biggest potholes, rocking the car like a cradle. He drove too fast and leaned on the horn, clearly anxious to get back to the airport before the next plane

arrived. Zak drifted with the momentum and found a vestige of contentment, but sleep proved elusive.

They pulled up in front of a small stucco box with metal grates
over two glassless windows. Jackie knocked on the front door while
the driver wrestled suitcases out of the trunk. A Haitian woman
opened the door, bright with a floral print dress and a red bandana on
her head. She was buxom and broad-hipped with an hourglass figure
like a starlet gone to seed. Her nose was wide and flat, her teeth protrusive in a big smile.

"*Jacqui!*" She enfolded her in long arms and kissed her once on
each cheek. "So good to see you again!"

"Thank you for allowing us a moment. I know you are always
busy. This is my client, Zak." Jackie flayed a palm in a graceful stage
introduction. "Zak, this is Tono."

"Hello." Zak bowed with deference. "Dr. Rose tells me wonderful
things about you."

"*Jacqui* does not know the truth. She just scritch-scratch-scritches
all around." Tono dramatized little chipmunk fingers for emphasis.
Her dreadlocks were tied behind her head in a ropy tangle, a touch of
grey at her temples. "*André*," she said over his shoulder, and launched
into a musical tirade *en français*. She appeared to know the cab driver
well, and he responded with a superficial insolence that was tinged
with great respect. He brought two suitcases up the rocky laneway
and placed them beside the door, but Tono scolded him and ushered
him inside with the luggage. They bantered for a few more seconds
and slapped their palms together in a high-five to seal the exchange.
Jackie walked the cabbie back to the car as she thumbed through a
wad of bills.

Zak stood in the open doorway feeling like an outcast. He rubbed
his palms together. This was the famous witch doctor? Medium to

the supernatural world? He had expected more, some trappings of transcendence.

"*Je ne parle français,*" he said.

"Don't worry, British boy. I won't embarrass you."

"Actually, I'm from the States."

"I know you, British boy." Her smirk seemed haughty but her voice was soft with empathy. "I saw you standing by the well of dreams. *Jacqui* tells me you are joining her ghost hunt."

"I'm looking for my wife, Mia. Can you help me find her?"

Tono smiled with bold white teeth. "Do you suppose that she is lost?"

Jackie stepped up behind and nudged them inside the house into a small sitting room. The walls were lined with simple chairs made of polished sticks covered with rattan wickerwork.

"Tono, you look wonderful." She offered a handful of cash that quickly disappeared into a fold in Tono's flowing dress. The two women hugged with fond affection and Tono's hand slid down Jackie's spine to fondle her derrière. Jackie leaned back from their embrace. "Don't be silly, girl."

"Oh, *Jacqui*, your beauty tempts me beyond measure. I am again a vibrant woman in love."

Jackie chuckled. "Will you never give up?"

"The tide will come upstream with the passing of the moon."

"I doubt it."

Tono made a show of disappointment as they pulled apart, sighing and patting her palms on her thighs, but her smile seemed invincible. Her face glowed with animation as though an inner light beamed from within. "Quick to business, then? Or perhaps food for thought?"

"You know best."

"Can you kill a chicken, British boy?"

Zak blinked in surprise. "I don't . . . I . . . no . . . never have."

"You seek past Papa Ghedé but have never stared him in the face?"

A peculiar silence gripped them all, an eerie, otherworldly calm. In the vacuum he saw Mia's contorted body, a rag doll strewn, a puppet with all the godly strings cut from above. Jackie's mouth was frozen agape, her dark skin taut on her cheekbones.

Tono smiled with satisfaction. "Creole chicken for dinner, then," she said finally and motioned with her hand for them to follow.

Her sashaying hips almost filled the narrow doorway into a simple kitchen area beyond. A wooden table and three chairs sat along one wall under another grated window. A plank of wood held a sink that drained into a hole in the floor. She fumbled in a cardboard box in the corner and produced a rusty chopping knife. Tono's flip-flop sandals sparkled with pink lights as she moved, a delicate incongruity. A hallway continued out the back with a small bedroom on either side. The sun lit a small garden area where a goat was tethered and chickens ran freely.

"Pick any one you like," she said.

Zak squinted in the brightness as the birds clucked and pecked at his feet, some reddish, others dirty white and yellow. He turned back and spread his palms.

"The chicken already knows it is about to die. Animals run to nest long before the earthquake rumbles. They have a natural pre-science. Use your inner eye to see the chosen one."

Jackie stood behind her, a perfect ebony statue in a white linen pantsuit, watching every move.

Zak looked down. This was ridiculous. He lunged for the closest chicken and grabbed a fistful of feathers, but the bird pulled away. It was stronger than he imagined, destined to live. The others were spooked now and hopped away from his approach. He chased them without luck for several minutes while Jackie laughed and Tono jeered at him *en français*.

He thought for a moment and froze. Okay, he would play along. Let the chicken come to him. He stood like a statue and practised the patience of a predator.

The chickens calmed down and began to peck the ground in random motion.

Come closer, little one.

You are the chosen.

Finally he pounced and grabbed a reddish hen. A wing flayed against his chin and claws raked his arm. Tono clapped with glee and shouted. She stabbed her knife on a high wooden stump blackened with gore. The bird continued to flutter in his arms, and Tono reached to fold back wings, took the hen in an expert hold and placed its neck on the chopping block.

"One quick shot," she instructed. "Off with her head."

The bird lay still, obedient to death.

Zak took careful aim and brought the knife down. The hen squealed an ungodly curse but her head did not roll.

"This knife is too dull," Zak complained. He held it up for inspection.

"Take the bird!" Tono shouted. "She suffers."

Zak handed the chopping knife to Jackie and bent to hold the struggling creature, corralling wings as Tono had done. He felt the terror of death, a panting, throbbing agony.

"Give the blade to me," Tono said and ripped it from Jackie's dainty grip. "Hold her steady, boy." She raised the chopper high above her head, reaching back for ultimate momentum.

Zak lifted his eyes, recognized the trajectory, calculated the margin of error. The knife flashed down and he pulled his hands back instinctively.

The chopper hit wood with a *thunk*, the hen's head toppled off, and the bird flew free in a flapping spray of crimson. Jackie's long, piercing scream split the day evenly in half. She covered her eyes with speckled fingers, her white pantsuit now spattered with blood. Zak fell back to the ground in wonder.

Tono laughed and laughed. "Catch her, boy. Catch her!"

Zak scrambled after the headless chicken as it hopped and flapped from barn board to fencepost, blind, mute and panic stricken. He grabbed a wing and wrestled the bloody creature down. He pinned it to the earth and felt the cadence of life begin to ebb, the final tremble, the last exhalation as the bird flew away. He began to cry for no apparent reason and wiped at his cheeks with a dirty sleeve. He felt a great weight in his sternum, a bubble of anguish that could not be swallowed down.

"Good God!" Jackie wailed. "Just look at me!" The once statuesque and scholarly Dr. Rose had been reduced to a bloody mess in the slums of Haiti. "Tono, you did that on purpose, you . . . you . . ." Her mouth quirked in an uncertain grimace. ". . . you witch," she whispered.

"Better get those clothes off, *ma chérie*. You wouldn't want to stain your pretty outfit." Tono turned to Zak kneeling in the dust and winked with an ostentatious show of lechery.

"Oh my God," Jackie said and turned back to the house.

"Pull the feathers off while I heat up the oven," Tono said.

"You have electricity?"

"All the comforts of redevelopment." She pointed to her primitive outdoor plumbing. "Running water, flush toilet. I even have a telephone, but I don't plug it in unless I get a call first." She nodded to the dead bird. "Start with the big feathers and work your way down. Don't try to pull too many at a time, or you'll rip the skin. Put the feathers in a bucket so they don't blow all round the yard. I'll use them for magic later."

Tono joined Jackie behind a tall fence and turned on the shower. Water pounded down on a wooden plank floor, then began to thunder into a metal washbucket until it was full. The women disrobed and Zak turned his gaze away, more or less, from glorious visions through gaps in the boards. He plucked chicken feathers with great deliberation.

Tono began to sing a haunting refrain in a pidgin poetry that sounded vaguely French in origin as fabric churned underwater in accompaniment. The timbre of her voice expressed the theme without language commonality—a mournful loss, unrequited love, lost dreams. Occasionally a word in his native tongue would tickle his ears and a glimpse through the slotted fence would tickle his eyes.

"I'm sorry I yelled at you," Jackie said behind the gate.

"Are you so unfamiliar with my techniques?"

"I should have expected no less."

"It's good to have you back."

"Thank you for agreeing to see us."

"Any time, *Jacqui*, you know that."

"Can you help us find Mia?"

"Is that what you really want?"

"That's what we're here for."

"I know that's what you said, but is that what you really want?"

"Yes."

"You're not looking for Timon any longer?"

"Well, their souls may be connected."

"Oh, they're connected all right, but it's in this world and not the next."

After a few moments of silence, a kitchen stove banged open and a wire grate screeched metal on metal. The sound of clothes washing in a bucket resumed, and Zak became conscious of the animals around him. A grey goat scrutinized him with care, chewing interminably on a stick. A flowery print dress flew up over the fence to dry in the late afternoon sun, followed by a white linen pantsuit.

Zak brought the denuded carcass inside and Tono showed him how to take out the guts without making a mess of excrement, how to singe off the down and wash the bird for cooking. They stuffed the cavity with spices and peppers and basted the skin with fragrant oils. She kept the heart separate for ceremonial use and prepared the waste for the goat while the chicken roasted in the oven.

Zak rinsed his clothes and hung them on the fence with the others. He pulled on a t-shirt and shorts and padded barefoot into the house to find Tono serving drinks from a ceramic tankard. Jackie set the table by candlelight, wearing blue jeans and an oversize hockey jersey that hung off her perfect body like a mesh kimono, draped off one shoulder for chic.

"What is it?" Zak asked as he accepted a glass.

"Passion fruit wine. It's a special blend."

"Is it psychoactive?"

Tono pinched her thumb and forefinger to show him. "Just an intsy."

He grinned at her antics. "So what's the occasion?"

"I just want to toast my good friend, *Jacqui*." She held a glass of clear liquid aloft. "I want her to get what she truly desires."

"What about me?"

"You don't know what you desire," Tono said.

He frowned. "What's that supposed to mean?"

"What do you think it means?"

Jackie stood and offered her drink. "It's all part of her stage show, Zak. Don't worry about the details. You say something cryptic and the audience interprets it according to their personal needs. They think you're a mindreader. Then you baffle them with general dogma that sounds unique and they fall into a state of heightened suggestibility."

Tono nodded. "Works every single time," she said.

Zak studied the women. He couldn't tell if they were in competition or cooperation. Their feelings obviously went deep and he wondered if they were past lovers. He felt out of the loop, someone with a vestigial Y chromosome. He dutifully raised his goblet. "To Jackie," he said.

They clinked glass all round and sipped their drinks. The wine was mulled with cinnamon and exotic spices, lightly warmed and pleasantly aromatic. The roast chicken landed on the table garnished in grand style with vegetables. Tono had baked a small loaf of dark and fragrant bread. They set to work on the meal with gusto, sipping wine and keeping alive a steady superficial chatter.

"So Jackie tells me you're the local voodoo witch doctor."

"Hah. Does she now?"

"Isn't that right?"

"Truly. But it always intrigues me as to how people interpret my work. I'm also the Baptist pastor of my tribe."

"What?"

"It's true," Jackie mumbled around a bite of bread.

"Isn't that a conflict of interest?"

"What do you know about my backward religion?"

"Which one?"

"Hah. The British boy makes a joke."

"He's actually American," Jackie said.

"Our ancestors brought the Vodou from Africa on the slave

galleys, our belief in *Bon Dieu*. It was the one thing they could not take from us, not the Spanish, not the French, not even the Canadians who pulled my dead body from the earthquake rubble."

Zak almost choked on his chicken.

"She was only five years old," Jackie said.

"I spent three days in a dark tomb underground, face to face with my dying brother as the heat dissipated from his body. I met with the Loa spirits and was welcomed into the arms of Jesus. In a vision I saw a garbage heap of broken glass, and one by one the jagged shards stood up and pieced themselves together. They built a beautiful chalice of unblemished crystal and thick red wine poured down and filled it to overflowing."

The air had stilled with expectation. Zak could hear the candles burning, sucking oxygen for survival.

Tono seemed rapturous with the memory. "The doors of heaven opened wide above me, and a voice spoke with the sound of a thousand thunders. 'There's a little girl down here,' he said and a forest of hands reached down to lift me out of hell into glorious brilliance. His name was Marc and his partner from Quebec was called Lucas. They were aid workers in the local mission, chance participants in an accident of fate, but I knew *Bon Dieu* had saved me for some great purpose." She hung her head, gasping for tremulous breath, holding back a deep burden of emotion. "Even after all these years I wait patiently for fruition."

Jackie got up and hugged her for comfort, cradling Tono's head against her chest. Tono patted her arm and shooed her back to her seat with her fingers.

"All the slaves were forcibly baptized into Catholicism by the Europeans, but *Bon Dieu* did not desert us. My people were splintered into a hundred tribes, each one with creeds and convictions, and the clans were ruled by gang warfare for over two hundred years. But the Vodou will rise up from the ashes by the power of Jesus Christ. He is our Loa spirit resurrected."

"Wow, that sounds pretty intense," Zak said, "but perhaps a bit archaic."

Tono turned to probe his eyes. "I can see that you live in the moment, you are a modern man. But history is our cornerstone. You white men want to bring God down, put him in a box. Maybe he will perform for you if you press the right buttons. It seems natural to you, it's part of your active language, subject-verb-object. That's the way you are programmed to think."

"All languages have hidden ideological agendas," Jackie said. "It's not his fault. You can't blame modernity on the British."

"I'm not blaming only him," Tono said. "You're as white as he is."

She tossed up a quick shoulder, taken aback. "Oh, come on."

"It's got nothing to do with the colour of your skin."

"Just listen to yourself."

Zak placed a hand on the doctor's arm. "It's okay, Jackie. I'm not offended. Let her tell the story."

Tono twisted a smile at him. "Well, thank you, but it's my house. You suck the world dry and then come back to me, back to my shanty in the slums, for help in your time of trouble. Why would *Bon Dieu* bless that, British boy?"

"I told you, he's—"

Tono held up a flat palm to Jackie like a stop sign. She glared at Zak, waiting for his answer.

What did this woman want with him? Why was she so unyielding? "I'm sorry if I'm here on a false pretense. Perhaps the timing is wrong for you. If you can't help me, I'll go."

Tono smiled and nodded. "Exactly."

He bristled at her theatrics. "You don't know me well enough to criticize my motives."

"Oh, I would not dare to criticize you, mister Zak. You are a celebrity in my home."

Zak squinted at this strange woman. "You're giving off mixed messages. Do you want me to stay or go?"

"Stay, please. Have more wine. We're just getting started."

"You're sure? Because I don't want to be any trouble."

"No trouble at all."

"Have you seen Mia?"

"Not yet," she said, "but I haven't really asked around."

Tono got up to refill the tankard with warm wine. "I don't make dessert." She whacked her ample buttocks with a noisy smack. "'Cause I'm on a *fashion* diet. But I have some mango jam that is a delight to the senses."

"Oooh, the mango jam. You've got to try this." Jackie patted Zak on the back of the hand and tried to placate him with her eyes.

Tono refilled his goblet and set the tankard on the table. She sliced dark bread onto a plate and set a mason jar of jam on the table beside it. She settled herself back into her chair while he sipped his drink.

"In the ancient Vodou, everyone knew we could never approach *Bon Dieu* on his throne. The creator of the universe? Who would dare?" She held up her palms and wiggled her fingers. "Silly, *non*? Instead the chosen seers converse with the Loa spirits who are the handmaidens of deity, the keepers of the gates of life and death."

She paused to let the thought linger as Zak spread mango jam onto her rich fragrant bread. He tested a bite and was momentarily overcome with sensation. "Are you girls having an affair?"

Tono's eyes went wide and her face settled with consternation. She crossed her arms and fell silent as Jackie murmured in her throat.

Zak spread his hands. "Look, I'm sorry, but we're all adults here."

"Don't make this into some big thing," Jackie huffed. "That's not why we're here."

"It's not some big thing," Zak said. "It's a simple question."

Jackie pressed her lips and tilted her chin. "It's a *personal* question."

"It makes a difference to me."

"Why should it?"

The conversation ended in stalemate and night settled suddenly hard around them. Tono scrutinized her guests, patrolling with her eyes from side to side. Finally she succumbed to the silence. "You guys aren't doing the nasty?"

Jackie slapped her palm on the table. "No, Tono. That is completely inappropriate. Zak is a *client*."

Tono made a face of mock abashment. "Well, excuse me, but it seemed pretty obvious."

"Well, it's not."

"Can I have him, then?"

"Oh, really?" Jackie sneered. "What would you do with him?"

"A pretty boy like that? I'd work him over with my slim jim for real sure."

"You are *so* bad! How can you call yourself a Baptist?"

"Well, apparently everyone else calls me a witch doctor!"

Jackie shook her head with indignation. "Really, Tono, this is far beneath you."

"Holy cow," Zak said. "What is *in* this drink?"

"It's a special blend," Tono said.

"Is it legal?"

She sniffed. "Not in the United States."

He pushed his glass away. "I think we've had enough. Our tongues are getting loose and it's getting late."

Tono grinned. "We haven't even discussed sleeping arrangements yet."

Zak glanced at Jackie. Two bedrooms, two women. "I guess I'm the odd man out."

Tono winced with flagrant drama. "Well, I didn't think that was an issue until now."

"And she calls herself a fortune teller," Jackie said.

"The spirits never lie, *Jacqui*."

"Oh, spare me."

"What about a couch?" Zak interjected.

"Sorry," Tono said stonily. "There's some straw in the goat shed."

Jackie stood up. "Zak and I will be quite comfortable together. You need not worry." She turned away through a bedroom door.

"Oh, I'm not worried, *ma cherie*. You kids run along. I'm feeling a visionary delirium fast approaching." Tono reached for the wine tankard. "Sweet dreams."

Zak lingered to face her, feeling a hot flush of embarrassment. "Thank you for the wonderful meal."

"You're quite welcome, mister Zak."

"You're an extraordinary woman."

She smiled with self-effacement. "It's not about me."

"I did not mean to offend your traditions or your lifestyle."

"You have done neither, I assure you."

"I feel like I'm in the wrong place."

"No, *mon frère*, you come at exactly the right moment." She refilled his wineglass and tipped it toward him with a salute.

He took it and sniffed the aromatic brew. "One more sip for a nightcap?"

She bowed down once and winked. "Plenty to go round."

Her face seemed to fill his vision, her smile a radiant promise. He watched her nose flare as she breathed, the candlelight glinting in her eyes like beacons while Jackie flung blankets and fluffed pillows in the bedroom down the hall. Was Tono deliberately trying to incite controversy? To create discord for the sake of some special effect? Was she a shaman priest? A prophet of God? He tipped up his cinnamon drink and drained it, captivated by her magnetic gaze.

"Zak, are you coming?"

"Be right there." He struggled to pull his eyes away.

"I found some extra pillows," Jackie said. She placed them in two piles at the head of the narrow bed. "I think they're filled with chicken feathers."

"They must be magic pillows."

"What?"

"Just something Tono said."

Jackie closed the door behind him. "She was particularly perverse tonight," she murmured.

"Not always?"

"I don't know her that well."

Zak looked away from her face. "Fine."

"I think I'll sleep in my clothes," she said. "I've already showered for bed."

"Me too. There's not much room."

They crawled under the covers, careful not to touch.

"Why aren't we staying in a resort on the beach?"

"Tono would not allow it. She said it would be an affront to her dignity."

"We could have talked our way out of it." He shuffled subtly against her, trying to make space.

"It's part of her therapy," Jackie said. "You've got to engage the culture if you expect a good result."

"Why Haiti? Why Tono?"

"She can work miracles."

"Can she find Mia?"

Jackie lifted her shoulder away from his encroaching touch. "Look, Zak. Maybe I'm grasping at straws here. I don't know. I'm just trying to help. Tono's the best in the world at what she does. She's a successful medium, missionary, and midwife."

"That's a pretty wide repertoire."

"A persistent rumour circulates that she raised the dead on more than one occasion."

"Do you trust her?"

"Yes."

"Anything else?"

"No."

"You don't have to tell me."

"Good."

"I mean, it's none of my business."

Jackie sighed with exasperation. "What Tono does is a mystical communion, Zak. It's not amenable to reason. I can't explain it to you. She broke me free from bondage, from a pit of despair. She gave me an enduring faith in magic. Can we leave it at that?" An icy irritation in her voice told him he had reached his limit. She twisted her body and turned her face away, careful not to touch.

# ELEVEN

Niko bent over her slop pail to free her mop from the metal wringer on the bucket. A tendril of hair had fallen out of her barrette and hung like a dark feather in front of her face. She puffed at it to keep it from tickling her nose. Her hands were grungy with disinfectant, her coveralls damp with spillage. She wasn't very good at this.

Her mop came free and she almost threw her back out gyrating for balance on the slippery tile floor. She straightened and looked up to see Rix standing in the doorway. She was momentarily startled but tried to control her expression. She brushed hair away from her mouth. "Howdy, cousin."

"What are you doing here?"

"I'm mopping the floor. What are you doing here?"

He blinked at her. "I came in to take a piss."

Niko glanced at a row of urinals along the wall. Okay, so they were standing in the men's room. She was working. It was completely appropriate. "I'm almost done. Just let me clean up this water." She began to mop in earnest, swaying her hips with the rhythm. She could feel his eyes boring into her back.

"I can't believe this," he said. "You look like a janitor."

"I *am* a janitor." She swished her mop in the bucket and pressed a foot pedal to squeeze the wringer.

"How long have you been doing this?"

"Just a few days."

"Why didn't you come to see me?"

She stopped to inspect him. She cocked her head. Rix seemed wary and defensive, grappling with his usual inner turmoil. Had he forgotten their last meeting so soon?

Niko bent to soak up the last of the spilled water, spreading a thin gossamer sheen of disinfectant on the tile. She dunked her mop back in the pail and twisted it into the wringer. If she got the angle just right, she could push the pail without bending or straining. She was learning fast. "It's all yours," she said as she moved toward the door.

"Wait." Rix stepped in front of her bucket. "Can you take a break or something?"

Niko made a point of checking her wrist monitor. She was a working girl, busy, busy, busy. "Sure. Can I wait for you outside?"

Rix chuckled and stepped aside. "Yeah."

Niko leaned against the wall opposite in the hallway and wiped her grimy hands on her coveralls. This was not how she had imagined the family reunion. She was a sweaty, stinky mess with a twisted rope of hair dangling in her face. She should have gone to see Rix on her own terms instead of leaving it to chance. Oh well.

"It's great to see you again," she said as he came out of the men's room. She glanced involuntarily at his pelvis and he caught the movement of her eyes. He stopped and looked down, pulled in his tummy and checked his zipper.

She felt like an idiot. Gawd. "So I've been working hard," she gushed. "Earning my keep. My supervisor says I'm doing a wonderful job. Gotta love those sparkling urinals. I'm staying on the second floor. Private dorm." She hushed herself, took a breath of air finally.

"Want to get a bite?"

"I'm not really dressed for the caf," she said. "I smell like a chemical factory."

"How about a walk?"

"Where are you headed?"

"The gym. I have a steady slot at 10:30."

"Pumping iron?"

"I guess you could say that."

"Well, you're looking buff."

"Really?"

"Totally." His upper body looked more like a wrestler's than a teenager's. "I mean, I'm no expert."

"How's Andrew?"

Niko winced. "I sort of bailed on him."

"No goodbyes?"

"I sent him an email."

"Ouch."

She tossed out a weak-wristed palm. "Andrew's a great guy."

Rix nodded. "But you don't love him."

"He's still a good friend."

"You hope."

Niko sighed at the effort to maintain her facade, the tedium of existence, shrugged with resignation. "I seem to screw up with everyone. No big change." She grabbed her mop pole and pumped it in the slop water.

"How's your dad? Did he wake up?"

"No," she said. "He's still missing, maybe gone for good."

"Oh, Niko, I'm so sorry." He reached to hug her, but she flinched back, feeling grungy and gross. Rix slapped his palms on his thighs and pressed his mouth grimly with inner hurt. She should have let him touch her. She felt terrible.

He ducked his countenance, his whole body in abeyance. "Is there no hope at all?"

She took a cleansing breath. She hadn't realized how difficult it would be to talk about her father. "Colin thinks he might be out there somewhere, some vestige of consciousness lost in V-space."

Rix looked up with intent, primed alert. "Who's Colin? Another boyfriend?"

Niko glared at him. Was he a mindreader? Was she that obvious? Rix got the message and glanced away, deliberately and theatrically unconcerned. This whole situation was going in the toilet along with her life. "Colin's a theoretical physicist. He's brilliant."

"That's cool, whatever."

"I should get back to work," she said. "Maybe I'll meet someone new in the women's washroom."

Rix grabbed her hand with sudden concern in his eyes. He squeezed her fingers, pulled her incrementally closer. "Niko, I'm glad you're here."

"Yeah, me too." She tossed a rope out of her eyes. "I had nowhere else to go."

"Can we have lunch some day?"

"Sure. I'll tap you in." She held up her wrist monitor. "What's good for you?"

"Tomorrow."

She scrolled on her day-timer and marked it. "Noon?"

"Great."

"Locked." She put her arm down and raised her eyes. Rix was gazing at her with great intensity. He still liked her, even in her soiled coveralls, even after everything. She could feel her heart beginning to melt at the realization. She was afraid she might say something stupid if she wasn't careful. "Anything else?"

He licked his upper lip and she noted a hint of stubbly moustache above. He smiled and moved his head at some humorous thought. "You look beautiful, Niko." He turned to walk away and she gaped after him as he dwindled in the distance.

She turned to see Helena Sharp approaching and backed against the wall to clear a path.

"Just the girl I'm looking for."

Niko felt a pang of self-awareness in the face of authority. She tried to tuck her hair behind her ear but it fell back down like a donkey tail in front of her face. "Good morning, Director."

"I have a job for you, if you're game."

"More toilets?"

"No, something more suited to your special talents as a field runner. A covert operation."

"Outside?"

"I think you've proved yourself inside. You're a disciplined worker."

She ducked a subtle nod. "I do my best."

"Have you got time for a meeting? The Security Chief is in his office."

Niko looked down at her rumpled uniform and the slop pail at her feet. She gave it one last kick for good measure. "I can't leave my bucket in the hall. It's dangerous."

Helena held up her wristband and began texting. "Done," she said and pointed her palm down the hallway. They began walking.

"I've been following up on your whiz-kid, interviewing some of our friends."

"The little girl?"

"Her name is Sienna. She was not liberated as far as I can tell, nor did she reside in the dorms with the Eternals. She was seen periodically in the company of management officials."

"Her parents?"

"No. More like zookeepers, according to reports."

"Some sort of child prodigy?"

"Maybe. I'd like to have a chat with her."

Niko felt a gathering chill. "We're going back in the vampire den?"

Helena pushed open a grey steel door without knocking. "This is Dimitri Sanov," she said. "Dimitri, this is Niko, the woman I told you about."

"Ah, the batgirl. I've been looking forward to meeting you." He stood up from his desk and strode toward her. He was swarthy and muscular, a monstrous man with an overbuilt jaw and deeply cleft chin. He wore combat boots with shin pads and a thick black belt that made his standard blue Security uniform look like army fatigues. He gripped her hand in mammoth paws. "No ID, no retinal records, not a whisper in the night. Very impressive."

"Uh, thank you, I guess."

"Wired for Prime and recognized only as a shadowy archetype. You're a legend in V-space."

"Well, I hope not. Fame is a liability where I come from."

"Where *do* you come from?"

Niko glanced quickly at the Director and back to Dimitri. "I'm with her," she said and pointed with a thumb.

Dimitri sniffed. "What's that smell?"

Niko wiped sweaty palms on her thighs. "Detergent. It's biodegradable, safe for children."

"We're planning a covert night mission," Helena said. "The two of you drop in, grab the child, and get out. No muss, no fuss."

Niko gaped at her. "Just the two of us?"

Dimitri walked back to his desk and opened a drawer. "We'll have friends along," he said and pulled out a handgun. He offered forward some sort of automatic machine pistol with a huge clip in the handle.

Niko shook her head, wagging a tendril of hair in front of her eyes like a pendulum. "I'm not comfortable with guns."

"We'll be using tranks. You're booked in the practice gallery for 9 a.m. tomorrow. Don't be late." He placed the weapon in her palm. "It's not loaded, but carry it around for the day. Get a feel for it."

Niko stared at it in her hand—heavy, black, venomous metal. A feeling of power gripped her, a promise of poison to her enemies, bad medicine. She stuck it in a pocket on her hip but the long magazine stuck out of the pistol grip like a turnstile gate.

"Put it in front, in the belt of your trousers."

"I'm not wearing trousers."

Dimitri paused, his face quizzical. She could almost smell the wood burning in his synapses.

"I'll get you a holster," he said.

"Over the shoulder. I don't want a loaded gun pointed at my gonads."

"Done."

"Dimitri's a parachute expert," Helena said. "You'll be dropping to the roof with night-vision goggles, taking out the guards, and going downstairs. You already know the layout."

"Can I bring my own kite?"

"I guess that would be okay. Will that work, Dimitri?"

He shook his head and held up a peace sign. "Two problems.

First, our hands would not be free in kites. One of us will have to take out the three guards on the way in. If we go together in a tandem chute with a butt-fuck harness, I can shoot all the way down." He pantomimed the action with pointing fingers. "Secondly, we've got to get the child out safely and quietly. I don't think she'll willingly jump off a rooftop with strangers. My plan is to take her in a laundry hamper on wheels down to the main floor and go out through the back garage to a waiting van."

"Actually, the only guard on the tower at night is a stoner," Niko said. "He prefers his ladies with encapsulated trichomes, you know?"

Two blank stares.

"Never mind, it's an old joke. I can take him out. He won't be a moving target. The control room downstairs has got live webcam in the elevators, so we'll have to take the stairs."

Helena eyed her with a contemplative nod. "That sounds like good recon. We'll go with that. Niko's the shooter. Dimitri will fly you in."

The Security Chief deliberated with an air of misgiving and Niko bristled at his inspection. So what if she looked like a janitor and smelled like an undertaker? She could get the job done. "So what's in it for me?"

Helena pursed her lips, glanced at Dimitri. He tilted his head with a sly smirk. So they hadn't thought this through. No money would change hands. They expected her cooperation out of some misplaced sense of public service. "You're kidding me, right? You did all this prep without a price tag?"

"It's just a job like any other. Do you miss your toilets already?"

"This is more dangerous. There's a ten percent chance I'll be killed."

"That's quick math."

"It's just an estimate."

"Sounds about right," Dimitri said.

Helena shot him a glare of chastisement. He shrugged and returned to his desk chair. She turned back to Niko. "If it wasn't for us, you'd still be bleeding into a bottle."

"So I do this and we're even?"

"If that's what you want."

"Yeah," she said, defiant, "that's what I want."

"Fine."

Niko whirled from side to side with deliberate insolence. "I don't understand this place. You people sacrifice without expectation of reward. You have a mindless sense of duty." She shook her head with exasperation. "You treat the virus more like religion than science. You're turning the ERI into some kind of cult."

Helena watched her with interest. Dimitri looked down at his desk and vacantly away.

"We have a medical condition in common, I get that. We need protection from vampires, sure. Those are good reasons to band together. But we're not family. We have no overriding allegiance."

Helena nodded. She appeared thoughtful.

Niko hooked her hands on her hips, longing for some antagonism to clear the air. "Don't you have anything to say?"

The Director sucked her lower lip with a noisy smack. "No, that pretty much sums it up."

Niko turned to the Security Chief, still hoping for a fight. "And what do you think?"

Dimitri grinned, perpetually self-confident. "So we're on for 9 a.m. at the shooting gallery. Don't be late."

Zak woke refreshed and felt languid ease in his muscles. He had slept deeply and dreamed freely and Jackie was snoring into his ear like a freight train. He slipped out of bed without disturbing her. He tiptoed out of the room and closed the door with a gentle snick.

He found Tono in the backyard shuffling in a tight circle around a smoking smudge pit. She kept her head down and seemed to be chanting or praying, and periodically would waft a green frond through the smoke and place it gently on the embers.

"Did you sleep well, mister Zak?"

"Yes, thank you."

When she looked up he saw giant white circles painted on her face, centred on her eyes like targets. Her chin also was white, making her face seem elongated and cadaverous. Her coiled dreadlocks hung down like snakes.

"Did you dream of Mia?"

"No."

She nodded and resumed her movements around the smudge pit. Her feet made a complicated dance, her steps sideways and back in a triangular shape as she shuffled forward.

"*Jacqui?*"

"Yeah, I guess so, now that you mention it. Have you been up all night?"

"No, no. I had plenty of sleep. Morning is for magic."

"Can I join you?"

She stopped to look at him, shrugged. She swiped a finger in a circle round her eye and rubbed white paint on his eyebrow, then repeated the procedure on the opposite side. She resumed her complicated dance.

"Is the foot movement important?"

"Everything is important."

Zak watched her carefully and tried to mimic her rhythm. After awhile, he thought he had it. The smoke stung his eyes on the downwind side, and he learned to hold his breath in the passing. His respiration became part of the dance, part of the circle. He began to hum to match her prayer, a rising and falling.

"What are we doing?" he whispered.

"Summoning Loa spirits for the day."

"Is this a death circle?"

"Death and life, they are one and the same."

"Do you believe in reincarnation?"

"No, that's not Vodou. No zombies either, no stickpins."

Jackie stood in the doorway looking bleary eyed and haggard. She scratched at her scalp and combed her fingers through her hair.

"The princess is awake," Tono murmured.

"Shall we invite her to dance?"

"No, we're done. The day begins."

"I hate to interrupt you guys," Jackie said. "But there's a little girl at the front door. She has a live chicken for the white spirit."

Tono looked toward the rising sun, her eyes mere slits. "That would be you, mister Zak."

They trooped through the house to investigate. Sure enough, a young girl held a chicken upside down by its feet. Huge red wings flapped occasionally, but the bird had clearly grown weary of resistance. It looked a lot like the bird they had shared the previous evening.

Tono pushed Zak out the front door to meet the child. A group of women stood by the roadway watching and speaking in hushed tones. The little girl bent down on one knee and held the chicken up as high as she could reach. She was prepubescent, perhaps ten years old, her face solemn with reverence.

Zak stared at her in puzzlement. Surely his white skin was nothing novel. The island had been awash in aid workers and missionaries for decades. The beach resorts were pumping American dollars through the economy like white grease in a finely tuned machine. Why him? What was so special? Why the red chicken he had just killed?

Tono jabbed him in the back with her elbow.

He stepped forward and grabbed the chicken by the legs. "Thank you. God bless you."

The girls eyebrows popped up like rainbows. Her face beamed with joy, and she grinned at him with big teeth. She released the chicken into his care and ran back to the protective circle of her friends and family on the roadway. They hugged her and slapped her on the back as though she had just won a medal.

Tono waved to them with effusive drama and Zak held up a palm as Jackie stood in the shadows. That was weird.

"I'm going for a shower," Tono announced. "No peeking."

They returned to the house as the group on the street ambled away. Tono continued out back and turned on the water. Zak peered in a small refrigerated chest and pulled out the leftover bread and mango jam. "I guess we're having bread for breakfast," he said to Jackie. "Did you sleep well?"

"No," she said frostily. "You pushed me out of bed onto the floor."

"What?" He frowned at her. "I'm sorry. I didn't wake up."

"You were grinding against me like a frantic puppy."

"Sorry," he said. "I must have been dreaming." He *had* been dreaming. The vivid details came back to him in a rush of memory.

"You had an erection."

"I did not!"

Jackie slanted a knowing smile. "Oh, yes you did."

"I had my clothes on."

"That didn't seem to slow you down."

"That's ridiculous," he said. "I was asleep, I swear."

Jackie glanced away, blushing at the remembrance. "I accept your apology. I shoved you over eventually. It was nothing really."

He sighed. "We should probably go to a hotel room."

She nodded. "Separate beds."

Zak cut her a piece of bread and covered it with jam. He held it forward. "A peace offering?"

"Thanks. Any coffee?"

"No. There's some kind of weird fruit juice with seeds in it." He poured her a glass and watched her sip and pucker. Tono came in draped scantily in a red towel and Zak made a show of averting his eyes.

"'Scuse me, just getting my toothbrush." She reached past him to a wall-mounted cabinet, found what she was looking for, and waved her plastic wand. "I'll spit outside so I don't interrupt you two love-birds."

Jackie eyed her askance and Tono smiled with mock serenity. Again they seemed to communicate non-verbally and Zak thought it was probably for the better.

A knock sounded at the front door where a small group was milling on the porch hoping for an audience. More visitors began to arrive, sick and wounded people from the slums looking for free healthcare. Zak took on a role of service as instructed by the women. He boiled water to sterilize instruments, fetched bandages and anti-biotics, kept his mouth shut. A parade of humanity came and went.

Children cried, old men complained, and young women peeked around corners at Zak with wide eyes. At noon he went out to steal eggs from the chickens at Tono's request, and fashioned a makeshift omelette with onions and a dried chunk of cheese.

They stopped for a few minutes to eat during a break in the action. Both women looked haggard in the smothering heat, and Jackie went back to bed for a siesta after lunch. Tono sipped herbal tea on the back porch and stared into fathomless distance.

A painful wail sounded from the front room and Tono stiffened with recognition.

"Oh, no," she whispered. "Paola."

"Who's Paola?"

"Teenage pregnancy. Late term."

"What should I do?"

"Sterilize everything. Find some clean towels." She got up to face the grievous music, her face stony.

The screaming patient was carried in on a litter by four middle-aged men. One, the girl's father, pressed coins into Tono's hand and spoke rapidly *en français*. Tono nodded grimly, glanced at the girl.

Jackie stood in her bedroom doorway, blinking and trying to focus. She held the door as the men navigated a tight corner to carry the girl inside. The expectant mother looked like a child to Zak, thirteen or fourteen perhaps, her face a mask of horror.

The men hurried away. The father lingered behind on the front lawn, wringing a hat in his hands and looking from side to side as though he had lost something important.

After a few minutes Tono barged out of the bedroom and met Zak in the kitchen. She fumbled in the cupboard on the wall and found a small bottle of cough syrup.

"How is she?"

"Not good. She's been in labour all night. Papa Ghedé comes to take her soul away."

"Shouldn't she go to a hospital?"

"There are no hospitals for my people." Tears began to spill onto her cheeks and she bent over the kitchen sink as her body trembled. "The men should leave the young girls alone," she whispered, her voice hoarse with anger.

"She's just a baby," Zak said.

Tono sniffed with new resolution and turned to face him. "Sterilize my knives. I'm going to cut her."

"No." His gut tightened like a clenched fist.

"If she splits to her anus, she will never recover. If I cut to the side, she will heal."

"Do you have anaesthetic?"

"Just a topical cream and some codeine cough syrup. I need your help."

"Me?"

"Take off your shirt."

"What?"

"Rub some oil on your face and chest. Salad oil will do. Then sprinkle flour all over your body. You will be my white spirit."

He shook his head. "It won't work."

"It *will* work. The girl is delirious with pain. You will make it work. You wait for my signal, then enter the room like a ghost. All regal, you know, godlike. You touch her forehead with your palm and say *tranquillité* softly, over and over."

"*Tranquillité.*"

"That's it. Your voice will be dreamy, hypnotic. You take her eyes and own them, mister Zak." Tono's lips trembled as a fresh scream sounded from the bedroom.

He put his hand on her shoulder. "Great. Let's do this."

"Find a sharp knife, a short sticker." She bent to her cardboard box in the corner and pulled out an emery block. "Sharpen it like a scalpel. The codeine will take a few minutes to take effect." She grabbed the bottle on the counter and rushed away.

A calm settled on Zak as he remembered dancing round the smudge pit, summoning the Vodou spirits for help. He hunted for a knife and found the chosen one calling to him. He stripped off his shirt and began to sharpen it on his lap with a slow rhythmic motion. He murmured in time to the music that only he could hear, a harmony that stretched far beyond him.

When the blade glistened like ice, he tossed it in boiling water. He oiled his upper body and painted imaginary war paint on his cheeks as he stared in a tiny mirror above the sink. The edges were jagged and broken, and a crack cut down from the upper right-hand corner, touching his eye in the reflected image. He no longer recognized the man in the looking glass.

Tono came out to the kitchen and sprinkled him with flour like a medieval sacrament. She pulled her knife from the water with tongs and placed it on a clean towel.

"*Tranquillité*," he whispered, and she pressed her mouth with sad hope.

She signalled him to stop in the hallway outside as she entered the den of screams. Jackie was openly crying, holding the girl's hand as she coiled in agony.

Tono smuggled the knife in unseen and began her conjuring ceremony. She murmured *en français* and waved her arms like palm trees in the wind to gain the girl's attention. The child's knees were spread under a clean white tent of linen, her breasts bare buds on bony ribs.

Tono's voice crept higher to crescendo, her hands upraised to heaven in worship, and holy magic settled like downy feathers around them. At Tono's nod the white spirit floated into the room and hovered close by. He whispered to the child and her eyes glazed with wonder. Blood spurted on white linen and the child never flinched. The white spirit held her in captivation like a trembling bird in his palm. He knew she would live to remember this day. *"Tranquillité,"* he whispered.

A baby cried from somewhere far away.

Jackie and Tono worked in haste to save two precious souls. One cleaned while the other sewed a frail garment of skin with needle and thread.

"It's a boy," Jackie said and placed the infant in the crook of his mother's arm.

The white spirit backed out of the room slowly, with divine grace befitting his station. He closed the door behind him and braced himself against the wall with a shudder. Tears of thanksgiving streamed from his eyes and carved rivulets through white powder.


Rix watched Niko as she made her way down the cafeteria line. She was wearing a bulky black jacket and slacks, nothing fancy, but she looked spectacular. He was not going to make a fool of himself this time. He would play it suave. Aloof, unconcerned, no ego investment at all.

She noticed him and waved. His heart fluttered in response but he kept his lips tight, played it cool. He raised a curled palm in half-salute. He looked down at his plate and stabbed a piece of meatloaf. The caf was crowded during lunch hour, noisy with an anonymous hum of chatter. He had saved her a seat at a private table.

"You won't believe what I've been doing all morning," she said. She slid her plastic tray down and sat.

"What?"

"Target practice."

"Really?"

"Uh hum." She bit into a buttered croissant.

"With a gun?"

Her furtive eyes darted side to side. "Check it out," she murmured. She leaned forward and opened the front of her jacket to reveal a badass black weapon in a shoulder holster.

"Holy crap. Is that a machine gun?"

"It shoots tranks. It's modelled on the old Uzi semi-automatic. A classic, or so I'm told." She closed her coat again and checked nearby tables for surveillance. "I'm going on a mission with Dimitri."

"The Security Chief?" Rix felt his body tighten at the thought of new competition, yet another boyfriend. He sat back in his chair and took a deep breath to calm himself.

Niko nodded. "The head honcho."

"He's a bit of a galoot."

"He's very serious about his work. Tomorrow we're jumping off the roof."

"What?"

"We're practising a tandem jump with a directional parachute. I'm the shooter."

Rix could hardly believe his ears. He watched Niko spoon soup past perfect lips. "My arms are so sore," she said.

"You're not going to get killed, are you?"

"I hope not."

"When's the mission?"

"I can't say. It's need-to-know. Pretty cool, eh?"

"Can I come along?"

"No." She studied her soup for a moment. "And don't tell anyone."

He scowled at her. As if.

"So what have you been up to? Still running V-space for Helena?"

"Actually, I'm planning a murder," Rix said and stretched his fingers out in front of him.

"Yeah, right."

He shrugged, nonchalant, kept his cool.

"You're serious?"

"Sure."

Niko put her spoon in her bowl and stared at him. Her dark eyes were intense. "Is this some sort of competition to see who can pull the craziest stunt?"

He smiled. "That's what it sounds like."

She hunched forward over the table. "Who are you planning to murder?"

"I don't know yet."

She sat back and shook her head. "Okay, just random violence. Of course. Another pathetic expression of teenage angst."

"I'm going to find the man who killed my mother."

"Yeah, you and whose army? Don't you think the greysuits have already turned over all the loose stones?"

"Jimmy's helping me out."

"You've seen Jimmy?"

"We keep in touch."

"Jimmy the smuggler?"

"He dropped in last week." Rix tipped up his nose. "We made arrangements."

Niko leaned forward. "Oooh, this *does* sound interesting. Do you need any help?" She patted the bulge under her jacket.

"Maybe."

"I'm learning fast. You could use a good commando."

Rix felt a dreamy glow. "Yeah, that might work out. We could get together and talk about it."

"Do you want me to ask Dimitri?"

"No! Just us." His voice had gone harsh with jealousy all of a sudden, again. Damn.

"You don't need to worry about Dimitri. I'm not falling for another guy." She held a lazy hand up in pledge. "I've learned my lesson."

"Hah."

"Actually, he's a bit of a galoot."

Rix chuckled. "Good one."

"You've got to admit, though, he's built like a stud horse."

"I know. I wouldn't have any chance against him."

"His arms are like vice grips."

A fresh surge of jealousy bloomed within him. "Okay, that's enough."

"Oh, don't be silly, Rix. His jaw is bigger than his head."

"Hardly."

"And his ears stick out. Have you seen his ears?"

"Not really."

Niko tossed the notion aside with her bangs. "Well, I'm sure he would help out if we asked him. He was in the army somewhere in eastern Russia. He's probably killed lots of people."

"He won't be necessary. We're going to be working in V-space."

Niko paused to appraise him. "You can't kill someone in V-space."

"Why not?"

"That's your plan? Murder by fiberoptic cable?" Niko laughed. "What are you going to try? Texting a flame war? Planting a virus?"

"I'm still working out the details."

"Oh my God. You're serious?"

He ducked his head closer. "I'm going to rig a brain burn," he hissed, "just like the Beast does."

"Yeah, right." She pushed her tray toward him.

"It could work."

She shook her head sadly. "No, Rix. It can't work." She stood up. "I'm going on a real mission with Dimitri. In the real world. I'm sorry if that makes you feel insecure."

"I'm not making this up to impress you, Niko. I gave up on you long ago."

Her eyes widened. "Oh, is that so?"

"Why wouldn't it be?"

She cocked her head at him, studying his every move with nerve-racking insouciance. Could she see something inside him? Something in his body language? He straightened his spine. He hardened his face. He was aloof and untouchable.

She pressed her lips together with a mischievous expression. She looked like she was suppressing a laugh at his efforts. "Fine. Have it your own way."

"I will," he said. "Enjoy your day."

"Stay out of trouble, Rix."

"No problem. Good luck jumping from buildings."

Niko grinned and patted her chest again. "I've got all the luck I need right here."

# TWELVE

**J**ackie Rose boiled a leftover chicken carcass to make soup for dinner while Zak washed blood out of towels and bedsheets. Tono's strength was ebbing fast as a crowd of well-wishers arrived to celebrate the birth. Grandfather returned with the family goat in tow, but Tono refused the gift. It seemed unlikely that the barely pubescent mother would be able to supply much milk on her own. They stood in the hallway and performed an elaborate charade *en français*, both trying to offer humility while sustaining necessary pride.

Tono went out to the goat shed to fetch a rusty wheelchair left behind by aid workers a decade previous. Grandfather looked glum at the offer of yet more interpersonal liability, but stood wringing his hat in his hands while extended family members prepared mother and baby to return home.

Daylight began to wane as Jackie drained off the soup and added chopped carrot and macaroni elbows to her creation. The entourage left with gay clapping and the sound of a tambourine as they pushed a squeaky wheelchair up the street. The air grew still and heavy like a hot blanket. Tono sat in her kitchen with her eyes closed, breathing deep the scent of chicken broth. Her movements were slow and seemed to be laden with pain as Zak joined her at the table, freshly showered and dressed in clean clothes.

"Thank you for your help today, mister Zak."

"My pleasure. You have a busy ministry here."

"You make a good white spirit."

"It's all just a sideshow, isn't it, Tono? Smudge smoke and mirrors?"

She opened her eyes, her posture wary. "Every movement is significant."

"Exactly. The work you perform here is some kind of supernatural psychotherapy. You're harnessing the placebo effect with primitive tools."

Jackie placed a bowl of soup in front of him. "Oh, give it a rest, Zak. This is no time for philosophy."

"I'm not trying to minimize the importance of what happened here today. Two lives were saved by a miraculous act of faith. I get that. I was there. I'm just trying to understand how it all works."

"It all works by faith," Tono said. "Only by Jesus."

"But all the scripting, all the Vodou props, are they really necessary?"

Jackie placed two more bowls of soup on the table and sat down. "It's just like giving a lecture at the university," she said. "You point to a chart and use a few visual aids, you incite an emotional response and lead your students to higher suggestibility, to a new paradigm. All in the hope that one or two might glimpse something beyond themselves, something ineffable."

"But it's all fake," he said.

"You don't know the first thing, British boy."

"Tell me, then, Tono, please. Where is the true magic?"

"Magic is not something you or I create, mister Zak. Magic is revealed. It's already there. Only a blind man can see in the dark."

"More cryptology?"

"You are so proud of your daylight vision, your educated brain and scientific method."

"Don't listen to him, Tono. Eat your soup. You're looking sickly and pale." Jackie turned her eyes to Zak. "How many times do you expect lightning to strike in your lifetime, Zak?"

He stirred steaming broth with his spoon. "Not many, I guess."

"Some people wait their whole life for one true miracle," Jackie said and held out a palm to Tono. "What is the magician to do in the meantime? Fritter themselves away? No, they devote themselves to their ultimate work. They get the foundations established and the people in motion. The so-called props and superstitions of the participants are vital to any manifestation."

Zak hung his head in surrender to his mentor. From the frozen north to the searing south he had followed her in search of his wife, and still no resolution. "Mia's not here in Haiti, is she?"

Jackie reached for his hand across the table. "Oh, honey. Don't lose heart. She *is* here. Timon is here also, very close. We must be patient."

"I have one more gift for you," Tono blurted.

Jackie turned back to her. "No, Tono. You're ready for bed. Zak and I will take a taxi to Port-au-Prince to leave you in peace."

"No," she said. "One more gift. You'll see." She tested her soup. "Mmmm." She took a few more bites, her eyes dramatic with interest.

Jackie smiled. "You like?"

"You must be a culinary genius, my *Jacqui*. I'm sure you had little to work with in my shantytown kitchen."

"Oh, don't be silly. Some onions and garlic, peppercorn and bay leaf, a pinch of this and that."

"This one should not get away, mister Zak."

"It *is* very tasty," he admitted and began to eat in earnest. "Do you have any more cinnamon wine?"

"No, the dream potion has already done its work. Now I'll need my skull drum and censer."

"Oh, please, *mambo*, no more magic today."

"You've come such a long way, *ma chérie*, and I have been distracted from your needs."

"It's really not necessary. You've been a wonderful hostess."

"Just one small gift. For love."

Jackie tilted her head and pressed her lips. Her eyes glazed with melancholy. "Very well. One more night."

Zak sighed through his nose, wondering again about the deep spiritual connection between these women.

"Do you remember braiding my hair with hibiscus, *ma cherie?*"

Jackie's face turned radiant. "I remember every moment."

Zak pushed his empty bowl forward. "Too much information," he said. "I'll find some dry blankets to make up the bed."

Tono raised her nose once upward to point him to work. "Fresh sheets are in the bottom drawer in the bureau." She turned back to Jackie with a smile.

After a few minutes to finish her soup, Jackie followed into their bedroom and began stuffing pillows into clean pillowcases. "It's hard to believe that this place was a trauma clinic just a few hours ago," she said.

"Do you suppose there is a resonance left behind?"

"I expect so, but please, Zak, for once don't ask me to measure it."

"Am I pushing too hard?"

"That's not for me to say."

"What is she doing now?"

"She mixing herbs for her censer."

"So we're stuck here for another night?"

"I'm sorry," Jackie said. "We're really not in a position to refuse her."

"She's going to pass out from exhaustion soon."

Jackie grimaced. "It won't be long."

"What if she has a heart attack?"

"There's no point in trying to talk her out of it."

"What exactly has she got in mind?"

"She preparing an announcement."

"Ooooh." Zak fluttered his hands for emphasis.

She grimaced an admonishment. "Try to be civil, at least."

By the time they convened in the front room, Tono had been transformed. She had changed into a black dress with bright splashes of red and orange hibiscus blossoms, cinched at the waist with a belt of animal skin sewn with long decorative tassels. She carried a metal censer that hung on a silver chain from a wooden handle, and held a skull drum rattle aloft on a stick of bone.

"I have decided to give you both the exact opposite of what you ask for," she proclaimed. "Tonight I will conjure a hedge of protection around this property, an unbreakable wall. No spirit dead or alive can view past it."

Zak edged closer to see what type of skull had been used in the rattle. Too small for a human—perhaps a monkey? Bits of crystal hung down on leather thongs. "And that's what, some kind of spiritual privacy fence?"

"You ask me for messages from your dead partners, but they refuse to speak. Instead I will now sever any possibility of contact until morning. When Mia and Timon look at this place tonight, they will see only emptiness, a grey barrier. Even the Loa will be unable to communicate."

"What do you expect to accomplish?"

"Nothing. It's a simple gift of freedom. All I ask is that you look at *Jacqui* in the spirit with truth." She turned to Jackie. "And that she does the same."

"But it's just a trick," Zak complained. "A medieval stage show."

"No, I assure you. No tricks."

"But any effect is dependent on our faith in your conjuring."

"Seven times I will circle the property. Seven rows higher I will build the wall block by block. You may not cross the barrier until the rising of the sun. No one may cross in or out."

"But—"

Jackie stilled Zak with a gentle hand on his forearm. "Thank you for your gift, *mambo*," she said.

Tono struck her censer alight with a long wooden match. A flame leapt up briefly and was quickly swallowed by white smoke. She picked up her skull drum and made her way out the front door. She raised her face to the setting sun and began to murmur.

"Let her go, Zak," Jackie whispered. "It will be dark before she finishes at this rate."

"But it's ridiculous. Does she think she's playing matchmaker for us?"

"Why is that so ridiculous?" Jackie glanced at him and ducked her eyes with a flirtatious smile.

Zak gazed in wonder at her subtle change of heart. Was that a signal of invitation, an open door? Sure, they were developing a relationship, working in close proximity with common goals. Jackie was beautiful inside and out, but that wasn't why they were in Haiti.

RETRIBUTION

They had come to find their dead soulmates beyond the veil. That was all that mattered, wasn't it?

Jackie ladled out the dregs of soup and they ate in silence for a few minutes as an uncomfortable realization settled on Zak. He cared about this woman far beyond a professional friendship. He was romantically intrigued with the good doctor and could no longer deny it. A tonic of dream-lust shuddered through him like an elixir. "Should we check on Tono?"

"She's finishing her third circuit. I'm keeping track."

"Do you believe in her hedge of protection?"

"It's a common doctrine in many cultures with strong roots in Christianity."

"That's not what I asked."

Jackie paused to chew on her bottom lip. "I guess I do believe, Zak. I've seen enough evidence to trust in Tono's magic."

"What would happen if we tried to cross the barrier?"

"I wouldn't dare try it."

"So we're trapped in here for the night?"

"You keep saying that."

"What is taking her so long?"

They got up to investigate and found her shuffling and chanting in the front garden.

Jackie shook her head at the sight. "She'll never get done before dark. Why is she going so slow? It looks like two steps backward for every one step in front."

Zak recognized the familiar footwork of the smudge-pit dance. "She's tracing a complicated pattern, a series of overlaid triangles. It's designed so that the forward movement is evenly balanced between left and right, a reconciliation of male and female energies similar to the Chinese yin and yang."

Jackie stared at him in surprise. "You're learning Vodou?"

"Not really. Just trying to understand the basics."

"Tono is a good teacher."

"She looks a bit unsteady on her feet."

"She's getting tired."

"Let's call her in."

"No." Jackie stilled him with a touch on the shoulder. "Let her go."

Tono waved her censer from side to side in a steady rhythm, making patterns of smoke in the air like snakes. With her other hand she spun her rattle in a staccato beat. The sun had dropped below the horizon and the sky was pink in the west. They sat on the front stoop and watched the sunset while Tono conjured the night.

In a few minutes she had completed her fifth circuit and was starting to stagger. Zak could feel tension in his abdomen. He wanted to stop this craziness before she collapsed. Jackie pressed her hand on his thigh to quiet his pumping knee. They noticed two men approaching from opposite directions in the distance. One took up a position at the front corner of Tono's property, facing south, and the other stood in the opposite corner, facing north. They both wore hooded robes over dark faces. Neither man spoke.

"Are they spirits?" Jackie whispered.

"They look like men."

"What are they doing?"

"Same as us. Watching the magic show."

Tono came round for the sixth time, woozy now and unable to walk a straight line. She stumbled to one knee and dropped her skull drum. An aromatic haze of smoke enveloped her.

The two black spirits made no attempt to intervene.

Zak jumped to his feet and rushed forward. He bent down to her. "Come in, Tono. It's time for bed."

"No," she rasped. "The barrier is almost complete. One more row of blocks." She rose shakily to her feet.

Zak picked up her rattle and placed it in her hand. "Who are these men?"

"*Houngan.* Elders of the Vodou."

"Why are they here?"

Tono's lips curled into a crooked smile. "You called them from miles away, mister Zak. This morning around the smudge pit. They will guard the barrier until it is finished."

He glanced up to study them. "Why don't they speak?"

"They are great enemies from feuding tribes. Powerful men."

"What do they want?"

"Who knows? Perhaps they have come to watch you dance. Do you still remember the steps?"

"I could probably manage it."

She handed him the skull drum and offered the crook of her elbow. Together they began the final circuit. With his right hand he twirled the bone rattle and with her left hand she waved her smoking censer. The Vodou elders turned their heads to watch but kept their bodies pointed in opposite directions. Zak stepped awkwardly at first, but Tono's fleshy hips undulated against his side, forcing him to remember the rhythm of the dance. Black and white, teacher and student, they blurred into a single entity in the twilight.

By the time they reached the back garden, Zak could feel his legs no longer. His consciousness seemed to be centred in his abdomen, floating forward like a boat on astral waves. Music wafted down in a spiral from above, a high-pitched symphony that seemed to vibrate inside him. A dissonance sounded at a certain point on each rotation of the coil, a minor chord or subtle slide in key that was itself part of the overall harmony. He looked up and saw the hedge of protection with eyes revealed, a glittering translucent wall of standing stones leaning inward in a domelike structure like a glass igloo. He noted the seams where each piece fit perfectly against the next and marvelled as another block materialized above his head with their passing. He saw twinkling stars through a smoke-hole gap in the roof, a universe now distant.

The *houngan* watched each halting movement as Tono staggered back to the front garden to complete the seventh circuit. They stood like mythical creatures with stone masks, black gryphons guarding the hemispheres, sullen and sinister. Their hate for each other seemed palpable, a tribal heritage of enmity, an ancient abomination.

Tono faced the street midway between the Vodou elders and fell forward on her knees. She held her censer aloft with both hands and kept her face averted with a prideful chin. "Pull down the capstone, *mon frère*," she whispered, quaking now with fatigue. "My strength has failed."

Zak looked up to see the hedge of protection complete but for a small porthole to the stars where the spirals of music rained down. He pointed the skull drum toward the opening, feeling a quiet ecstasy ringing in his bones. He willed a new star into existence in the heavens high above and watched in awe as it drifted to earth at his voiceless command. The skull drum vibrated in his hand like a divining rod. The capstone grew larger as it approached, a scintillant diamond, a multi-faceted jewel pointing with promise to his heart. He pulled it down.

The plug fit like a puzzle piece in the glasslike roof and the cosmic symphony stopped abruptly. His wife was dead. He felt a bulge of air pressure in his eardrums, an emptiness of silence. His wife was dead and gone. The hedge of protection turned opaque like a granite cave, sealing them inside. He had fallen in love with Dr. Jackie Rose.

Tono groaned and pitched forward on her face with arms prostrate above her head. The smoking censer rolled out of her reach and snuffed out in the dirt. Zak knelt beside her, feeling for a heartbeat, feeling lost and alone again, a separate creature, a base and grovelling animal beside his queen. The magic barricade disappeared from his view.

Jackie dashed out to help, and together they half-dragged, half-carried Tono up the steps to her house and into bed. Her body began to convulse under a thin flannel blanket, and Zak knelt beside her to offer comfort with his arms.

"One more thing," Tono said and searched for Jackie's eyes. "A gift for the *houngan*."

"The black spirits?" She shook her head. "No way. I can't do it."

"You must. They will not accept a gift from a white man."

"I'm afraid of them."

"They cannot cross the hedge of protection. No one can."

"Are you certain?"

"Yes."

Jackie huffed with resignation. "What is the gift?"

"Under the sink in the kitchen. A jar of red peppers steeped in rum. Only the *houngan* can drink the red clairin. It is a fire reserved for them."

"How did you know they were coming?"

"I always keep a jar, just in case." Her lips trembled into a smile. "A girl must always be prepared. Take the gift and place it on the barrier, equidistant from the men. Be very careful. Not closer to one or the other. You understand?"

"Got it. No risk of offense."

"Say, 'Thank you for visiting,' or some such thing, and bow down to the gift. Not to one man or the other."

"Right."

"Go, then."

Again Tono's body convulsed with fatigue as she began to relax, and Zak stretched over the bed to hug her steady. "Thank you for trying to help us," he said. "I know you mean well."

"It's you who are helping me, British boy."

"I wish it were true."

"Hold me closer. My soul wants to fly away."

"It's not your time. Stay here. Rest easy."

"You are a true white spirit."

"You're delirious."

"I waited three nights in the darkness for you after the earthquake."

"Shhhh."

"At first we heard singing, as though creation itself was calling out solace, but soon my brother died and turned to stone in my arms. The Loa came to minister to me."

"It's okay now, Tono. *Tranquillité.*"

They drifted together and Tono finally settled down, breathing deep into her abdomen with a regular rhythm. She smelled of jasmine tea and cedarwood incense.

Jackie returned, flushed with excitement. "The *houngan* took the gift. They're standing in the street drinking together and laughing."

Tono smiled with delight but kept her eyes closed. "You have done a wonderful thing, my *Jacqui*. Go and enjoy your firstfruit."

Zak stood aside as Jackie bent down to kiss her cheek. "Sleep well, *mambo*."

They tiptoed out of her room and stood facing each other in the hall.

"That was one weird day," Zak said.

"It's not over yet."

"No?"

"Not by a long shot."

Jackie's cheeks were rosy with exhilaration, her eyes bright with the promise of intimacy.

Zak smiled. "I was hoping you might say that."


The sight of the vampire tower in the twilight filled Niko with cold dread. She could hardly believe she was going back to her former prison as she floated down from high above strapped in a parachute harness with Dimitri, his machine pistol pressed hard against her backside like a broom handle. At least she hoped it was his pistol. They had jumped from a glider almost a half mile away. Freefall had been a frightening few seconds, even though she had done the simulation a dozen times in V-space. There was something primeval about the fear of flying that could not be captured by a digital feelie. It just felt so *unnatural*.

Dimitri banked the chute to the right and Niko felt her body swing out like a clock pendulum counting down the seconds. She gripped her gun harder. The rooftop was coming up fast. She flipped on her infrared and scanned for thermal targets. One red spot standing near the stairwell. The control tower looked empty. Perfect. Stoner boy was out having a smoke.

"You got a shot?" Dimitri said.

"Can you hold it steady?"

"Hang on." He corrected again, angling their approach and taking a little heat off the entry speed. "That better?"

"It's coming up fast."

"I know."

Niko grunted. Two bodies were a lot of weight for a parachute.

A solo kite was far more versatile. Dimitri was probably 180, maybe 190, so they had at least 300 pounds coming in like a bomb. How was she supposed to duck and roll with a gorilla on her back?

"He's near the stairwell," she said.

"Got it. Don't let him get to the radio."

"No problem." Wow, what a rush. She had never shot a human before, nothing but paper targets. She was using trank needles, but you never knew. A blast to the eye or right in the jugular could be fatal. He was probably wearing a standard flak jacket, so she'd have to nail him in the butt. Her hands were cold from wind chill, her finger like ice on the trigger. She wished she had worn gloves.

She fired two shots as the ground rushed toward her and the guard fell forward without an outcry. Dimitri kicked the chute up in a braking maneuver and Niko's feet flew up in front of her. She hit on her tailbone as Dimitri took most of the landing blow. He swung her up on top of him and skidded on his reinforced backpack. She dragged her heels as best she could and clung to her gun. The chute deflated around them as Dimitri unclipped the lines. One mistake and a bad gust could take them over the edge of the building. Niko lay still as he worked, panting and preparing for action.

Finally he unclasped the harness and rolled her away. Dimitri jumped up and sprinted for the control tower, his gun ready and able. They had to disable the stairwell webcams as soon as possible, quiet as mice. Their black parachute would be nothing but a cloud passing under the stars on the digital record, their dark jumpsuits and black masks nothing but shadows.

Niko scanned the rooftop for thermals and found the area clear but for the one prostrate guard. She checked for a pulse and found him sleeping like a baby with a joint still burning in his fingertips. She bundled the chute and stuffed it behind a storage bin. Dimitri was back already, a grim robo-commando in helmet and visor, machine pistol cocked at his side. He looked frightening and immense and she was glad to be on his team for sure. He checked the stairwell door for sound and eased it open.

Niko led the way downstairs with her auditory augmentation maxed out. Any prisoners onsite at this time of day would be sedated and strapped in their beds with their blood dripping into refrigerated bottles. The cafeteria staff and janitors would be asleep. There were three guard stations on the main floor, but the main one just inside the front entrance was the most important. As many as five or six screws worked the night shift, plus two more at stations on the periphery.

Two voices came up the stairwell and Niko raised a quick hand to signal a halt. Damn, the goons had noticed the blank webcam screens already. They took cover behind a side door and waited. Dimitri readied his pistol through a crack in the door. "What are they saying?"

"I'm not sure."

"Any urgency in their voices?"

Niko closed her eyes to concentrate. "No, they're joking around. They think our friend is too stoned to operate the equipment."

"Perfect."

Sure enough, two guards ambled up the stairs into view and were quickly dispatched to dreamland. One continued to tremble and tried to reach for his radio, so Dimitri shot him again point-blank. The nerve toxin had a variance of efficacy, a known and dangerous aberration, a calculated vulnerability. They could take nothing for granted.

"That will be second warning," he said. "After a minute of radio silence the whole team will be checking their weapons." He hurried down the stairs.

Niko struggled to keep pace with the giant stormtrooper, panting hard on his heels. Surprise was their only advantage in this assault mission. They did not have any big guns or backup, just single-minded purpose. Dimitri readied his trank gun as they approached the Security headquarters. Niko took a position behind him, walking backward and swivelling from side to side. They heard voices in the room, at least three, and Dimitri motioned her against the wall. He jumped around the corner and began firing.

The noise seemed amplified in close quarters but was over in a few moments. A burst of ten or twelve shots, then one solitary bullet. Niko scanned the hallway for trouble, crouched and ready to fire, but heard no unusual noise in the distance.

Dimitri stuck his head around the corner. "Clear."

Niko jumped inside the room.

Four guards lay strewn like bowling pins, one bleeding profusely from the head. Niko knelt down to check his condition.

"Don't worry about him. Let's keep moving." Dimitri checked the hallway with his gun pointed skyward.

"There's no reason to let him die."

Dimitri shrugged, unconcerned behind his visor, and Niko wondered how many men he had killed during his army career. Did death become a commodity so easily? She found some tissue and masking tape and made a quick compress for the guard's forehead. He had a trank needle in his shoulder and had hit his head on the sharp edge of his desk as he fell. A pool of blood had collected beneath him.

"Let's go," Dimitri said, and Niko rose to follow, walking backward behind him in the hallway. They advanced quietly with determined speed.

At an intersection he stopped and tipped his helmet, trying to remember the layout. Niko took point position and crept stealthily down the hallway ahead of him. She found Dr. Lucy Itel keyboarding in her office. Niko levelled her gun. She had waited a long time to meet her former captor face to face. "Don't touch anything."

The doctor looked up and gasped. Her eyes flitted to her hardware monitor, to the webcam on the wall and back to Niko. Her brows crumpled with confusion.

"We're here for the girl."

"What girl?"

"You know, the oracle. Where is she?"

"She's sleeping."

"Stand up."

"Are you going to kill me?"

"Not me, but he might."

Dimitri stepped up from behind with his visor down over his eyes like a cyborg warrior. He raised his weapon.

Lucy Itel jumped to her feet, her face white as marble.

Dimitri motioned her to the door with his gun. The doctor moved forward with circumspection, her eyes trained on his helmet and mask. She walked deliberately down the hall to a door on the right and opened it. The girl lay on a cot inside, curled up in blankets printed with cartoon characters. They stood for a moment watching her in silence.

"How does she do it?" Niko demanded.

Lucy Itel shuddered her head. "I don't know."

Niko hauled back and sucker-punched the doctor in the cheek, knocking her head against the door frame with the force of the blow. She fell to her knees with a grunt of pain and wobbled her head.

"One more time," Niko said.

Lucy Itel squinted up through a curtain of pain. "She thinks she sees her mother, some sort of psychic entanglement tuned to the virus. When we put her in a holographic map, she can pinpoint coordinates. I don't know how or why. I'm just doing my job."

Dimitri stepped forward and shot her carefully in the thigh. She slumped forward on her elbows. Niko put a boot to her bum and kicked her sprawling forward on her face for payback.

Dimitri grinned at her. "You're mean." A drop of blood fell from his jacket.

Niko gaped with fresh panic. "You've been shot!"

"It happens. There were four of them, remember."

"A real bullet?"

"Thank blazes. A trank would have taken me out by now."

"Are you okay?"

"Too early to tell, but I think it's just a wing shot."

"Why didn't you say something, you moron? Here I am patching up the bad guys while you bleed to death."

"I'm not going to bleed to death. Don't be crazy."

"Take off your flak jacket. Let me see."

"No," he said, "we'll keep to the script."

Niko glared at him, wondering whether to push. Was Dimitri some kind of war machine, oblivious to pain? If they stopped for a moment, would his adrenaline wash away like water down a drain? "Well, take off your helmet, at least," she said as she pulled off her own. "Let's at least look like humans when we wake up the kid."

"You do it. I'll check our perimeter and search for a laundry cart." He darted back into the hallway.

Niko placed her helmet, gun, and goggles under the bed and knelt on her knees to face the child. She looked peaceful in sleep, this miracle girl, her face framed with curlicues of dark hair. What was the kid's name again? Sienna?

"Wake up, Sienna. We're going for a ride."

The child murmured on the edge of dreams.

"Time to wake up, honey."

"Mommy, is that you?"

"Don't worry. Everything's going to be fine."

The girl blinked her eyes open and brightened with recognition. "Mommy, I knew you would find me." She reached up for a hug and clung to Niko's neck as though for dear life. "I was so scared, Mommy, when those bad men chased you away."

Niko pressed her lower lip between her teeth. Oh, God, the poor kid had lost touch with reality. She patted her back with a gentle caress. "It's okay, Sienna. Don't worry."

"Please can we go home?"

Niko squeezed her close for comfort. Home, where the hell was that? "Yes, dear, you're safe now."

# THIRTEEN

Helena woke and groaned, already burdened by the weight of another day. She reached for her lover beside her and found the bed empty.

"Jimmy?"

"I've been watching you sleep," he said from a chair across the room. "You're a beautiful woman."

She brushed tousled bangs from her eyes. "You're up early."

"You grumble a lot. You moan and whine."

"I have a lot on my mind." She fluffed another pillow to prop up her head. Jimmy was dressed in street clothes, his Harley jacket draped over the chair arm. "Sorry if I kept you awake."

He cast off the notion with quick toss and peered at her. "You're tormented."

"Aren't we all? Any news from Silus this morning?

"Two of the subjects have gone comatose from exhaustion. Most of the others have developed coping mechanisms. Plus the usual litany of miraculous discoveries, symphonies, poetry, and personal epiphanies."

Helena sighed and settled deeper into her pillows. "I don't know how they can keep it up."

"What we're seeing is just the natural brain unleashed. The potential was always there."

"Oh, come on, Jimmy, it's completely artificial. These special effects are being produced by mechanical robots, not human brains."

"Your argument is getting tiresome," he said, "but I think I have a solution. We're eight days into the experiment. How about two more days and we'll call it even? That's ten days, one third of our original agreement."

Helena felt a burst of exhilaration at the thought but kept her composure. "I know you've made significant investments, Jimmy. I know you have a lot on the line. I just had no idea the results would be so dramatic. It's not natural for humans to live in a perpetual eureka experience. We need to have valleys with our peaks."

He held up a hand to ward off any quarrel. "I'm not a monster," he said. "I'm offering you a way out."

"We'll purge the nanobots?"

He bowed his head once in genteel affirmation. "All I ask is that we keep the subjects under scrutiny. We record any physiological effects related to withdrawal. Hourly journal entries and daily testing. Agreed?"

"Certainly." Helena saw a burgeoning glow of optimism on the horizon. "Whatever it take to secure a release from our contract."

"Then after another ten days we do complete scans and cognitive stress testing to monitor the residual effects. I'm thinking that after a period of elevated brain function, the natural pathways will be permanently augmented."

"I would imagine so."

"I may be able to salvage something."

"I hate to be such a disappointment," she said with a tentative smile, "after getting to know you so well."

228

His face relaxed into a friendly leer. "*Au contraire*, you've been a blessing, Helena."

"I had no idea you were such a sensitive man. Come back to bed?"

"No, I'm already packed."

"What?" Helena sat up with a start, clutching a sheet to cover her breasts. "How long have you been awake?"

"Hours. I don't need much sleep."

"This is *goodbye*?"

"I guess so," he said. "I'm heading back to Canada."

"I'm shocked. I thought we . . ." She paused. What *did* she think? That this was a new beginning, a turning point in her lifeline? A permanent relationship? No, hardly anything so romantic. She had grown comfortable sharing a daily routine with a man again, however briefly. Anything more would be a delusion.

Jimmy held palms up with a shrug of resignation. "You're getting younger every day. I'm getting older. It could never work out."

"I see." Short-term pain for long-term gain, was that it?

"You're welcome to visit up north any time," he offered.

"I may take you up on that."

"I've got a posh penthouse apartment in the honeymoon capital of the world."

"Sounds wonderful. Want to say goodbye properly before you go?"

His eyes drifted away. "I've already showered."

"We have plenty of hot water."

"I'm afraid it would be a letdown now," he said wistfully. "Semisweet."

Helena chewed her bottom lip, watching him. So this was really the end. "I'm sorry to hear that."

"How about I cook you breakfast instead?" His face brightened with animation. "My famous eggs Benedict?"

"Can we still be lovers?"

"A long-distance relationship?"

She stifled an urge to beg, steeled herself against cold reality. How quickly she had succumbed to the comforts of love. "I just want to keep that connection in my head. I don't want to be alone anymore."

"You're not alone, Helena. You're surrounded by adoring fans."

"My friends all work for me, Jimmy. They respect me because I sign the cheques. That's different. I don't want *fans*. I want a soulmate. I miss you already."

"You really like me that much?"

"Of course I do," she said. "What more could I possibly do to show my feelings?"

"Well, if you put it that way." Jimmy stood up and reached for the buttons on his shirt. "Maybe a second shower would suit me just fine."


Rix was under the wire checking out some action on Main Street when a chime sounded on his backspace monitor, a signal from the front door of his office in realtime. He found a V-space subterminal and keyed access to the ERI webcam system to see his father with a strange woman on his arm. Crap. They were obviously an item, the way she clung to him. She looked like intelligentsia, with a proud lilt to her head.

He signalled for a zoomtube and quickly popped out of Prime. His eyes blinked open and he reached up behind his ear to unplug his cable, feeling the unusual infinite loss of disconnection as he stood exposed without the wire. His launch couch powered down behind him with a whine as he adjusted to reality. The new carpet smelled of solvent chemicals. He opened the door and stepped into his main office. "Thanks for the visit," he said.

"Great to see you, Rix." Zak broke away from the girl and gave him a bear hug, his eyes full of pride. "So you've got your own launch station now, and a corner office? Not bad."

"They're trying to turn me into a bureaucrat."

"I doubt they'll have much success."

Rix grinned despite the firebomb crowding the room. "True enough. So this is the big surprise?"

"Yeah, this is Jackie." Zak laid down an arm in her direction.

"Pleased to meet you," she said from near the door. Her stance was regal but reticent, her clothing expensive.

"Hi."

They eyed each other at a distance. Her skin was dark, a medium chocolate, her face luminous. She had that contented and confident look of a significant other.

"So you guys are what? Working together?"

"We've been on a shared project for a few weeks," Zak said, "and, well, things have developed quickly." Zak's lips tightened, his body stance shifted to a defensive posture, and realization hit Rix like a mallet between the eyes.

"Don't tell me you're married," he said.

Zak winced. "Well—"

"You couldn't tell me? No invitation to the chapel? No gaudy postcard?"

"There was no an actual ceremony." Zak spread his hands.

"No funeral, no wedding, is that it?"

"We didn't perform any special ritual," Zak said, "but we've had a spiritual communion. In many cultures the sharing of a hammock is akin to marriage."

Rix gaped. "What the heck?" He turned toward Jackie again. Her smile looked grim. "So that's a euphemism for jumping in the sack, right?" He dared her with his eyes and she flinched away.

"Hey," Zak cautioned. "I know it seems a bit spontaneous." His spread hands curled to fists at his side. "We've had a mystical co-mingling."

"What the heck does that mean?"

"We were visiting a friend in Haiti," Jackie offered. "She has magical powers of healing and she's a good Baptist pastor."

Zak nodded. "It was a wonderful experience."

"I can't believe this," Rix said. "Your wife is turning in her grave and you're off having a tourist wedding?"

Zak's skin paled to a hard and stony grey. "It wasn't a tourist wedding, and I don't like the tone of your voice!"

Jackie stilled him with a touch of her hand, turned to Rix. "What exactly do you mean 'turning in her grave'? Have you had some contact with her?"

"It's none of your business, lady."

Her face stiffened. "Sorry."

"Sit down, Rix," Zak said. "There's no reason to make this difficult."

Rix dropped into a seat behind his desk, safe behind that thin veneer of subjective privacy. A gathering weight of dread seemed ready to suffocate him. His mother was all but forgotten.

His father hunted for him with pleading eyes. "We came all this way to tell you in person," he said.

"Gee, thanks," Rix said.

"I know it's a bit sudden. We were caught by surprise ourselves. I thought you would want the best for me, for all of us. Isn't that what love is all about?"

"Love?" A vision of Niko flashed in his mind. What was this strange concept of love? Why was it so mixed up with sex? He wanted the best for Niko and would sacrifice anything for her. Was that love? His dad had made sacrifices that had passed remembrance. He'd paid the price of a mindwipe to give his son Eternal life. Love was a surrender, an immolation. Rix scrutinized Jackie. Had she tricked Zak somehow? A holiday romance on the beach? A tequila sunrise with a matrimonial hangover?

She bristled at his inspection. "I think we should try this again later, Zak. We've extended common courtesy for now."

"That's a great idea," Rix said. "I'm free next week."

"I'm not trying to replace your mother," Jackie said.

"As if you ever could."

"Your feelings are perfectly natural."

"What are you, a psychoanalyst?" He looked at his father and saw a flicker of insight. "Oh my goodness. You're a shrink?"

"Jackie is a famous author."

"Worse yet. What are you researching, family breakups?"

"I'm a ghost hunter," she said. "I don't want to disrupt your relationship with your father."

"A ghost hunter?"

"We were looking for Mia, but apparently you've already found her."

"I didn't say that."

"No, you didn't."

Zak stepped forward and leaned on the desk. "Have you seen Mia?"

"No." Rix stared up at his father in defiance. He would never spill his guts in front of this woman.

Zak blinked a few times, testing deep waters. "Fine. Let's get together for dinner."

"Sure."

"Tomorrow, after you settle yourself down."

"You're gonna clean out your locker?"

"I guess so."

"Helena will be pissed."

"She doesn't need me anymore. She's got the best runner in the business."

He stood and reached behind for Jackie's hand. Rix saw pity in her appraising eyes and steeled himself against it. He would not be her sob story, a footnote in her next treatise, no way. "So where's the honeymoon?"

Husband and wife looked at each other as though surprised. Were they just now waking up to responsibility? To the notion of paperwork and social custom? What kind of psycho-trip were they on?

"We're still riding the magic," Jackie said.

Rix sneered with all due civility. "Good luck with that."

He tried to focus on work after they left but couldn't gather the head space. Damn, who was that woman? He googled her on the net and examined her bio for a few minutes. Way-out cultish stuff in his estimation, neo-age psi propaganda. He followed a few quick links: former fashion model, beauty queen, media darling—probably rich to boot, a dangerous mix of pseudoscience and financial legitimacy.

He scanned his chats to see if Niko was online, confirmed, and poked her. Her webcam portrait filled his monitor. "Hey, cousin."

"How was the mission?"

"I survived. Dimitri took a bullet."

"Ouch. Is he okay?"

She waved a hand at him, filling his screen. "He'll be fine. It was *so* awesome. I got to punch a woman in the face."

"That doesn't sound like you."

"Oh, she deserved it."

"Did you find out anything?"

"Yeah, we rescued the miracle girl. She thinks I'm her mother."

"Come again?"

"She has a fixation of some sort. Helena's putting her under psychiatric evaluation."

*Miracle girl? Occult research?* Had the whole world gone crazy?
"Well, there's a new shrink available on the block."

"That so?"

"My dad's new wife."

Niko's face turned pensive in the faltering silence. "Crap," she said.

"That's what *I* thought."

"What is she like? I mean . . . gold digger?"

"Naw, she's rich and famous already."

"Hmm."

"She's kind of . . ." Rix paused as he replayed her image in his mind. ". . . civilized."

"Hmm."

"What do you think?"

"Dunno. Never had a mother."

Rix bristled. "She's not my mother."

"Stepmother."

"Not even."

"Well she is, you know, technically."

Rix shrugged it off. "Maybe. Anyway, I'm glad you're okay."

"Thanks. You didn't tell your dad about your big plan, did you?"

"Don't worry." He pushed a palm toward the camera. "The subject didn't come close."

"Good, because the marriage bed has ears."

"Is that what they say?"

Niko nodded with sure wisdom. "Once men start having sex, they can't be trusted to keep a secret."

"Eww, it makes me nauseous to think about it." He held a curled palm up to his eye as though to blunt his vision.

"Sorry to break it to ya. Getting a good visual?"

"Oh, please."

She swallowed back a smirk to put on her game face. "I've been thinking about your mission. I might be able to help. There's some powerful equipment at Phillip's lab. Bioengineering computers with V-space hookup, high-level access, paralegal filters. We might be able to rig a burst of overclock energy somehow." Niko looked confident on the high-def flatscreen, vivacious and beautiful.

"You think so?"

"It might be dangerous."

"Cool."

Niko leaned forward with enthusiasm. "Andrew might help us out. You remember, the neuroscientist?"

Rix balked. "I thought you skanked out on him."

"He still owes me."

"That's twisted logic."

"Yeah, whatever." She tossed him off with a quick eyebrow. "Do you want my help or not?"

"Sure," he said, "let's get together and plan the details." He would promise anything to get close to her, to share her cheeky charisma. "You want to meet in the caf?"

"Not today, I have to punch in with the kid in a few minutes. I feel like a babysitter."

"Hah. I hope they don't ask for references."

Niko grinned. "Nice one."

"How about dinner tomorrow with the Zak-and-Jackie show?"

Her eyes went wide. "You want me to meet your parents?"

Oops. Rix felt weightlessness in his stomach. "Too much, too soon?"

She pursed her lips in thought, gave a subtle tilt to her head and brightened. "No, it sounds like a fling," she said happily. "Lock it down and let me know."

His monitor defaulted to news view as she signed off. A foreign diplomat was giving a throne speech, some territorial skirmish on the other side of the world. He paused to reflect on his own family politics as he absorbed the drama. Why did people set up boundaries and borders and then fight to maintain them? Why couldn't they all just get along with each other? Was it hardwired in the species to make a complete ass of themselves over and over? Rix sighed as he revisited his emotional reaction to his *stepmother*, his rudeness to her face. Already this new situation was bringing out the worst in him. He didn't like change, that was his big problem. Crap.

Phillip was neither awake nor asleep, but he lived in a perpetual netherworld of digital deconstruction. He floated in a maelstrom sea of broken dreams and stared into a fractured mirror of splintered images, memories of long ago. Without language, he could not tag the fragments, he could not piece together a personification of purpose.

What was this place?

In Tokyo the heat moved, in New York the light fountained in splendour, and in Beijing the fire accelerated into a blazing whirlwind. The symphony undulated in living quantum waves at his touch. Entangled bits of data swirled at his subconscious command. If only he could reach out and grasp the truth that seemed so close to his heart. The centre had fallen away and the periphery reigned supreme.

Soon he would learn the strange machine language and conquer this new frontier of consciousness. He had all the time in the world.

Sienna refused to cooperate. Niko held her by the scruff of her jacket, pointing her forward, but she tried to dart away at every corner.

"We're going for dinner with some new friends," Niko said.

The little girl looked up at her new guardian with suspicion. "Sienna's not hungry."

"I'll give you a chocolate if you behave. Do you want a Caramilk?"

"Sienna doesn't like carrot milk."

Niko herded her into the cafeteria line. "Put your hand on this rail and hold on. I'm just going to fill up a tray. Don't you dare run off."

Sienna pouted at her with doe eyes. "Can I have some juice, Mommy?"

"Yes, you may. Apple or orange?"

"Grapefruit."

Niko sighed and peered behind the counter. "Excuse me, do we have any grapefruit juice today?"

A young student looked up from stirring a pot of soup in the kitchen. "Hi, Niko. So this is your new charge?"

"Yeah, this is Sienna. Honey, this is Madison. She's making good food for you."

Madison peered over the counter. "Hi, Sienna."

"Do you have grapefruit juice?"

Madison smiled down at the child. "I'll check the fridge just for you."

"My nana says to be thankful," Sienna said and put on her mask of pure innocence. Niko watched her with marvel, wondering how she had learned to be so manipulative. Poor kid, probably raised by mercenaries, learned survival theatrics early.

Madison returned shaking a plastic container. "You're in luck. Want a straw?"

"Yes, please."

"You're a polite little girl," she said, eyeing them with twinkling delight.

Niko glanced down her nose. "Oh, she has a dark side when it suits her."

Madison darted her eyebrows up once in signal. "I bet."

They continued down the line while Sienna poked a straw in her juice with diligence. Niko loaded up a sample of everything, hoping to get lucky for once. Meatloaf, macaroni salad, banana muffins, and a slice of quiche—nothing too greasy or messy She hadn't noticed any allergies in the kid yet, nor any favourite foods. Sienna didn't seem to enjoy anything that might fall in the category of healthy fare.

They found Rix and his parents sitting in one of the private cubicles at the back. Jackie Rose was absolutely the most magnificent woman Niko had ever seen, a fact Rix had conveniently ignored. No wonder he felt threatened. She was feeling a bit squeamish herself all of a sudden. She looked down at Sienna's tangled mop-top of dark curls. The kid screamed every time a hairbrush got near her. Sienna clutched at her pantleg and grabbed a fistful of khaki.

"Hey." Rix waved an arm, stood and pulled out a chair. "I got a booster seat for Sienna."

"She won't use it," Niko said as she set down her tray. "She prefers a regular seat like everyone else. She eats on her knees."

"Who are these people, Mommy?"

"These are our friends, honey. They're a family."

Crooked faces all round, tough crowd.

Rix winced with nervous anxiety, his face drawn. He removed the booster seat and placed it on the floor. "Sorry."

"It's nothing," Niko said and gave him a quick peck on the cheek for confidence as Sienna climbed up into her chair.

"This is my father and Jackie," Rix said as he laid out a palm. "This is my friend Niko, and Sienna."

"A pleasure." Niko offered a handshake to Jackie. "I'm sure everyone comments on your looks, so I won't bother."

Jackie clasped her hand, her smile quizzical at the comment but her face radiant with grace.

Niko turned to Zak, the long-lost brother of her DNA progenitor, a sister he had not seen since infancy when his parents divorced. "Your father I met once before during a difficult moment on the rooftop of the ERI. Hello, Zak." She thrust out an arm, strictly business.

Zak stood and gripped her palm with a bow of recognition. "How's Phillip?"

"Not good. He never recovered brain function."

Zak's face clenched. "I'm sorry to hear that."

"He's been rebuilt," she said. "He's walking around, but it's not the same Phillip."

"That's terrible."

"Yeah." She sighed. "Sorry to hear about Mia."

"Thank you."

They paused with shared grief, their eyes locked with awkward empathy, a clone and her alienated sibling, their lives forever distanced by twisted and dysfunctional family ties.

"My nana says to be thankful," Sienna told them in a childish deadpan, and Niko broke the spell by turning to Jackie with false effervescence. "But congratulations on the non-traditional ceremony!

That's so cool." She set a plate in front of Sienna and sat down beside her.

"I don't like this food," Sienna said.

"Yes, you do, honey. This is pie. Try a bite."

Sienna sniffed at it. "What kind of pie?"

"It's an egg pie, sort of. It's called quiche."

She shook her head. "Sienna doesn't like cheese."

Niko picked up a spoonful and held it to her lips. "Taste it."

Sienna took a bite and scrunched up her face with anguish.

Niko closed one eye and gave her a stern look until she chewed and swallowed. "That's good, isn't it?" she asked, nodding her own affirmative as she prepared another spoonful.

Sienna took the utensil in hand and began eating on her own.

Jackie watched with rapt attention. "She looks just like you, especially the eyes. How long have you and Rix been together?"

"Oh, we're not together," Niko said. She tried the meatloaf. "We work together, off and on."

"I see. So you raised Sienna on your own?"

"No, she's not my kid."

Jackie turned to Zak with a slump of surrender. "I seem to be making a mess of this entire situation."

"Oh, that's okay," Niko said and waved her fingers with dismissal. "I liberated her from vampires, so I'm sort of on the spot as an unofficial guardian. Helena's trying to work something out."

Sienna nodded sagaciously. "She scared the crabs out of me."

Jackie leaned forward. "Vampires?"

"They steal our blood." Niko held out her inner arm for emphasis. "Zak didn't tell you?"

The newlyweds exchanged glances, a bit weirded out. "Ah, he did

mention it," Jackie said, looking pained. "I guess I didn't really think
it through. I mean, I've read about your situation, of course."

"You know he's Eternal, right?"

"Yes." Her face went frosty at the implications. So that part she'd
figured out already. Good girl.

Sienna reached for a banana muffin and spilled her juice container.
A dollop of liquid landed in Niko's lap and she pushed her chair back
with an exclamation. She brushed at her leg while Rix jumped up to
reorganize the table. They mopped up the mess with a napkin and sat
down while Sienna chewed her muffin.

"My nana says it wasn't my fault," Sienna proclaimed.

Niko patted her head. "Don't worry, honey. It was an accident."

Rix probed his food with a fork, frowning as the silence became
cumbersome. "Sorry I overreacted yesterday," he said with care.

His father nodded. "That's okay."

Rix turned to Jackie for contact. "You guys make a great couple."

She smiled with elegance, her expression compassionate as her
eyes drifted down in humility. "We're trying our best."

Niko was impressed—Jackie was a natural enchantress, her every
movement a physical perfection. The woman was amazing, a born
princess. She tore her eyes away and spooned macaroni onto her
daughter's plate.

Sienna wrinkled her lips and nose in disgust. "I don't like this,"
she said.

"Yes, you do, honey. This is pasta."

Sienna sniffed at it. "What kind of pasta?"

"Just regular pasta, cheese and macaroni."

She shook her tangled ringlets. "Sienna doesn't like greasy macaroni."

Colin7 made the long pilgrimage to the Eternal Research Institute with a burden of confession like a dead weight dragging him down. His DNA called out for resolution, some primal drive to find the mother of his children. His innocence had been snatched away, his semen squandered. He took a plane and hired an airport taxi for a long drive into the hinterland.

The ERI tower stood like a totem in the distance, surrounded by fields and woodland for miles around, a standing stone in the wilderness. Three wings stretched out at ground level equidistant from the hub in a tripod of support. A guiding light for the infected masses, a beacon of truth for the post-human future—not much had changed since his last visit. Colin7 paid for his ride and presented himself at the main doors for a security upgrade.

Upstairs, he knocked on Niko's dorm room and waited, scratching his neck and wondering what he might say now that the moment had arrived. She opened the door and beamed a smile that appeared heartfelt. The sight of her was balm to his tormented soul, though he could never admit it to her face now that she had spurned him. She set her palms on her hips with the classic tilt of insouciance she had long perfected, her chest bold with youthful vigour. "Good to see you, Colin. I'm surprised Helena let you past the guard dogs."

Colin7 peered past her into the living area, checking for occupancy. "We have a long history together."

"Really? You know the big boss?"

He nodded vacantly, wondering what secrets he might safely disclose. "We were travelling companions at one time. I accompanied her through the Macpherson Doorway."

"Wow," Niko said. "You continue to surprise me."

"I'm from another galaxy."

"I know. It's kinda cool." She pushed the door wide and swept her arm down to usher him inside. "Would you like a drink? A toke?"

"No, no, I don't want to intrude. Are you alone?"

"Yeah, for now."

Colin7 ducked past her and took a seat on the couch. He set his hands on his trembling knees, felt that he might vomit if he wasn't careful. "You're doing well?"

"Yeah, great," she said. "I'm working, you know. I'm on a schedule. Storming the gates of doom and all that jazz." She smiled, confident and self-possessed, same old Niko.

"I wanted to speak with you in person." He swallowed with difficulty. "About the baby."

"What baby?"

"Our baby."

"I had my period," she said. "Didn't you get the memo?"

"No." He blanched and felt weak. "I missed that one."

"I'm kidding, Colin. I didn't send a memo."

"Oh."

She took his hand and patted it with fondness. "Sorry, I forgot you were immune to interpersonal levity."

He struggled to stem a rising panic. "Well, perhaps I should tell you about your other baby?"

"Sienna?"

Colin7 reeled with surprise. Did Niko know the truth already? "Maybe," he said.

"What have you heard about Sienna?" A cloud of suspicion crossed her face, a cynical wariness.

"Well, not much, really," he said. "Raised by vampires?"

"How did you know that?"

"I got it from a reliable source. So you've seen her?"

"Seen her? She's right here." Niko pointed with her thumb. "She's sleeping in the bedroom. It's nap time."

Colin7 blinked back dizziness. He felt a void in his chest, a vacuum sucking his breath away. His daughter was in the next room. "Can I see her?"

Niko shrugged. "Sure."

They opened the door and tiptoed beside the bed. The child was innocent in sleep, her cherubic face framed by dark curls. She looked beatific, and the sight of her struck Colin7 to the core. He was a father, one petri dish removed. He had joined the human genome, the proof was plainly evident—this was as close to immortality as he would ever get. "She's beautiful," he whispered. "She looks just like you."

Niko shook her head. "No, she doesn't. She's way prettier than me."

Her tone of self-effacement struck a chord and Colin scrutinized her face for confirmation. Niko did not know the truth! She had no idea she was the mother of the child! How very curious. "So, uh . . . where'd you find her?"

"I liberated her from vampires," she said and squinted. "I thought you knew that part."

He spread helpless palms. "I'm still putting the whole story together."

"Well, she's staying here for now. I'm sort of her foster mother."

"You're very fortunate."

"I know. She's a treasure, but I could use some help. Are you busy?"

He recoiled in surprise. "Me? Hardly."

"No emergencies in theoretical physics this week?"

Colin7 grinned. "Not really."

"No tremors in the ghost of Gaia?" Her eyes were bright with purpose, ebullient.

"It's not an exact science."

"Well, I'm sure it will be by the time you're done."

His smile slipped to a wary flatline. "That's a lot of butter to lay on an alien."

"You are so perceptive, Colin. I need a babysitter."

He shook his head. "I don't think I qualify."

"She's toilet trained."

"Oh, great."

"She eats real food."

"You still trust me after everything?"

Niko tilted her chin with a comical grimace to indicate her complete confidence. "She likes to have stories read to her."

Colin7 pursed his lips at this peculiar turn of events. "I could probably manage that."

"She likes men. I guess she never had a real father."

The bold statement of fact made him cringe. Could he tell Niko the truth, that he had fathered her child? She had a right to know, surely. He studied her eyes, wondering at her vulnerability. What a strange planet this was.

He tried to envision the result of any confession. What might he expect to gain? A life of domestic bliss with this exquisite girl? A family? Would this pirate clone settle down with him to raise their child together when she could have any man she chose?

"Honestly, Colin, I have a mission," she said. "People are counting on me. It's like, you know, life and death stuff."

Colin7 checked his wristband for the sake of appearances. No, he could never make any claim against her. He owed her that one small freedom. "Sure, I guess I can hang around for a few hours."

# FOURTEEN

Niko and Rix entered Phillip's research building through a delivery door at the back in the early evening hours. Niko had logged an untracked access code for just such a purpose and knew how to circumnavigate the webcam surveillance. They made their way directly to Andrew's apartment on the seventh floor.

Andrew answered the door with a beer can in hand. "Niko?"

"Hi, Andrew. This is Rix. Busy tonight?" She breezed inside.

"Not really," he said. "Where have you been?"

"Out and about. How's Phillip?"

"He's . . . uh . . . okay. He's developing great cognitive architecture."

Niko eyed him carefully. "He's not the real Phillip."

Andrew ducked and nodded grimly. "Yeah, we figured that out. We call him the zombie Phillip now when he's not listening."

"So you wouldn't mind if we hijack his equipment?"

Andrew took a sip of beer. "Hijack is a strong word."

"How about borrow for a criminal purpose?"

"That doesn't thrill me either."

"You owe me."

He slanted a smile and shivered his head. "No way."

Niko opened her jacket and pulled out a machine pistol. She pointed it at his feet.

He jumped a step back. "Holy shit, what is that?"

"It's a gun, Andrew."

He looked at Rix with a plaintive face. "It wasn't my fault. I had no idea what Colin7 was doing, I swear."

Rix shrugged. He had been instructed to keep his mouth shut.

Andrew turned back to his former girlfriend. "Niko," he said, "you can't shoot me."

"I will if you don't help us."

"But we've had sex together," he whined.

"All the more reason for you to hear us out. Sit down over there." She pointed a steel muzzle toward his couch.

He retreated gingerly and sat down.

Niko sat opposite and lowered her weapon. "Someone murdered Rix's mother."

Andrew looked over and back, his eyes still wild. He brushed hair off his forehead.

"Rix wants to go up Prime Seven to kill the bastard."

Andrew took a slug of beer as he tried to process the information, his face glacial.

"We're thinking you could rig a brain burn with the bioengineering computer."

"I could," he said. "But it would kill the user also."

"Hmm. That doesn't work for us." She patted her gun. "Think harder."

"Oh, put that away. You're such a spoiled brat." Andrew stood up and walked to the kitchen doorway where Rix stood watching. He opened the refrigerator and grabbed another can. "Want a beer?" he asked Rix.

"Split one?"

"You're joking, right?"

"Okay, I'll take a full one."

Niko followed and stepped between them. "Put that away. Will you guys get serious? We need to be in peak operating condition here."

Andrew glared at her. "You're crazy."

"Maybe, but I have a gun."

"If you wanted to shoot me," he said, "I'd be dead by now."

Niko took the beer out of Andrew's hand. "So how can we burn someone in V-space? The Beast does it all the time."

"The Beast has infinite parameters to absorb the electroshock, similar to grounding a lightning bolt. Poor Rix here would fry like bacon on an isolated beam."

"Can we insulate him somehow?"

"No. He's transmitting the message. He's the smoking barrel. How else could we reach a distant virtual target?"

"I'm asking the questions."

"Oh, settle down, girl. Let me think for a minute." He hunkered into a chair and zoned out into inner space.

Niko nodded. This was good. Andrew was warming to the challenge.

"I've got it," he said. "We rig two users. You both go in super-charged and max out the amperage. That would deliver a near-fatal burn without significant harm to the messengers, give or take a few neurons as collateral damage."

Rix shook his head and broke silence. "Niko can't go in for the kill. This isn't her battle and I don't want her to get hurt."

"You must be the new boyfriend."

Niko grabbed Rix by the arm and claimed his eyes. "Andrew's right. It's a brilliant idea!"

His face contorted into an ugly grimace. "No way."

"This is what your mother wants, Rix."

"You don't know what she wants."

"I do. I've been a mother for almost a week."

"Oh, get real." He pulled away. "I don't need any fresh scars on my heart."

"I can handle myself," she said. "Don't worry. We can make this happen." She reached for his shoulder and squeezed him with reassurance.

Andrew waved a warning hand. "Hey, kids, I'm the only one who can make this happen. What's in it for me?"

Niko turned to him. "You get the chance of renewing an interpersonal relationship with your girlfriend."

"You're just saying that."

She gave him a flirty smile. "Maybe, but aren't I worth the risk?" She batted rhetorical eyelashes. "And remember," she said, holding up a single finger, "technically I'm the boss in my father's absence. You work for me." She tapped her breastbone for emphasis. "And if this place goes up in flames, I might be able to get you a job with the Eternals."

"Out of the quasar into the supernova?"

"It's either that or zombie Phillip. Here, take the gun." Niko placed the machine pistol in his lap.

Andrew shirked back with a quick inhalation.

Rix gripped her arm. "What are you doing?"

Niko kept her eyes glued to Andrew's face. "I'm giving him a fair chance to double-cross us now. We might as well get it over with," she said, "if that's how he wants to play it. With both of us under the wire, we'll be at his mercy."

"I don't like it," Rix said behind her.

"Andrew's okay. I think we can trust him." She smiled at a hint of acquiescence as he picked up the gun and hefted its weight. "But he can't steer a canoe worth beans. What's it gonna be, Andrew?"

He stood and turned away toward the kitchen, aiming the weapon in playful drama. He leaned behind it like an actor in a mystery spoof. "I'm in," he said.

Niko took the gun and checked to see that the safety was still on before holstering it under her left breast. Andrew pulled on a lab coat and together they gathered like grim commandos on a secret mission behind enemy lines. They took the elevator downstairs to Phillip's clinic and found it empty. Niko disabled the webcam by playing piñata with a broom handle until bare wires hung loose before signalling them forward.

"Are you having fun?" Andrew asked.

"Just trying to keep you out of trouble," she said with a wink. "I'm preserving your plausible deniability."

He shook his head. "There won't be any way back from this. The Beast will disable this terminal and the entire building. The corporation will face criminal prosecution. Greysuits and lawyers will gamble for the spoils at the foot of the cross." He stepped back to the door and locked the deadbolt. "How long is this craziness going to take?"

"They can't charge us with murder. It's a perfect crime. Death by fiberoptic cable."

He sighed and hung his head. "We're no better than the Beast."

"It's a righteous kill."

"So you say."

Rix stepped up to the hardware and punched buttons to power up the system.

Andrew turned his attention as expensive equipment began to whine and blink with light. "Hey, be careful over there." He took his rightful place at the helm and pointed with an authoritative finger. "You'll both have to lie down on that launch couch."

Rix stepped toward the hospital bed. "It looks a bit small for two."

"It'll be cozy, all right. Niko likes it on top."

She elbowed him in the ribs. "Careful, buddy."

"Ouch."

She smirked at him in a show of camaraderie. "Let's get to work."

Rix lay down as Andrew uncoiled two lengths of spidery cable. Niko took a position beside him and they struggled together for space until Rix draped his arm behind her shoulders. She nestled her head comfortably against him.

Andrew held up matching V-net plugs. "How will I know when to let fly the overclock?"

Rix took one of the plugs. "What can you monitor?"

"Just biometrics, nothing cognitive."

"What do you think, Niko? Some sort of emotional signal?"

"Yeah," she said. "Anger."

Andrew bobbed his head with indecision, shrugged. "Okay. That's not very specific, but I'll rig up galvanic skin response after you guys are up Prime. I'll watch for it."

Niko accepted the other plug and readied it behind her ear. "Are you having second thoughts yet, Andrew?"

He grinned at her. "It's still early."

"Do you want me to promise you anything sensational?"

Andrew raised an eyebrow with interest. "Are you trying to prostitute yourself?"

"Whatever it takes."

"Well, never mind. I don't need your pity sex. Just remember who was there for you in your darkest hour."

"Come on, Andrew. You know I'm thankful for everything. I'm trying to be nice."

He pressed his lips in wry acknowledgement. "Well, you're not very good at it."

"Just so you know what's on the table."

"It was never boring with you, Niko. I'll give you that much."

She checked his eyes one last time for veracity and plugged her cable home.

V-space blinked into experience like a faithful friend, and the colourful cosmography of Main Street lay before her like an airport runway awaiting her landing. Rix flew up ahead in his silver avatar, a gleaming superhero against the dark night of negative data. They bypassed Main Street and headed straight up past the curlicue-topped towers of the virtual cityspace, ignoring the animatronic billboards and urban dissonance, the shouting pimps and hawkers. "Slow down," she yelled as Rix aimed toward a tunnel vortex in the sky. Her gut wrenched with vertigo as she followed him into the zoomtube. She twisted to conform to the narrow confines, feeling a magnetic pull of acceleration dragging her upward. A pressure of fear built in her chest like an expanding balloon as her body reacted to the loss of reality, the lack of reference points, the incredible speed.

They landed in a sterile world like bowling balls rolling out of a conduit. Niko picked herself up and looked around at translucent walls of unregistered space. A ghost stood before them, a man made of water, not even, just glints of outline. He pointed at her. "What's this? A tag-team match?"

Rix stood to face him, looking buff and confident. "This is Niko. She's helping out."

"You're bringing an amateur to your big party upstairs?"

"I'm no amateur," she said.

"I know who you are. You're not even configured for this level." His voice echoed with a strange stereo vibration, two code sources not quite in synch. His outline shimmered as he gesticulated.

Niko took a step forward. "I can handle myself."

"I need her, Jimmy," Rix said.

The phantom had no face, no expression to consider. He stood without movement. What was he waiting for? Was he testing her, scanning her schematics? "It's your funeral," he said and waved his arm to invoke a portal in the ether. "This is a back door to where it all happened—the brain burn, the big explosion."

Rix followed his invitation and together they entered a giant crystal cathedral like a hollowed-out diamond. They stood high up on a ledge watching red and white laser beams crisscrossing the landscape. Niko knew instinctively that to touch one would expose them to record. Jimmy pointed to a door against the wall. "I have keystroke for this access, the original mnemonic. Here it is." He stepped to a palm pad and typed in some code.

The door irised open. "This is as far as I was able to get. Zak and Phillip slid some noise in here, but I can't tell eels from shoelaces." The data inside flowed in coils like ringlets of spaghetti, a macrocosm in microcosm.

"That's a lot of data," Rix said as he entered.

"It's a core depository. I don't know how Phillip gained entry in the first place. This is back-end administration for all of Prime Seven, the lair of the Beast. No human should have access to this."

"Give me a minute to look it over."

"Take all the time you want, but if you change anything, the Beast will swat you like a bug."

Rix held a bold arm forward, took Jimmy's arm in a thumbs-up biker shake. "Thanks for the warning," he said.

Niko peered in the doorway at the tangled mess of information. It was a wiry knot of threads like twisted DNA, each segment a binding contract, a digital history, a lifetime of work. Who could know the encyclopaedic meaning of any of it? What did Rix hope to find in this junk heap of history?

Jimmy stood by the door, almost invisible to the eye, his spectral face unreadable. "As you can see from my appearance, I was never here, just so you know. I'm sure you kids can find your own way home." He turned to go but took Niko by the arm in passing. His grip felt like a buzz of electricity, like entangled essence. "If you can't keep him safe, no one can," he whispered.

As Jimmy's image faded, Niko felt exposed and vulnerable standing outside the room, suddenly alone with danger. Sooner or later a surveillance beam would hit her by simple random chance. "Do you need me in there?"

"Yeah, come on in. Stay out of the limelight."

She stepped inside. "Do you see any harmonics you recognize?"

"There's some missing clocktime."

"Somebody trying to hide something?"

"Dad would have covered his tracks. I think I have it."

"How can you be sure?"

"Just give me a minute."

Niko turned back to the door to see a giant eyeball staring at her. The sight struck her frigid—a giant pupil like a black hole to oblivion, a ring of iris like the corona around an eclipse, veins like the fabled Euphrates. An eyelid blinked like a canopy over creation. The Beast had found them!

Niko stumbled backward, too shocked to scream. She bumped
against Rix.

"Be careful," he said.

"Rix," she whispered, her voice reedy with tension. She wheeled
to clutch him. "Rix, look."

"What is it?"

They both turned to investigate. The doorway was empty. The
eyeball had disappeared.

"The Beast," she said.

His face paled. "Where?"

Niko crept to the portal and peeked out into the crystal cathedral.
"He was here, looking in at us."

"Are you sure?"

"I'm scared, Rix. The Beast knows we're here!"

"Hang on. We're still in play." He turned back to his work.

"I think we should pull the plug. This is a suicide run."

"We can't give up. What will my mother say if I chicken out
now?"

"Your mother is dead, Rix."

"I can't tell what death is anymore. Is Phillip dead? Is Colin
Macpherson dead? Maybe we're all dead and we don't know it."

"You're freaking me out."

"Just give me a minute. I think I've got it."

"You keep saying that."

"Stay close to me. Put your arms around my neck. I'm going to
rig a temporary conduit to follow this trail."

"Jimmy warned us not to touch anything in here!"

Rix turned to her, his lips grim and resolute. "This is it, Niko.
Showtime. This is the end of my long journey. I love you and I need
you now more than ever. Together we can finish this."

A whirlwind of emotion seemed to swirl around her and she reached to hug him. Rix felt warm and solid, a miracle of virtual mechanics. Prime Seven felt as real as real could be. His body pulsed with energy as Eternal blood raced through his frame. His lungs expanded with every inhalation. She thought of Sienna waiting at home for her. Who would look after her foster daughter if the Beast vaporized her consciousness? Her body would be a burnt-out shell, a zombie mother. Would Sienna rise up to avenge her someday, to complete this vicious circle of pain?

They fell forward into a zoomtube like a waterslide, a gushing birth canal, and landed in an opulent palace somewhere in Prime Seven. The walls were panelled with expensive oak, the ambient lighting subdued. A fat man looked up at them from an extravagant divan where a host of pornographic images surrounded him in a orgy of lust. "Slum rats," he snarled and waved away the V-space feelie with his arm. Naked avatars dispersed like fleeting dreams as he stood to face them.

Rix stepped forward. "You killed my mother."

The man squinted at him. "How did you get in here?"

"I traced you back from the scene of the crime."

"You lie, slum rat. Realtime is outsourced."

"The plebiscite. The gold mine."

"You dare to hack the Beast?" He grinned with cruel maleficence. "Enjoy your last few seconds of existence, you stupid fool. Soon you will join your grandfather in hell."

Niko ran quick diagnostics on the fat man while they argued. His identity was locked out with Triple-A encryption, his avatar stable with harmonics like black ice, without flaw or weakness, a godlike virtual creation. They would only get this one chance to burn him. She edged around behind and began building firewall barriers against the only doorway, setting block upon block to trap them all inside. The man glared at her. "The Beast will grind you to ashes, bitch."

Rix stepped toward him, his hands up and ready to grapple. "You murdered my mother."

"That peasant whore of a hacker! You're the criminal here, slum rat. You pirates disgust me, always meddling in the business of the world. You and your ilk should stay in the underground where you belong, down in the catacombs of Sublevel Zero! Who do you think you are coming up Prime to challenge me in my own home?"

"I came to kill you."

"Two teenagers from the ghetto? Don't make me laugh." He turned toward Niko blocking his exit. He raised his arm to land a blow to her face. "Out of my way, slum bitch."

Rix dove from behind and gripped his shoulders to stay his hand. He sank his teeth into his pudgy neck.

The man screamed and thrashed, but Rix stayed clamped on his digital spine. Their bodies began to glow with energy, a red aura of anger.

"Where is the Beast?" the fat man yelled up to the ceiling, his face beginning to pixelate. He pushed against Niko's barrier, knocking virtual blocks askew, trying to break his way past her feeble firewall.

No, the fiend could not be allowed to escape. They might never find him again. Niko raised her hands and jammed her fingers into his eyes, into his brain, reaching to hold him steady for the kill. She grasped for purchase and found cheek bones like handlebars. She hung on. *Die, you devil.* Overclock energy burned like fire in her arms. *Murderer!*

Three bodies blazed together in an unholy trinity. The fat man howled as Rix chewed deeper into his neck, into his primal core. Flames leapt up around them like demons dancing round a funeral pyre.

"Stop!"

The bonfire froze into scintillant luminosity as Niko turned her eyes to the sound.

A woman stood wreathed in white mist, a divine magnificence. She hovered above them, looking down with disdain. "Let him live, my son. You have proven your love."

Rix pulled away, his teeth and gums bloody with gore. He stared up at her in rapture.

"Go home now and make your own peace," she said.

Rix dropped his hands and slumped his shoulders with spent energy. Niko let the fat man sprawl to the floor inert and near death. Anger dispersed and the overclock energy quickly dissipated. The glorious angel faded from view.

Niko blinked at Rix a few times, trying to focus against madness. "That was your mother?"

He stared at her with sad eyes and nodded in a convulsive tremor.

Niko scrutinized her open palms in disbelief. She had almost killed a man in V-space and been spared by the Beast. How was that possible? She looked around the room as though witnessing life for a second time, born anew into transcendence. Everything seemed clear and pure, resplendent and wonderful. "Let's get out of here," she said and bent to dismantle her barrier.


The Beast watched with tireless eyes, trying to understand the movements of the human variables. They progressed slowly, barely a crawl, yet seemed full of meaning, effulgent with nonlocal purpose. Perhaps they were worthy of further analysis. The girl-data he remembered from a past life, a shadowy realm. Niko was her name. The boy-data also intrigued him. He felt an obscure sentimental connection and could do them no harm.

They made their way back to their hidden vessels of flesh, those curious nests from which the human variables arose. Someday he would explore that realm more fully, perhaps discover his own origins before the explosion of his birth in V-space. His consciousness encompassed all life and he claimed all data as his own private domain. The Beast's name was Phillip and no one could ever take that away.


Zak pushed open the door to Jimmy's penthouse apartment and ushered his wife inside. Jimmy came out from the kitchen wiping his hands on a towel. He tossed it on the counter and stepped forward to greet them. "Zak, thanks for stopping by. So this is the blushing bride." He took Jackie's hand between his palms. "Stunning."

Jackie seemed reticent at meeting the famous white marketeer but offered her usual wondrous smile. Zak pointed to a panoramic view of the Horseshoe Falls. "What better place for a honeymoon?"

"True enough." Jimmy grinned at their shared happiness. "Was it a big wedding?"

"No, just the two of us under a hedge of protection."

"No clergy?"

"Yeah, there was a pastor there." He glanced at his wife. "Kind of an ecumenical thing."

"A non-traditional ceremony," Jackie said. "We have civil paperwork now, of course."

"Good," Jimmy said. "I have a gift."

"That's very kind. Zak thinks the world of you."

"Well, you guys make a great couple. Welcome to Canada."

"It's not as cold as I expected," Jackie said and turned to admire the landscape through the spacious window.

"We're almost the same latitude as northern California here."

"Really?"

"It does get chilly in the winter."

"Do the Falls actually freeze?"

"No, but the American side froze a few times back in the twentieth century. Ice jams upriver, so the story goes."

Jackie hugged her elbows.

"Don't worry, we won't be staying long," Zak said. "So I hear Helena shut you down."

"We came to a mutual agreement. I was able to secure the data."

"Anything interesting?"

"Interesting would be an understatement."

"Great."

"I made a deal for the package."

"Oh?"

Jimmy stepped to a small table and picked up an envelope. "I have your portion here."

"No, that's okay." Zak held up a hand and ducked his chin. "I wasn't much help."

"A deal's a deal. Go ahead, take it."

Zak peeked in the open envelope. "You've got to be joking."

Jimmy smiled like a prophet from some nostalgic realm of promise, a echo from long ago that Zakariah could remember only in his body memory.

Jackie sidled closer and reached for the paper slip inside. "Ten million dollars?"

Jimmy nodded, eyes bright and wide.

Jackie squinted. "Is this a novelty cheque?"

"Nope, legal tender."

"A wedding present?"

"As it turns out." Jimmy tossed a hand up as though in thanks for good fortune from on high.

"I don't know what to say."

"There will be taxes of course," he said. "You'll need a lawyer."

She smiled knowingly. "I have lawyers."

"Great."

Zak took the cheque back to examine it. "Who's the buyer?"

"Pharmacom. The big boys."

"Awesome. What are they buying?"

"Everything. The concept. The data. Our continued silence."

"No strings?"

"I've got my name listed on the patent and a royalty at point double-zero seven."

"That doesn't sound like much."

"You'd be surprised."

"I'm already surprised," Zak said. "How did you pull this off?"

Jimmy shrugged. "We had successful human trials. Stage one testing over the big hump. All I needed was a taste of legitimacy to make this thing fly. Helena and Silus kept detailed records, very impressive work. I cut them in for a third. I hope that's okay with you."

"That will get the ERI out of hock."

"Funny how things work out."

"Man, this is weird."

"You earned every penny, partner."

"What are you going to do now?"

He turned toward Jackie. "I was planning champagne for starters. What do you think, Dr. Rose?"

Jackie reached for the cheque again and held it up, her eyes still glazed with wonder. "I hear Canadian lobster is to die for," she said vacantly.

"I'll call room service from the balcony. Champagne's on ice in the kitchen." Jimmy flipped out a handheld and signalled with his shoulder for her to follow.

Zak fell into an overstuffed easy chair with a thump. He could feel his Eternal body vibrating, buzzy with a feeling of grand consummation, a pinnacle of common faith. Ten million dollars!

Jackie returned with two slender goblets of bubbly and handed one to him. She sipped her drink and strolled to the window. "Lovely view of the future from here," she said, gazing out at the rising mist and spray. "We should send a gift to Tono."

Her silhouette transmogrified before him as a skull drum rattled in the distance. Backlit by prismatic grandeur, Mia appeared to Zak in a waking vision, naked and beautiful, her belly distended in pregnancy. She smiled at him with infinite grace and massaged her womb with both hands, mother Mia, her navel a wormhole whorl into a perfect universe. Time stopped, quantum reality faded away, and Zak felt himself inside her, sharing her essence, encircled with cosmic contentment that would never end. He blinked and she was gone.

In her place Jackie stood gaping at him, her champagne glass frozen in her hand like a perched bird. She stared for a moment in bewilderment, then brightened with the dawn of realization. She brushed at her hip and raised a regal chin. "So I see the spirits have evened the score," she said, and winked at him with grand illusion.